W9-BZU-116

THE
WICKED
WINTER

WILLIAM K. SANFORD
TOWN LIBRARY
629 ALBANY-SHAKER RD.
LOUDONVILLE, NY 12211
TEL: (518) 458-9274

Also by Kate Sedley

Death and the Chapman
The Plymouth Cloak
The Hanged Man
The Holy Innocents
The Eve of Saint Hyacinth

137808

M

THE
WICKED
WINTER

KATE SEDLEY

ST. MARTIN'S PRESS
NEW YORK

THE WICKED WINTER. Copyright © 1996 by Kate Sedley. All rights reserved. Printed in the United States of America. No part of this book may be used or reproduced in any manner whatsoever without written permission except in the case of brief quotations embodied in critical articles or reviews. For information, address St. Martin's Press, 175 Fifth Avenue, New York, N.Y. 10010.

ISBN 0-312-20625-9

First published in Great Britain by Headline Book Publishing, a division of Hodder Headline PLC

First U.S. Edition: August 1999

10 9 8 7 6 5 4 3 2 1

THE
WICKED WINTER

Chapter One

It was bitterly cold. In the last few minutes a wind had arisen, blustering across the house-tops from the river Frome, moaning between the houses and rattling all their shutters like the teeth in an old man's head. My mother-in-law, standing beside me, reached across and pulled the woollen shawl closer about my sleeping daughter who weighed so uncomfortably against my shoulder. Elizabeth, now two months past her first birthday, as well as inheriting my fair hair and blue eyes also promised to have my height and build, and she was a heavy child for her age. I shifted her sleeping form as gently as I could from my right arm to my left, but even that, like the powerful voice of the friar who preached from the High Cross, failed to awaken her. But it disturbed several other members of the tightly packed congregation, who turned frowning faces towards me and bade me be still.

The reputation of the Dominican friar, Father Simeon, had preceded his appearance in Bristol by many months. It had already been one of the main topics of the marketplace when I returned to Margaret Walker's home, amongst the weavers and spinners of the city, the previous September. Now at last, in the first week of an icy January of the year of

Our Lord 1476, the great preacher had finally arrived; and on this Monday morning, braving the treacherous conditions underfoot, the citizens had left their work and flocked to hear what he had to say.

Reluctant to quit the fireside, I had offered to remain at home with Elizabeth while my mother-in-law went alone, but Margaret would not permit it.

'It will do you good,' she had retorted, 'to listen to a rousing sermon for a change. The Word of God is too little expounded in the churches nowadays. Not,' she added hastily, 'that I am accusing the parish priests of failing in their duty. Heaven's my witness that I meant nothing of the kind! It's just that the poor men are too overburdened with the rigours of office to find time to explain the Scriptures. They're content to leave that to the friars.'

'Oh?' I questioned the truth of this judgement. 'I thought the Church accused all the Orders of avarice, lechery and hypocrisy. You know the saying: "Friars and fiends be but little asunder."'

Margaret looked displeased. 'I pay no heed to common gossip and neither should you. It ruins the reputations of too many good people.'

I knew she had cause for her dislike of unfounded calumnies and gently squeezed her hand.

'Mother,' I said, although the title had always been inclined to stick in my throat, 'it's not just that I want to sit in the warm for a little longer on such an unpleasant morning, but surely it's unwise to expose Elizabeth to the bitter weather.'

She laughed mirthlessly. 'And what, pray, would you know

about what is and what isn't wise for the child? She's over a year old, and these past four months have been the longest time you've spent in her company since she was born. And you'll soon be off on your travels again. Oh, don't deny it! I recognise the signs. You've been restless for days now, peddling your wares from dawn to dusk. And since Christmas, as the days lengthen, you've ventured a little further afield each time. On at least three occasions you've travelled so far that you've been unable to return home at night.'

'I'm a chapman,' I protested. 'I have to go abroad to sell my wares.' But I could hear the note of guilt in my voice.

Margaret heard it too, and smiled acidly. 'There are enough villages and homesteads in the neighbourhood to keep you busy; and with ships from foreign parts constantly dropping anchor along the Backs, no shortage of supplies to replenish your pack. With the money I earn from spinning we don't lack for food or clothing, nor for a roof over our heads. We could settle down here very comfortably together until you decide to marry again – as a big, strong, handsome lad like you is bound to do one day. I'm quite prepared for that. But there are plenty of local girls who'd be more than willing to have you, and Alderman Weaver, after what you did for him, would doubtless let you have one of his cottages to live in. You wouldn't be far away and I could still visit Elizabeth whenever I wished.'

'I see you've been making plans for me,' I answered, trying to make light of my resentment.

Margaret gave an emphatic shake of her head. 'No, Roger lad, I shouldn't dare. I know they're only daydreams. You have the wanderlust in you. I accepted that fact very early on in our acquaintance. It was the reason you couldn't take your final vows and become a monk. It's why, in a way, I'm glad that Lillis didn't live beyond that first autumn of your marriage. She couldn't have borne all the partings, never knowing when she was going to see you again.'

'Forgive me,' I begged, once more pressing her work-roughened hand. 'I know it must be lonely for you, bringing up Elizabeth on your own.'

'We are as God made us,' she replied philosophically. 'We must do His will as we think fit. You were born a rover and you won't change yet awhile. However,' she added in a brisker tone, 'you aren't wriggling out of coming with me this morning to hear Friar Simeon preach. Elizabeth will do well enough if she's wrapped up properly, and you can carry her in your arms. It shouldn't be too difficult for someone as strapping as you.'

But she overestimated even my strength, for as I have already said, my daughter was not a delicate child. (Today, in her thirty-eighth year, Elizabeth has more than fulfilled that early promise. She is a big, tall, handsome woman, not easily roused to anger, but ruling her husband and children, and above all me, with a fist of iron concealed in a silken glove.) My arms were aching long before the friar had reached the halfway point in his dissertation.

Simeon was a tall, cadaverous man with the thin, dyspeptic face of the true fanatic. His arms flailed the air as he spoke eloquently of hellfire and damnation, and his eyes glowed like coals in their sunken sockets. Too little food and too much penance had made him feverish. Hectic spots of colour burned in either cheek and there was a bluish tinge around his lips. His black Dominican habit was mired and dusty about the hem with much walking of the winter roads, and the sparse brown hair hung lankly to his narrow shoulders.

At the end of half an hour my mind began to wander, going back over the extraordinary events of the previous year (which I have set down in detail elsewhere, but which at that time I judged it wise to keep to myself). By the end of another half hour I was unable to think of anything except the extreme discomfort caused by Elizabeth's weight. There was no feeling in either of my arms and I was in serious danger of dropping her.

But help was at hand. Friar Simeon was obviously coming to the end of his sermon. The crowd was hushed now, tense and expectant, as a great wave of elation seemed to wash through the preacher's body. He reached up into the heavens as though he could bring down God to fight on his side. Once again the impassioned tones rang out.

'Three things are necessary for the salvation of man! To know what he should believe, to know what he ought to desire, to know what he should do! Believe in God, desire God, serve God! Renounce the temptations of the flesh for they are the temptations of the devil! Prayer and purity, my children! These are the things we must strive after!'

Men were swaying now in a kind of ecstasy; women were weeping uncontrollably. The crowd was aflame, kindled by the spark of the friar's emotion.

'So I bid you all go forth and root out evil wherever you may find it! Perfect blessedness is a vision of God!'

There was a moment's profound silence, as if indeed we

had all been vouchsafed that vision. Then with a sudden concerted movement his listeners began to disperse, drifting away like people awakening from a dream, back to their humdrum existence. For a while they had touched the heights, each one capable of a place among the saints. Now the real world intruded. Anger, envy and greed reared their ugly heads once more.

I heaved a sigh of relief at the conclusion of my ordeal just as my daughter stirred and opened her eyes, blinking placidly.

'Heigh-ho, lass!' I said and swung her on to my back, her little arms clasped trustingly around my neck. I turned to Margaret. 'Can you tuck the shawl around her?'

But my mother-in-law had disappeared. Moments later I saw her stooping over the friar who had lowered himself to the ground, exhausted by his labours, his emaciated body hunched against a wintry blast of wind. She was smiling triumphantly, and I guessed correctly that she had beaten the two other local matrons who crowded at her heels in their bid to offer hospitality to the preacher. I sighed resignedly. I had hoped for a quiet dinner, during which I had intended to break it gently to Margaret that her suspicions, voiced earlier that morning, were well founded: I had to get away soon from the stifling domesticity of the cottage and travel the road for a while; not for long, only a sennight, or a fortnight at the most.

The need to go had become overwhelming. I had been fighting it for days, knowing from past experience that when the longing grew to be as powerful as this, God had work for me to do. Of course I argued with Him about it. I always did, although I knew that any priest would tell me that it is wrong to address oneself directly to the Almighty. He is too awesome, too clouded in glory, to be approached by lowly sinners. The multitude of saints, the Virgin Herself, are there to intercede on our behalf, to take upon their own shoulders the trivial burdens of our days. But I had always secretly rebelled against this notion. Throughout life I have found it better to speak directly, wherever possible, to the head man.

God, as usual, listened patiently to everything I had to say and then proceeded with His own plans as if I hadn't spoken. Naturally I'd known what the outcome would be, but protesting gives me a sense of independence and the prospect that one day I might even win.

Margaret returned, the friar walking beside her.

'Roger, Brother Simeon has done us the honour of agreeing to share our dinner. Brother, this is my son-by-marriage, Roger the chapman.'

'Master Chapman!' The pale blue eyes regarded me fiercely as if he knew that of all that crowd I was the only one who had paid his words scant attention. Fortunately, as my gaze shifted guiltily under his, he was diverted by the approach of one of the congregation, a fuller whom I knew by sight, bearing a purse full of money.

'A collection taken up amongst us, Brother,' the man said respectfully, 'to help you on your way.'

'Thank you, my son.' Friar Simeon stowed the purse away in the shabby leather pouch which hung from his girdle. 'And now, Dame Walker, shall we eat?'

An hour later, as the pale winter sun rose towards its zenith,

Friar Simeon scraped the last drop of stew from his bowl and drained the last dregs of ale from his cup before giving a contented sigh.

'That was an excellent repast, Mistress Walker.'

They were the first words he had uttered since saying grace, a silence which had inhibited both Margaret and myself from speaking throughout the meal. The only noise, apart from the sounds of eating, had been Elizabeth's baby prattle, which no one but her grandmother could understand. She sat, as good as gold, in her own little chair with the high carved back which a neighbour and friend, Nick Brimble, had made for her, sharing the contents of Margaret's dish. She was a quiet, mannerly child even at that young age.

'I'm glad you found it to your liking, Brother,' said my mother-in-law, preparing to rise from the table. 'If you've finished, perhaps you'd care to draw nearer the fire. It's a bitter day.'

The friar needed no second bidding, dragging his stool closer to the hearth and pulling up his shabby gown so that the warmth could seep into his bony knees. Margaret sat beside him while I lowered myself to the floor, among the rushes, cradling Elizabeth, now released from her chair, on my lap.

'Do you come from these parts, Brother?' I asked, thinking that I had detected a trace of local accent in his speech, but he shook his head.

'I'm from the north, the far north. From the ancient kingdom of Northumbria.'

His tone was abrasive as though I had somehow insulted him with my suggestion that he was from the south, where existence was safer and softer than in those harsher regions, governed solely by the laws of survival.

Margaret asked placatingly, 'Do you tarry long with us in Bristol?'

He shook his head. 'I slept last night with my fellow Dominicans beyond the town, but tonight only Our Lord knows where I shall take my rest.' Simeon crossed himself. 'His Will be done.'

Margaret was horrified. 'Surely you'll tarry another night at the friary in the broad meads? It would be most unwise to set forward with the day so advanced and the weather so inclement and, above all, yourself so exhausted from your morning's labours!'

The friar turned his burning eyes upon her. 'What God wills for us we must do without question, nor with any thought for our body's needs.'

I shifted a little uncomfortably at this, causing Elizabeth, who was crooning to herself and making a bed for her wooden doll among the straw, to glance up at me inquiringly. I bent my head and kissed her on one velvety cheek before asking boldly, 'What is your mission from God, Brother?'

Again the eyes glowed like coals in a furnace.

'To bring back sinners into the fold! This is a godless age, Master Chapman, but what can you expect with a king upon the throne who thinks of nothing but bodily pleasures, and a queen whose family are eaten alive by greed? The court is a stinking cesspit of iniquity and only one member of it, My Lord of Gloucester, seems immune from its cupidity and licentiousness. He at least has the sense to stay away, living as he does on his own estates and visiting London as infrequently as possible. His, if report is true, was one of the very few voices raised against this late ignominious débâcle in France. The roads of this country are even more unsafe to walk than they were six months ago because of the disbanded troops, who are all working off their frustrated martial spirits by murder and highway robbery.'

There was a great deal that I could have said on that subject had I been so minded, but I kept my counsel. Instead I reminded Brother Simeon that King Edward, far from spending his entire time in 'bodily pleasures', had been travelling the length and breadth of England meting out summary justice to the offenders.

The friar snorted. 'Maybe, when he can tear himself away from the embraces of this new leman of his, Mistress Jane Shore.'

I could not help retorting, 'You appear remarkably well informed.'

'I've come from London,' he hissed, 'where the talk is of nothing else. It seems that Lord Hastings and the King's elder stepson, the Marquess of Dorset, are also besotted by the creature, and are only waiting for His Grace's affections to wane before snapping her up for themselves.' He reached down and laid a claw-like hand on my shoulder. 'You think it wrong for a man of God to be concerned with such things? You fool! How else can I identify the evil which must be overcome? How else can I root out the sins which are destroying men's souls?'

His thin features which, in repose, looked like a parchment mask, were transformed by the light of reforming zeal. I recalled stories of the early Dominican friars who, in their

fanatical determination to stamp out heresy, had forced
families to testify one against the other, who had burned the
unrepentant at the stake and who had even exhumed the
bodies of those found guilty after death and burned them
also. Their Chief Inquisitor had been Saint Thomas Aquinas,
whose words Friar Simeon had quoted in his sermon this
morning. Plainly, in the same spirit, he was carrying out his
own crusade against lechery and debauchery, the sins which
gave him most offence.

I thought it time to change the subject. 'Where do you go
when you leave the city, Brother?'

'I go as far as the coast, to Woodspring Priory, where
Father Prior has sent word, asking me to preach to his flock.
But between here and there, I shall spread God's message
wherever men will heed it.' He leant towards me, the pale
blue eyes seeming to change colour until they were almost
black. 'Lead a pure and untainted life, Chapman. Resist the
temptations of the flesh.' He drew back abruptly and rose to
his feet. 'Thank you for your hospitality, Mistress Walker,
and God's blessing on this house.'

He wrapped himself in his thick frieze cloak, nodded in
my direction as Margaret and I respectfully rose to our feet,
laid a perfunctory hand on Elizabeth's fair head and then
was gone, letting in a short blast of icy wind as he first opened
and then closed the door behind him.

The atmosphere inside the cottage lightened perceptibly
with his departure. Even my mother-in-law felt it, although
she said gravely, 'A saintly man.'

I grunted and resumed my seat upon the floor beside my
daughter. It had often crossed my mind that saints caused as

much trouble in this life as sinners, but I did not speak my thought aloud. Margaret would have been scandalised at the idea and I needed her to be in a good mood. I was wondering how to break the news of my imminent departure, but she forestalled me, sitting down once more and regarding me with a shrewd, unwinking gaze.

'So,' she remarked, 'you're leaving tomorrow morning, early.'

I jumped. 'How . . . how did you know?'

'I told you this morning, you have been restless for days.'

'But – you couldn't have known exactly when I meant to go. I only made that particular decision a moment or two since.'

Margaret laughed. 'Roger, yours is not a difficult mind to read. I had only to watch your face when Brother Simeon was speaking of travelling on to realise that his example had fired you with an immediate desire to follow in his footsteps. It was, however, unlikely that you would be off without apprising me of your plans and taking a proper farewell of Elizabeth first. It therefore seemed improbable that you would leave today. But tomorrow, at first light, yes, then you will take your pack, your cloak, your cudgel and we shall not see you again for weeks. Months, maybe, if the wanderlust grips you.'

I looked at her with respect. 'You're a clever woman, Mother.'

She made a vigorous denial. 'I can't read and write as the monks taught you to do. I just use my common sense.'

I smiled and heaved myself up off the floor and on to the stool which the friar had vacated, slipping an arm about her still trim waist.

'I'm lucky to have you to look after Elizabeth for me,' I said. 'Don't ever think that I'm ungrateful, or sorry that I married Lillis.'

She sighed. 'No, not now that she is dead. No, no! That's not meant as a reproach. You didn't love her, and I know that what happened between you was not your fault alone. Lillis was always a wayward girl, determined to get what she wanted. And now,' Margaret added on a more practical note, 'I must see to it that your spare shirt is ready and take your boots to the cobbler by Redcliffe Church. You'll need a stout pair of soles on them in this weather, and Matt Cordwainer will mend them while I wait.'

I gave her a hug. 'You're far kinder to me than I have any right to expect. I shan't be gone more than a couple of weeks at the most.'

'Don't make promises that you might not be able to keep,' she admonished me, standing up. 'Give me your boots and I'll be off directly. While I'm gone, you can draw some water from the well and refill the barrel. Also replenish my store of logs from the common pile. Tie Elizabeth to her bed with this strip of linen so that she can't crawl into the fire when you're not here to watch her.'

She put on her cloak and hood, slipped her feet into their pattens and clattered away down the street. I was left with my deep sense of guilt and the rapidly mounting excitement which I always felt at the prospect of approaching freedom. And mixed with that excitement was apprehension, wondering where that freedom would lead me.

Chapter Two

Margaret had shown great foresight when she told me not to make promises that I might not wish to keep. I had already been on the road for ten days, and although I was less than a dozen miles from Bristol as the crow flies – and could indeed, with steady walking, have been home within the allotted span – I was still moving in a south-westerly direction towards the coast and the broad channel of water which is the Severn estuary.

In spite of the bitter cold and the iron-hard ground, I was savouring my freedom. I had not hurried, searching out every settlement, however small, within a two-day journey both north and south of the main pack-horse track. And everywhere I had been welcomed and fêted as one braving the hazardous weather to bring a little pleasure and distraction into people's lives. For the winter months are a dreary, dead time in isolated villages and hamlets, with nothing much for the inhabitants to do except work and sleep once the festivities of Plough Monday are over. Even on the larger farms and holdings the lambing season keeps the men busy out in the fields all day, and the women are glad to see a fresh face and hear city gossip, as well as being able to replenish their stocks of

15

needles, thread and other such haberdashery.

But that particular January there was another diversion for the good folk of north Somerset to talk about. Wherever I went, however remote the homestead, the name of Friar Simeon seemed to be on everyone's lips, either as having not long departed or as being expected within the next few days. Those who had just heard him preach were distinguished from their fellows by being somewhat more subdued in manner and paying a greater attention to evening and morning prayers. I could not help wondering how long this new-found piety would last; and, in those places where he had preceded my arrival by several days, I noted that the after-effects of his sermon were already beginning to fade. Nevertheless, his message was generally applauded by members of the older generation who deplored, as had my mother-in-law, declining moral standards amongst the young.

By noon on the tenth day the weather, which had improved somewhat during the past week, once again turned bitterly cold. It had been a morning of heavy frost, and the grass crunched under my feet as I descended a steep slope towards the huddle of cottages at the bottom. On the opposite side of the valley the round-shouldered hills sparkled here and there with rime as a thin winter sunshine, cold as steel, penetrated the gathering clouds. Now and then a spatter of rain stung my face, and above a distant swathe of woodland I could see the bitten-off stump of a rainbow, which sailors call a wind-dog.

The children of the village, those not needed by their elders to help in the home or out of doors, were keeping warm with a game of camping, the two 'armies' drawn up at either end of a stretch of level ground beside the stream whose bed was the valley floor. Their 'gauntlet' was an old shoe which had seen better days, judging by the way its sole gaped from its upper. But it proved to be an excellent flier as, with a shouted challenge, it was hurled by the captain of one side high over the heads of his opponents, to land in the stunted scrub and whin behind them. And while the 'enemy' searched desperately to retrieve the token, their numbers rapidly diminished as they were taken 'prisoner' and dragged off to the other end of the field. At last, however, the shoe was discovered and flung back with a cry of triumph, to embed itself in a clump of willows growing close to the bank. The challenge was thus reversed, and while I watched, the 'enemy' managed to recover several of its own side and take captive a couple of their opponents as well. I smiled to myself, recalling the many games of camping played in my youth, but I could not wait to see which side was victorious. With sufficiently skilful players the business of capturing all the other team might last for hours.

The goodwives of this isolated community were as warmly welcoming as their sisters had been elsewhere, and so overpowering was their hospitality that I eventually found myself forced to refuse some of the food and drink being pressed upon me. I wondered briefly if I were sickening for one of those ailments so common in winter months, but there are, after all, only so many oatcakes and so many stoups of ale that anyone can eat and drink within a certain time. And after an hour or so I had reached my limit, reluctant as I was to say so.

The last place I visited was the home of the miller and his wife where I lingered unduly, eventually allowing myself to be persuaded to stop to dinner. I had intended to press forward while the weather held, for several of the village greybeards, country-wise in all such matters, had predicted snow within the next few hours, and before that happened I wished to find shelter where my presence would prove less of an embarrassment were I to be holed up there for many days. These people were poor, and the addition of an extra mouth to feed for more than a single meal would quickly deplete their store of winter provisions.

But the miller and his wife had a daughter, a pretty, dark-haired girl with sparkling black eyes and a buxom figure who, I was certain, must attract the local youths like bees to heather. She was the most attractive young woman I had seen for quite a while, and although there could not possibly be anything between us – apart from the accidental brushing of hands and touching of feet beneath the table – it was nevertheless a pleasure just to sit and watch her eager face bent over the contents of my pack. She fingered the ribbons longingly and tried to cajole her mother into buying one, but the goodwife was adamant in her refusal.

'We can't afford it, child, and that's a fact. And it's no good appealing to your father,' she added as the miller, dusty with flour, came in from the mill, ravenous for his dinner. 'He'll tell you the same.' And she glared threateningly at her husband, daring him to gainsay her authority.

The miller tousled his daughter's head regretfully, but tried to make the best of things.

'What occasions do you have, lass, for the wearing of

such finery? I doubt if that great lout, Mark Wilson, will think you any the prettier for a ribbon in your hair. He's besotted enough already.'

The girl looked so crestfallen that I pushed the bundle of ribbons towards her.

'Here, choose one,' I said. 'It will pay for my dinner.'

Her delight, and the more restrained but no less warmly expressed gratitude of her parents, amply rewarded me for the loss of the ribbon's value, even though she selected an expensive one of dark red silk which I had purchased from a Portuguese merchantman, anchored in the Backs, before I left Bristol. Moreover, the two bowls of fish stew (it being a Friday) which I ate, washed down by several cups of homemade ale, made up for any regrets I might have harboured for my impulsive gesture.

The two women were anxious for news of the outside world, and the information that I had been in London as late as last September was greeted with breathless inquiries regarding anything to do with the court. Had I ever seen the King? Or the Queen? Or any member of the royal family? What were the latest London fashions? Was it true that the women there painted their faces with white lead? At this point the miller snorted and remarked thickly through a mouthful of stew that much good it would do either of them to know the answers to such questions, but that did not deter his wife and daughter. The set of a sleeve, the shape of a bodice, the fall of a skirt were as meat and drink to them here, in their isolated little world.

I disclaimed any detailed knowledge of, or indeed any interest in, the subject of women's fashion; but as for the rest, and as with Brother Simeon, there was a great deal I could have told them had I been so minded. However, it was doubtful that they would have believed me even had I felt at liberty to do so. Instead, I satisfied their curiosity with a story about the Duke of Clarence who, sitting on a Commission of Oyer and Terminer in Westminster Hall, noticed that the Mayor had nodded off during the proceedings. My lord had thereupon observed jeeringly to the next witness, 'Speak softly, sir, for His Worship is asleep!' A remark which had caused near rioting in the streets.

'For no one, not the King himself, can insult the Mayor of London and get away with it. The Londoners won't stand for it. Their Mayor and Aldermen mean more to them than any member of the royal family, and the Corporation's dignity and rights are jealously guarded. In the end, the Duke had humbly to beg Mayor Owlgrave's pardon – but only after King Edward had intervened and ordered his brother to make his apologies.'

'They say there's little love lost between King Edward and the Lord Clarence,' the miller's wife put in. 'At least, that's the gossip that reaches our ears from passing travellers.'

I thought about this. At last I answered carefully, 'He surely doesn't have the regard for him that he does for Prince Richard, and he certainly doesn't trust him. But that's not surprising considering the number of times that Prince George has turned his coat. Yet the King has also forgiven him on an equal number of occasions, so I'd reckon he must be fond of him. Indeed, I'd say that there's a strong bond of affection between all three royal brothers.'

The miller laid down his spoon and looked thoughtfully at me across the table. 'You seem remarkably well informed for a chapman.'

I had grown so accustomed to this accusation that I had my answer ready and replied easily, 'No more than any other man who listens to alehouse tattle and is aware of what's happening in the world around him. I'm capable of drawing my own conclusions with the best of them, though they might not agree with those of Hob or Jack.'

Fortunately my host seemed happy with this explanation. He cut a slab of ewe's milk cheese and crammed it into his mouth, thus making any further conversation with him impossible for several minutes. I rose to my feet.

'I must be on my way,' I said, going to the door and glancing up at the sky. 'Judging by the position of the sun, it's less than an hour short of noon, and the days draw in so quickly at this time of year. How far is the nearest village to this, if I continue travelling westward?'

The miller's wife joined me at the door, but before she could make answer our attention was diverted by the sound of hoofs, and then two horses and their riders came splashing through the icy stream. The animals snorted, tossing their heads, their breath hanging on the air in clouds of steam. Feet slithered on the frozen grasses as the men drew rein and slid, shivering, to the ground.

They were both clothed in warm but modest homespun and wrapped against the cold in thick frieze cloaks. Their boots, although well worn, were of leather, come by, I guessed, at second or third-hand. Round, well-fed faces were at present nipped and pinched by the biting wind, but sturdy limbs and the beginning of a paunch on the shorter of the two suggested a master who nourished and looked after his servants. Both men were young, about my own age, and had the dark Celtic colouring of the Welsh, a common enough occurrence along the borders between England and Wales, where the two races have met and mingled for centuries. But when they spoke it was in the flat, rough-edged tones of their Saxon forefathers; true Wessex men.

The slightly older and thinner of the pair addressed the miller's wife.

'We're lookin' fer Friar Simeon. Has he been 'ere? We know 'im to be in these parts.'

It was the miller himself who answered, having joined us at the door.

'The friar were here more'n a week since. Why? Who wants t' know?'

The younger man said, 'Our mistress. She as is wife to Sir Hugh Cederwell. She wants to see the friar most urgent. We've instructions to ask him to come to my lady as soon as he can.'

The miller shrugged. 'Well, 'e ain't here, as I told you. Said he was bound fer Woodspring Priory, so I'd seek in that direction if I was you.'

The two men grunted their thanks and remounted, declining the goodwife's offer of a cup of ale.

'We'd best get on while the daylight lasts. It may take us some time to catch up with him if we've to ride all the way to the Priory.'

They again forded the stream, the horses' hoofs sending up a spray of iridescent drops which hung for a moment on the bright, clear air. I went back into the millhouse to collect my things.

'Who's Lady Cederwell?' I asked.

'Like they told you,' said Mistress Miller, helping me to gather up the rest of my wares and restore them to my pack, 'she's the wife of Sir Hugh Cederwell of Cederwell Manor. That lies some five, six miles west of here and within sight of the River Severn, or so I understand. I've never been that far myself, but,' she added proudly, 'I know people who have.'

'Ay, more fools they,' grunted the miller as he disappeared once more through the door leading into the mill.

'I don't know about that,' his wife sighed regretfully. 'Mark you, I'm not saying as I'd want to go as far as Cederwell Manor, for it's nought but a small place from what I gather. But Lynom Hall, now, I wouldn't mind seeing that. For it's the biggest house in these parts and closer to us than the other. And the Widow Lynom's a fine, handsome woman by all accounts. Red hair and not a trace of grey they say, even though she's past her prime.'

'Maybe she uses alkanet plant to colour it,' suggested her daughter. 'After all, when the roots are boiled the water's used to redden cheese. Why shouldn't it do the same for hair?'

But the miller's wife was unwilling to allow that here, in Somerset, a lady of birth and quality could be capable of practising such deception. In London or Bristol – well! The shrug of her shoulders implied that in those dens of vice and iniquity anything was possible; and while the foibles of city dwellers made excellent hearing over a plate of fish stew, they were not seriously to be considered as general practice among the more godly denizens of the countryside.

I wrapped myself in my cloak, hoisted my pack on to my shoulders and grasped my stout cudgel – my 'Plymouth cloak' as Devonshire people call it – firmly in my right hand.

'If you can give me some general direction towards Lynom Hall,' I said, 'I should be grateful. Mistress Lynom sounds as if she might be a lady interested in buying my wares. Lady Cederwell, also.'

The miller's wife pursed her lips. 'The Widow Lynom would probably welcome your arrival, for she sounds to be an open-handed lady when it comes to her personal adornment. I've heard her described as vain. But as for Lady Cederwell, you mayn't be so lucky there. Common report says she's a very pious young woman, a devout daughter of the Church, more often to be found at her prie-dieu than staring at her reflection in a mirror.'

'Well,' I answered philosophically, 'the female members of her household may be in need of needles and thread or twine or laces. And as you saw, I have some very good pewter knives and spoons.'

'True.' The goodwife considered for a moment, then turned to her daughter. 'Joanna, I've no need of you here for a while. Put on your cloak and pattens and accompany the chapman back to the main track. Show him which way to take at the crossroads; the path to Lynom.'

'There's no call to send the child out on such a day,' I protested, but was overruled by both mother and daughter.

'I shall be glad of the air,' Joanna Miller said, slipping her feet into wooden clogs. She flung a serviceable woollen cloak about her slender figure and pulled up the hood.

It was by now bitterly cold, too cold in fact for snow but promising an extremely sharp frost by the following morning. Joanna trod composedly by my side as we ascended the slope out of the valley, not needing my proffered arm and unhampered by her heavy-soled shoes. Away from the mill she seemed less of a girl and more of a woman; and when she told me that she was but fifteen years of age and the only child, I realised that the miller and his wife must have come late to the blessings of parenthood. I also realised that while they struggled against the temptation to be too doting a mother and father, Joanna possibly found it rewarding to play the little girl for their benefit.

We talked desultorily of this and that until we reached the summit of the hill and had walked a short distance along the pack-horse track to the crossroads. Here Joanna pointed out the path to Lynom Hall and prepared to leave me. Just before she did so, however, she gave a knowing little smile and said, 'You may meet Sir Hugh Cederwell there.'

'At Lynom Hall?' I queried, puzzled.

She nodded and smiled her cat-like smile. 'Gossip has it that the widow is his mistress, although my mother would be angry to hear me admit it.'

'Indeed,' was all that I could think of to say. I stood there looking at her, feeling as I so often did in the presence of women, bewildered and rather stupid. For it has been my experience throughout life that whereas a man is always himself whoever he may be with, a woman is capable of changing her character to suit her mood or the person she is confronting at that present.

'Indeed, indeed,' she mocked with a little laugh, sending me an enigmatic glance from beneath the close-drawn hood which framed her delicate features. Then she turned and vanished around a bend in the track beyond which was the narrow, barely discernible path which led down into the valley. I looked after her for a moment before swinging on my heel and starting along the road in front of me.

I walked for the next hour without meeting anyone or hearing any human voice other than my own, as I whistled in my usual tuneless fashion to keep up my spirits. It became increasingly colder as the afternoon wore on and the shadows lengthened, and with the absence of habitation I became anxious as to where I should spend the night. It was necessary to get under cover before darkness fell, and for the first time since leaving the shelter of my mother-in-law's roof I questioned the wisdom of this winter expedition. Had I for once confused my desire for freedom, my dislike of being confined within four walls, with that sense of being used by God for His Divine Purpose? Had there, I wondered, shivering and drawing my cloak tighter about me, ever really been any purpose other than my own desire to escape from the restrictions and rules imposed by living in close proximity to other people? Was I, as my mother had often accused me of being, selfish? Did I search for excuses to ignore the claims which those nearest to me had upon my time and person? I could find no answer.

Against an overcast sky the leafless branches of the trees raised knotted arms in a silent, defiant gesture, and overall was that peculiar soundlessness which I could remember from winter days in my youth, around Wells. To the north of the track the distant vista of hills hung like a dirty grey shroud and were devoid of any signs of life. All the animals had been driven indoors to share the warmth of smoking turf fires with their owners.

The track broadened out a little and another opened up on my left. I paused, staring along it as far as I could see, wondering where it led and whether I was meant to go that way or no. But Joanna Miller had made no mention of deviating from my present path, and as this second track plainly ran southwards through thick wood and scrubland, I decided to proceed straight ahead, but I wished that I could meet with some other foolhardy traveller, out and about his business on such an unpleasant afternoon.

Almost immediately my wish was granted as the rattle of wheels and the clop of horse's hoofs sounded behind me. I turned my head to see a cart approaching, a solid brown cob harnessed between its shafts, carrying a load of firewood. The driver was bunched forward over the reins, his head well down and concealed beneath its hood, his hands mottled red and blue by the cold. I stepped out almost into the middle of the track and hailed him, hoping for a ride, but either he did not hear me or he was too intent on getting home to stop and help a stranger. Whichever it was, he chose that moment to flick the reins and increase his speed, forcing me to step back hurriedly. I trod on a loose stone at the side of the path and went down heavily, twisting my left foot beneath me as I did so.

For several minutes I was unable to move, conscious of nothing but the pain in my ankle. When at last this was bearable enough for me to drag myself upright with the aid of my cudgel, which by the grace of God had fallen close to my hand, I let rip with all the blasphemies at my command, cursing the retreating form of the carter. Then having somewhat relieved my feelings, I gingerly put my left foot to the ground and tested my weight on the ankle. A searing pain shot up my leg, causing me to swear yet again with even greater fluency than before. I glanced wildly around me, wondering how far it was to the nearest habitation.

And then I saw it, a boulder house built into the steep bank on the right of the track some yards ahead of me, a thin wisp of smoke spiralling through the hole in the heather-thatched roof. I dragged myself the short distance and had to stoop almost double, such was my height, to get my head beneath the lintel-stone of the narrow doorway. Inside, the hovel was so dark that even the single rushlight was momentarily invisible to me and I failed to realise that the floor was several inches below the level of the road. Consequently I missed my footing and pitched forward on my face. As the bare, beaten earth came up to meet me, the red-hot pain once more shot up my leg and I lay there, writhing and groaning in agony.

Chapter Three

I must have lost consciousness for a moment, because the next thing I knew I was lying on my back with a face swimming above me, illuminated by the pallid glow of a rushlight. It was a narrow, etiolated face, with very pale blue eyes and lashes so fair that they were almost white. The impression of the skull was very strong beneath the paper-thin skin and a few tufts and strands of hair, as colourless as the eyelashes, grew from the balding pate. Yet those seemingly fleshless arms needed to have a greater strength than their appearance suggested in order to have shifted my bulk.

I lifted myself on to my elbows and tried to get up, but immediately my left leg protested and I sank back with a groan.

'Still! Still!' the man ordered in a hoarse voice which barely rose above a whisper. 'Wait.'

He turned, setting down the rushlight and its holder on the ground. Then with a little help from me, he pulled off my left boot and began gently to prod the ankle, grunting softly to himself as he did so. At last he raised his head.

'Swollen,' he said. 'Bone not broken. Rest two days. Maybe three. All right then.'

He picked up the rushlight again, holding it above his head, and so perilously close to birch boughs which supported the heather thatching that I cried out in alarm. He seemed unperturbed however, pointing with his free hand to the farther wall. I twisted my body to look behind me and, my eyes now having grown accustomed to the darkness, I saw a bed of dried straw in one part of the semi-circular embrasure dug out from the bank.

'You lie there,' my rescuer invited.

And while I dragged my painful way across the floor, he gathered up my pack and cudgel, placing them carefully in a corner. After that, he made his way to his storage shelves, three of them, also cut out of the bank, one above the other. From the top one he took a small earthenware pot; then indicating to me that I should remove my jerkin and hose – a feat I was unable to accomplish without his assistance – he knelt beside me, dipped his fingers into the jar and began to rub some of its contents into my burning flesh. I instantly recognised the salve from its smell. My mother used to make it, a mixture of rue, borage and honey; an ointment invaluable for reducing swelling. My ankle began to feel better almost at once.

'What's your name?' I asked.

He did not answer immediately, and I was just beginning to wonder if he had heard me when he glanced up and muttered briefly, 'Ulnoth.'

'That's a Saxon name,' I said.

'Yes. Saxon,' he repeated.

'And what was your father's name?'

After another silence he grunted, 'Wolf. Me Ulnoth Wolfsson.'

I nodded. 'And do you have children?'

There was yet further delay before he answered, as if it took him a while to absorb and understand words. But at last he muttered, 'No. No *kinder*. No Ulnothsson. No Ulnothsdaughter.'

I had met one or two people like him before on my travels. Although it was now many hundreds of years since our Norman masters had conquered us, and although in general Saxon and Norman blood had become so mixed that only the bastard word 'English' would do to describe our race, here and there, in isolated places, could still be found true descendants of the Saxon tribes.

When he had finished attending to my ankle, Ulnoth helped me back into my clothes before gathering up an armful of brushwood from a pile stacked against one of the outer stone walls. After rekindling the fire on the hearth, he erected an old and rickety tripod from which he suspended an equally ancient iron pot, seemingly already filled with water from the rill which trickled sluggishly down the bank outside. Into this he threw various dried herbs, which hung in branches from the ceiling, followed by the dismembered carcass of a rabbit taken from his larder, a hole in the freezing ground.

The resulting stew was delicious, and I swallowed it down along with any scruples I might have had about eating meat on a Friday. I suspected that my host did not even know which day of the week it was, but I was wrong. When we had both eaten our fill – in my case three bowls of stew to

31

his one – Ulnoth took the dregs of home-brewed mead with which we had washed down our meal, and poured them as a libation on the threshold of the hut.

'For Frig,' he said, noticing my curious stare. 'Today Frig's day.'

Of course. Frig, mother of the Nordic gods. And the wife of Woden? I didn't know. I couldn't remember. Furthermore, I did not at that moment care. My eyes were beginning to close and my body felt heavy. The straw bed on which I lay, though verminous, was warm, and the salve had soothed away the worst of my pain. Before I knew it, I was sound asleep.

Ulnoth proved to be right. My ankle had sustained no serious injury; I had merely given it a bad wrench when I fell. Under his gentle ministrations it was better within two days, but that bringing us to the Sabbath, I waited until the following day and then lingered one more, in order to make sure that I was really fit to continue my journey. But on Tuesday – or, as Ulnoth called it, Tiuw's day, Tiuw being the ancient god of war – I could tarry no longer. For one thing I was rapidly eating my host out of house and home, and for another the silence and inactivity were becoming oppressive.

The sparseness of Ulnoth's conversation, the fact that he was obviously unaccustomed to using words fluently, had at first made me believe him a simpleton, but as time wore on I realised that this was not so. One day, talking idly to him about my visit to the neighbouring village and not certain whether he were listening or no, he suddenly interrupted me with, 'Miller. You visit mill.'

'How do you know that?' I asked him.

For answer, he put out a hand and brushed my sleeve. Then, holding the rushlight closer, he showed me the tips of his fingers which were lightly powdered with flour. On another occasion he said, 'Your wife dead.' It was not a question, and once again I demanded how he came to his conclusion.

He smiled his faint smile. 'You speak of child. Daughter. You speak of mother. Not speak of woman. Why?' He shrugged his thin shoulders. 'Because dead.'

It was, I suppose, something that anyone might have worked out for himself, but in Ulnoth I had not expected such powers of deduction, for he mingled hardly at all with his fellow men. This was plain from the way he shrank back into the farthest recesses of the house and waved me to silence whenever any traffic passed on the road. It was very light at that time of year, but only that morning, we had already heard the slap of shoes on the iron-hard ground and, a little later, the clop of hoofs as someone rode by in the opposite direction. He lived on small animals and birds which he trapped in the woods, but he attended to his snares and filled his water pots at the rill very early in the day, before anybody else was about.

But when he was forced into company, as he had been into mine, he revealed a kindliness and sweetness of disposition often found lacking in a lot of people who have more to be grateful for than he. He did not forgo companionship because he doubted others – on the contrary, I thought him if anything too trusting – but because solitude was his way of life. I managed to prise out of him that his parents had died 'long, long time gone'; probably, I surmised, when he was still a child. There was no means of telling how old Ulnoth really was, and it was likely that he was younger than he looked. Nevertheless, he had spent many years on his own, and it was only natural that after all that while he should prefer it.

Before I said my farewells I asked for directions to Lynom Hall. Ulnoth led me outside and pointed back along the track, the way I had come four days earlier.

'Road,' he said, pointing to the right, and I recalled that other track which, as I approached the boulder house, had branched off to my left. 'There along.'

I thanked him for all he had done, my gratitude the deeper because he had refused to accept any payment from me, either in money or in goods from my pack.

'What need?' he had asked, spreading wide his skeletal hands. And indeed, I could see that by his standards he wanted for nothing. Nature and his own ingenuity provided everything, including homemade needles and thread.

I embraced him, hoping that I might perhaps claim him as a friend; but I had gone only a yard or two along the track when, turning to glance over my shoulder, I found the road behind me already empty. Ulnoth had not waited to see me on my way, but scuttled back into his house like a frightened coney into its burrow. I smiled to myself with a little shake of my head, then set out, my left ankle as strong as ever, to discover Lynom Hall.

It was as cold, if not colder than it had been on Friday, and I was thankful not only for my thick, hooded frieze cloak, but also for my leather jerkin, lined with scarlet, which a widow woman had parted with some years earlier in exchange for necessaries from my pack.

I retraced my steps to that other, south-bound track and turned the corner, searching the landscape ahead of me for any sign of habitation. But the last in a range of hillocks obscured the view, causing the path to swerve first right and then left as it curled around its base. Once this double bend had been negotiated however, a broad plain opened up in front of me, and the sharp, salt tang of the sea was borne inland on the wind. In the near distance I could see the outbuildings of what promised to be a sizeable building and which I thought must certainly be Lynom Hall.

And so it proved. A moated, stone-built house with a large undercroft and surrounded by bakery, dairy and laundry, chapel, stables and byre could be no other. A wooden drawbridge, wide enough for the passage of a large wagon, spanned a moat which I discovered to be very deep and filled with brackish water. Two men, who were busy carrying hay from the undercroft to the stables, gave me a cursory glance as I crossed it.

'Is your mistress at home?' I called.

One said, 'She is, but you'd best not disturb her, Chapman, at this present,' and looked at his companion and sniggered. There was plainly some significance in the remark.

'Then maybe I can see the housekeeper or the cook or one of the maids,' I suggested. 'Any woman of the household will do. I've plenty still in my pack to interest her.'

The man who had so far not spoken put down the sheaf of straw he was humping.

'I daresay the old lady 'ud be glad to see you,' he admitted, and his fellow nodded in agreement.

'Always glad to see anyone, she is. Finds the days hang heavy. Well, they do when you're old and confined to the house I reckon.' He eyed me up and down, his head tilted consideringly to one side. Wisps of red hair protruded from beneath his hood. 'You're a big, stout-looking lad. Give us a hand with this hay and we'll introduce you to the housekeeper ourselves, with a recommendation that she takes you up to see Dame Judith. What's your name?'

I told them, and in return learned that the red-haired man was called Hamon and the other Jasper. I laid down my pack and stick, seized a bale of hay and carried it easily enough into the stables. A fine red chestnut with a pale mane and tail fixed me with a beady eye and blew gustily through its nostrils as I entered.

'Better leave Belle Amie to us,' Hamon said over his shoulder. 'The mare's Mistress Lynom's pride and joy, but to my mind she's a nasty nature. Feed the cob and Jessamine there.' He indicated a raw-boned grey. 'They're both quiet and gentle.'

'What about him?' Jasper demanded with a jerk of his head towards a big handsome black with white stockings and a white blaze on its forehead. 'Did we ought perhaps—?'

'Nah!' Hamon interrupted decisively. 'Why should we waste our winter fodder on a stranger? He'll have hay enough waiting for him in his own stable. Great overfed brute!'

'The mistress might expect it,' Jasper demurred. 'How long's he going to be here?'

Hamon gave a ribald chuckle. 'How do I know? As long as his master, and how long's that? In such circumstances, there's no saying.' And they both laughed immoderately, nudging one another in the ribs.

I made no inquiries as to their meaning, judging it wisest to remain ignorant, but half guessing at the truth. Had not Joanna Miller informed me that I might meet Sir Hugh Cederwell at Lynom Hall? 'Gossip has it that the widow is his mistress.' But if that were indeed the case, the less I knew about this illicit liaison the better. I hoped, the weather holding, to travel as far as Cederwell Manor.

When the horses had been fed, Jasper dropping a little hay into the black's manger while his companion wasn't looking, and I had again taken up my pack and cudgel, the two men led me around to the back of the house and into the kitchen. In contrast to the extreme cold outside, the heat in there was almost overpowering, emanating from a huge fire on the central hearth and a number of ovens set into the thick stone walls. A big woman in a gown of grey burrel and a linen coif and apron, wielding a large ladle as if it were her wand of office, as in a way I suppose it was, dominated the room and sent the kitchen-maids scurrying in all directions to carry out her orders.

'What are you two great oafs doing in my kitchen?' she demanded, when she saw Hamon and Jasper. 'Out, before you carry the muck from the yard and stables all over my swept and scrubbed floor!'

'Here's a chapman,' Hamon said sulkily, 'come hawking his wares. We thought the old lady might be glad of his company.'

I stepped forward with meekly lowered eyes for inspection by this she-dragon, who gave me a basilisk stare. But after a moment her expression softened somewhat and she nodded.

'Very well.' Her blue eyes narrowed. 'Are you hungry, my lad?' And when I assured her that I was, she instructed a tow-headed girl to give me one of the apple pasties which were cooling on a marble slab close to the half-open door. 'Best give him the large size with a frame like his.'

The child shovelled a pasty on to a wooden platter and handed it to me with a self-conscious giggle. Hamon and Jasper immediately began to moan that good looks and a fine physique gave a man an unfair advantage over his fellows.

'Oh . . . give them a pasty apiece, Bet,' the cook instructed at last, pursing her lips in exasperation. 'But you eat them outside, the pair of you. You reek of horses!'

The two men seemed to take no offence at her tone but, grinning broadly, accepted their apple pasties from Bet's hands and vanished through the kitchen doorway. I was allowed to eat mine in peace, sitting beside the fire and warming my chilled bones by its leaping flames. When I had finished, not even a crumb of pastry remaining, Bet was told to conduct me to Dame Judith.

'The late master's mother,' the cook explained, basting a couple of fat chickens which were roasting on the spit, 'complains of being neglected since her son died, three years since. And it's true that there's not much love lost between her and the mistress. But,' she added judiciously, 'old people do tend to exaggerate their hardships in my experience.'

'Is Dame Judith upstairs or down?' asked Bet, and was

told that the old lady was in the solar.

She led me out of the kitchen and into a narrow passageway where the draughts from open doors lifted the rushes on the flagstones; and the sudden chill, after the heat we had just left, made us both shiver. As I followed Bet, I could see into the various rooms on the opposite side of the corridor, the counting-house, justice room and parlour, all their windows facing frontwards to the track beyond the moat. The reason I was able to see this was because the shutters in the parlour had been set wide in spite of the inclement weather, and Lynom Hall had no surrounding walls for protection. In this remote corner of the world they plainly did not fear attacks from their neighbours.

'Someone in this house is fond of fresh air,' I remarked to Bet as she preceded me up a twisting staircase.

'Oh, that's the old mistress,' she said with another giggle. 'She don't seem to feel the cold, not even when it's bitter. Leastways, she says she don't, but it's my belief she's just nosy. She likes to sit by the window and look out to see what's going on. Makes the young mistress fair mad, I can tell you. I'd best close them shutters when I come down again, before she discovers they've been opened. Dame Judith was in the parlour earlier,' she added by way of explanation.

At the top of the stairs, I was conducted into the solar, as dank and chilly on this bleak winter's day as the rest of the house. But it was a comfortable room with many indications of wealth from the candelabra of latten tin, supporting a number of pure wax candles, to the tapestries which decorated the walls and the cushions strewn across the window seat. Two of the windows were glazed – a greater rarity then than nowadays, when you, my children, take so many of these modern luxuries for granted – and a third had panes of horn. A fourth window of stretched and oiled linen had been set wide to the elements. Bet at once hurried across and closed it.

'You d' know what the mistress says about openin' windows this weather, Dame Judith,' she scolded. 'You'll catch yer death, you will surely.'

The upright old woman, seated in a chair near the fire, sniffed scornfully.

'And what if I do, pray? That's what she hopes will happen. The lying jade just pretends to be concerned about me, but nothing would suit her better than to be rid of me. Where is she, eh? Not a soul's been next nor nigh me since I was brought up here earlier this morning. What's she up to? Why hasn't she been to see me?'

'The mistress is busy,' Bet answered, colouring. 'Look, here's a chapman come selling his wares. I've brought 'im to visit you.'

Dame Judith peered at me with short-sighted, faded blue eyes, but for the moment evinced no further interest.

'Don't change the subject,' she ordered Bet sternly. 'You tell my daughter-in-law to come and see me.' She added to the network of wrinkles already lining her face by screwing it up in disgust. 'I know what she's at, the harlot! She may think she's pulling the wool over my eyes, but you can tell her that she ain't. I wasn't born last September! That Sir Hugh Cederwell's here again. It's no use your denying it, girl! I saw him ride in this morning not long after breakfast, while I was still downstairs in the parlour.' She gave a sudden grin, grinding her toothless gums together. 'I see a lot of things that people don't reckon on me seeing.'

'That's 'cause you sits with the shutters wide open,' Bet reprimanded the old lady. She beckoned me forward. 'Here's the chapman, like I told you. You talk to 'im fer a bit and look at what 'e's got to sell you.'

Bet whisked herself out of the solar before Dame Judith could protest or hinder her further. I was left alone with this indomitable old lady whose fragility made me feel even gawkier and more overgrown than usual. In her grey gown and slippers, untidy locks of white hair pushing out from beneath her hood, she was like a wisp of smoke waiting to be blown away by the first puff of wind. She eyed me sharply.

'They think I don't know what goes on in this house,' she snorted. 'But I do. Oh yes, I do indeed. That Sir Hugh Cederwell! Lovely young wife by all accounts, but he prefers a maturer woman with more experience between the sheets.' I felt the blood steal up under my skin. Dame Judith saw it and laughed. 'Embarrass you, do I? Why does a little plain speaking make you uncomfortable? I'm sure a good-looking lad such as you is no virgin, and you must have exchanged plenty of ribaldry in the alehouses and taverns. But you don't care to hear it on a woman's lips, is that it? Ah well! I shouldn't chide you. It's good to know that you hold womankind in such esteem. So!' She clapped her dry, fleshless hands together. 'Show me your wares. I promise I'll buy something, even if I don't really want it. It'll be payment for your time and company, which are the two things I chiefly need.'

She was seated in a high, carved armchair and instructed

me to draw up a flat-topped oaken coffer which stood against one wall. It would serve, she said, as a table on which to display my goods. But when I had spread them out, she showed no immediate inclination to look them over, but folded her hands in her lap, leant back in her chair and began to reminisce about her youth; a youth spent, as a young and beautiful woman, at King Henry's court before what she called 'all the troubles and upheavals'.

'From time to time he was completely mad, poor man, like his grandsire, the French king that his father beat at Agincourt. And when he wasn't mad, he was on his knees praying, or exhorting all us women to cover our breasts. Low-cut gowns, he said, were the work of the devil. And Queen Margaret wearing the most daring of any of us! When he first saw his son, Prince Edward, him who was killed a few years back at Tewkesbury, he said the boy must be the child of the Holy Ghost.' Dame Judith cackled with amusement. 'The child of the Earl of Wiltshire or of Somerset more like! At least, that's what the rest of us thought. We—'

The door of the solar opened and the old lady broke off her narrative at once, snapping her jaws together like a pair of tongs cracking nuts. An authoritative voice demanded, 'Mother, what are you up to? Who is this man? And what is he doing in the solar?'

Chapter Four

Dame Judith drew herself up to her full height – not an easy thing to do whilst sitting down, but the old lady managed to give that impression – and said coldly, 'Bet brought this chapman to see me. She thought I might wish to purchase some of his goods.'

'Bet has no right to think,' was the terse response as the mistress of the house advanced further into the room.

The Widow Lynom was indeed, as the miller's wife had said, a fine woman with a high, broad forehead, slate-blue eyes, a long and impressively straight nose and a full, voluptuous mouth. In spite of this there was a hardness about the features which, to my mind at least, prevented her from being truly handsome. She wore a red woollen gown trimmed with squirrel fur at neck and wrists, and caught around her waist by a green leather belt studded with jewels. Her slender fingers were heavily beringed, but of the red hair, which might or might not be dyed with alkanet, there was no sign, all being concealed beneath a hood of fine, crisp lawn. Her skin was carefully whitened, her lips stained with a salve made from the distillation of strawberry juice – I was by now growing wise in the wiles and deceptions of women – and she carried herself well, as befitted someone born to command. Yet nothing could disguise the fact that she would never see forty again. Nevertheless, I could guess her attraction for any man tied to a sober and pious wife, however young. There was a raffish gleam in the blue eyes which suggested that she would not be niggardly with her sexual favours.

'Oh, I'm fully aware that you'd deny me anything that gives me pleasure,' Dame Judith snapped, her bony cheeks growing pink with outrage. 'Fortunately I have a few friends left in the household.' She turned to me. 'You needn't think I was treated like this when my son was alive. Then I was accorded all the respect that is my due.'

The widow sighed and tapped one leather-shod foot in exasperation.

'Don't be mendacious, Mother! You know very well that no one denies you anything you wish. We wouldn't be so foolish, knowing the tantrums we'd be subjected to if you were thwarted.'

'Tantrums is it?' Dame Judith was fairly spitting with annoyance. 'I'd have you know, Chapman, that I'm one of the most reasonable, sweet-tempered women living, but what I have to endure would try the patience of a saint!' The widow raised her eyes ceilingwards and appeared to be praying for strength, but her mother-in-law ignored her. 'For one thing, why am I forced to remove up here every morning instead of being allowed to stay downstairs in the parlour, where I can at least look out of the window and watch who's passing on the road? Not,' she grumbled, 'that there's much traffic at this time of year. The only people I saw today were a holy man and a carter with a load of tree trunks bound for the sawmill. Oh yes, and the blacksmith, accompanied by a young girl muffled to the eyes and who looked to me as if she were keeping a tryst of some sort with him.' The old woman's sharp nose quivered. 'I must get Bet to discover if he's courting. But who could it be from hereabouts?' She tittered. 'Aren't I a nosy old woman?'

'You're brought up here to the solar, Mother,' the Widow Lynom interrupted forcefully, 'for that very reason; to stop you sitting with the parlour shutters wide open and catching your death of cold. In the summer you may stop there as long as you wish, and well you know it, so don't pretend that I ill treat you.' For the first time since entering the room she turned to look at me properly, and her forbidding gaze softened slightly. 'Well, Chapman, as you're here, you can show us both what you have to sell. We don't often get pedlars around in the depth of winter. You must be a hardy young fellow to be on the road in January.'

Dame Judith let out an unpleasant cackle. 'You've discovered he's both young and good-looking, have you, Ursula? You want to be careful, my girl! What if Sir Hugh found out that you've a wandering eye?'

Her daughter-in-law flushed scarlet. 'I don't know what you're talking about, Mother. What has it to do with Sir Hugh, pray? He has a wife of his own to look after.'

The older woman sniffed derisively. 'Little Mistress Good and Saintly. Well, he's not likely to have any worries concerning *her* on that head. But he'd do well to look to his own conduct – and to that of his precious son – if he wants to escape trouble in his household. Jeanette Cederwell's not one to brook misconduct lightly.'

Contrary to all expectations, I began to feel sorry for Ursula Lynom, so much the victim of her mother-in-law's scathing tongue. I tried to divert the old lady's attention.

'I didn't think, from what I've been told, that Lady Cederwell is old enough to have a grown son.'

'Lord bless you, he ain't her child! Jeanette's only two years older than Maurice. No, no! He's the son of Sir Hugh's first wife, who died when he was born.' Dame Judith leaned back in her chair and smiled expansively, delighted with the chance to gossip. 'We all thought Sir Hugh was going to remain a widower for life – or until such time as he could gain his heart's desire.' Here, she stole a sideways glance at her daughter-in-law, but the widow began to examine my goods with exaggerated care. The dame continued, 'But then, nigh on six years ago, he went up country to visit a cousin of his who lives in the neighbourhood of Gloucester, and came back married to a child young enough to be his daughter; a wool heiress recently orphaned.' The old woman's smile broadened into a malicious grin. 'Wealthy, but not so wealthy as Ursula here became when my poor son, Anthony, died two years later.' She threw up her head and gave a high-pitched whinny of mirth.

I rapidly reassessed my ideas of Sir Hugh Cederwell. I realised now that he must be roughly the same age as Ursula Lynom.

'That will do now, Mother.' The younger woman turned away abruptly. 'Buy what you want from the chapman and then you must sleep for half an hour before your dinner.'

'I'm not a child to be ordered around,' Dame Judith

snapped. She added spitefully, 'I was mistress in this house long before you.'

Ursula Lynom sighed. 'A fact of which you are never tired of reminding me. Nevertheless, you will do well to remember that it is *I* who am in charge here now.' There was the slightest undertone of menace, and I saw the old lady suddenly wither and withdraw into herself. My sympathies, which had been in a constant state of flux, somersaulted back to her. I should have known, though, that she was fully capable of standing up for herself.

After only a momentary silence, she counter-attacked with, 'Sir Hugh must have left early this morning. I hadn't expected to see you until noon.'

Colour once more tinged the widow's cheeks, but she answered calmly, 'We had completed our business. He has advised me against buying the extra land to the south of the eastern pasture.'

Dame Judith let out a sound like the hoot of an owl. 'Business, she says! There's only one kind of business you and Hugh Cederwell carry on, and it's got nothing to do with land south, north or west of the eastern pasture!' And while her daughter-in-law struggled to find her breath, the older woman continued, 'A pretty hash the pair of you have made of your lives between you! When he and Anthony went a-courting you, twenty-odd years and more ago, you chose my lad, even though it was plain to everyone but yourself that you were in love with Hugh. And as for him, he's as big a fool as you are. Having lost his own wife after only a year of marriage, he waits fifteen more in the hope that you might one day be free, only to shackle himself to a child almost young enough to be his daughter, a mere twenty-two months before Anthony succumbs to a putrid fever. Bunglers, both of you!'

The widow's face was by now scarlet with rage, and I couldn't altogether blame her. Dame Judith should not have aired the family linen before a passing stranger, as Mistress Lynom now roundly told her.

'You're a prattling, meddling, evil old shrew who deserves a ducking! How *dare* you discuss my affairs like this in front of a pedlar! You have a loose tongue, and one day it will get you into serious trouble.' She bent down, breathing hard and short, advancing her congested face to within an inch of the older woman's. 'It could even be the death of you, so be careful.' I must have made an inarticulate sound of protest, for the widow straightened herself abruptly, realising how her words might be interpreted. 'What I mean is,' she floundered, 'you can't gossip about people without making enemies, and sitting by that open window of a morning you see too much of your neighbours' business.'

It was a lame apology for her threatening attitude and had no relevance to Dame Judith's recent revelations. The old lady looked cowed, however, and seemed anxious to make her peace.

'I know, I know,' she mumbled. 'My tongue runs away with me at times. But the chapman won't pass on what he's heard, will you, lad? You don't appear to me to be the chattering kind.'

'Mistress Lynom's affairs are none of mine,' I answered briskly. 'I promise I shan't repeat anything you've said.'

'There you are, Ursula,' her mother-in-law pleaded. 'I

can recognise a good man when I see one, so you'll let him stop and talk to me for a while, won't you? You know how starved of company and news of the outside world we are during the winter months.'

I could tell from the expression on Ursula Lynom's face that she would have liked to order me off the manor at once, but she was sensible enough to see that such conduct might antagonise me into breaking my word. So she said, with as much grace as she could muster, 'You're welcome to remain with my mother-in-law for a little, Chapman, and afterwards you may go to the kitchen and tell Jane Cook to give you some dinner.' Her eyes strayed to the goods displayed on the top of the coffer, coming to rest on a set of silver buttons, inlaid with mother-of-pearl. One long, slender hand reached out and fingered them. 'They're beautiful. I'll have them whatever their price. You may go to the counting-house when you've finished here and collect your money.'

The door of the solar closed behind her and Dame Judith let out a sigh of relief.

'She'll give those buttons to Hugh Cederwell,' she mourned, and then, in childlike fashion, clapped a scrawny hand over her mouth. 'There I go again. She's right to be angry with me, you know, although I wouldn't give her the satisfaction of admitting it. My tongue does run away with me, but gossiping's my only pleasure nowadays. It's hard, Chapman, being a dependant in a house where you once wore the keys at your belt and had the running of it all.'

I agreed that indeed it must be, and placed several items which I thought she might like immediately in front of her, in order to distract her mind from its woes. In the end, she bought a pair of enamelled girdle tags and a length of fine lace, but that was all, suddenly losing interest in the proceedings. Like all old people she tired swiftly and easily, falling asleep without warning. Quietly, so as not to disturb her, I packed away the rest of my wares, took what had been purchased downstairs to the counting-house, where the household treasurer paid me my dues, and then made my way back to the kitchen.

'Where do you go from here?' Bet asked as we finished the stewed mutton and apple pasties which made up the lesser servants' dinner. (The chickens had been served in the dining hall, leaving the tantalising smell of onions and sage and cinnamon to linger on in the kitchen.)

'I hope to get as far as Cederwell Manor, where I shall beg a fireside corner for the night. How far would you reckon it to be from here?'

'Two mile. Maybe more,' Bet said with a stifled giggle. 'An hour's good walking.'

The other three kitchen-maids and the pot-boy were also suppressing sniggers which the mention of Cederwell Manor had prompted, one eye on the cook as if fearful that she might admonish them. But although she failed to join in their general merriment, she did no more than remain aloof.

'You'd better get started as soon as you've eaten, Chapman,' she advised. 'It'll take you more'n an hour at a steady pace, and the ground's treacherous at this season. Moreover, snow's been threatening all day and I reckon it'll start to fall before evening.' She went to the kitchen door and stared out. 'Sky's full of it. Grey as a shroud. When it does come, it's going to be heavy.'

'How do I get there? To Cederwell Manor?'

'Where'd you come from? North from Woodspring? This is the Woodspring road.'

I shook my head. 'No, south from the main pack-horse track which runs along the high ground from Bristol to the mouth of the Severn.'

Jane Cook came back and sat down again at the kitchen table.

'Then retrace your steps to the junction of the two roads and turn westwards when you get there. Keep walking and you're bound, sooner or later, to arrive at the manor. But a word of warning.' She cupped her chin in her hands. 'Don't ask for Lady Cederwell. She'll not be interested in any fripperies you might be hoping to sell. I'm told she wears a plain wooden cross on a string about her neck and that is her only adornment. As for household necessaries, you might as well deal directly with Sir Hugh's housekeeper, Phillipa Talke, who's run the manor for him since Master Maurice was born and left motherless, the poor little lamb.'

Bet sucked her fingers clean of the last vestiges of food.

'My cousin, Audrey Lambspringe – who's maid to Lady Cederwell,' she added for my benefit, ' – says Mistress Talke was hoping to marry Sir Hugh herself one day.'

Jane Cook snorted but, somewhat to my surprise, did not discourage this idle chatter. But then she, too, I supposed, must find winter in such an isolated homestead as dull as everyone else.

One of the other kitchen-maids observed with a giggle, 'She's waited a mighty long time then with nothin' t' show fer it. An' now 'e's married again.' She lowered her voice and glanced furtively over her shoulder to make sure that none of the upper servants was within earshot. 'An' what about our own mistress? If anythin' were to 'appen to Lady Cederwell, I reckon she'd 'ave first bite o' the cherry, not Mistress Talke.'

'She's 'avin' more'n 'er fair share o' bites already,' the pot-boy put in, reducing them all, including Jane Cook, to helpless laughter.

I decided it was time to be on my way if I was to arrive at Cederwell Manor before darkness fell, and which at that time of year descended in mid-afternoon. The female servants had chosen what they wanted from my pack before the meal, so there was nothing further to detain me. I therefore said my farewells and left. Passing the stables on my way out, I paused to glance inside, hoping to wish Hamon and Jasper goodbye, but they were nowhere to be seen. Nor, now I came to think of it, had they been at dinner. I reflected that perhaps they were permanently banned by Jane Cook from eating indoors because, as she had pointed out earlier, they smelled too much of horses. But as I was about to set foot on the drawbridge, I was forced to beat a hurried retreat in order to avoid Hamon, mounted on Jessamine, the raw-boned grey. Horse and rider came clattering across the wooden slats as though Old Scratch himself were after them, and both, by their appearance, in a lather. At the same moment, Jasper materialised from somewhere behind the stables, inquiring in a whisper, 'Did all go well?'

Hamon was already sliding from the saddle, tossing the mare's reins to his fellow groom as he did so.

'Here, stable her and rub her down. I must go speak to my lady.'

He ran towards the house, almost tripping over his feet in his hurry.

Jasper stared after him with a thoughtful look, which gradually settled into one of avid and ill-contained curiosity. My own interest was also aroused and I turned back to speak to him.

'Your friend seems in a mighty rush,' I said. 'Where's he come from?'

The groom started a little at the sound of my voice.

'Where's Hamon been?' I repeated.

Jasper hesitated, then shrugged. 'I know where he's supposed to have been; to Cederwell Manor with a present for Sir Hugh. He was sent there by my lady just on the dinner hour. At least that was the excuse.'

'What do you mean, the excuse?' I asked him.

Jasper blinked once or twice in confusion before again lifting his shoulders.

'I meant nothing by it. I was just talking for talking's sake, the way you do sometimes.' He looked me up and down. 'Hadn't you best be going? It'll be dusk pretty soon.'

I agreed, but reluctantly. My nose, like Dame Judith's, was twitching with the desire to know more, but there was no way that I could reasonably stay. And then suddenly I realised that the answer to the mystery might well lie at Cederwell Manor, if that was indeed where Hamon had been ... But of course that was where he had been! Ursula Lynom had sent him after Sir Hugh with the silver and mother-of-pearl buttons. They were a gift for him, just as her mother-

in-law had predicted they would be. I bade my companion a
cheery 'God be with ye!' and set out once more on my way.

Leafless trees, like so many hobgoblins, crouched against
the leaden-grey sky and every now and again a snowflake
floated down, to lie for a moment before gradually dissolving
into the iron-hard ground. But soon they would begin to pitch.
The snowstorm which had threatened for the past few days
was now upon us and I must get into shelter before the hours
of darkness. I quickened my step, my pack considerably
lighter than when I set out from Bristol two weeks earlier.

I reached the end of the Woodspring road and the junction
with the main pack-horse track almost before I realised it,
my mind busy with the events of the day since leaving
Ulnoth's dwelling that same morning. And, upon that
thought, I found myself once again drawing abreast of the
boulder house. On impulse, I stooped and went inside, calling
out, 'Ulnoth!'

For a few seconds, standing there blinking in the gloom,
I could not see him, and had just decided that he must have
gone to attend to his snares when a slight shuffling noise
sounded from the furthest corner.

'Ulnoth!' I repeated.

He crawled forward. 'Chapman,' he said with such a note
of relief in his voice that I immediately grew suspicious.

'Who did you think it was? Have you had another visitor?'

He shook his head a little too vigorously. 'No. No. Ulnoth
frightened.'

'Why? If no one's been here, who or what is there to be
scared of? Have you seen something from your doorway?'

'No, no! Nothing.'

I suspected him of lying. Clearly something or someone had upset him, but however hard I probed, he refused to say any more. I did what I could to calm him, settling him in the farthest recess of the house, in the embrasure cut into the bank, and gave him some water. When he stopped trembling I offered, 'I'll stay with you if you wish. Spend the night here.'

But he did not want this, giving me a shove which almost caused me to lose my balance. For the second time I realised that he was stronger than he looked.

'Go. You go,' he muttered.

'Very well, I shall. I must be on my way at once if I'm to reach Cederwell Manor before dark.'

Suddenly, he started to moan, rocking backwards and forwards and muttering to himself, 'Death. Death. Death.'

'What about death?' I demanded. And then, when he did not answer, 'Whose death, Ulnoth? What are you trying to tell me?'

But not another word could I prise from him however long and patiently I tried. At last, when he turned his back to me, hunching in on himself, I realised that I could ill afford to waste more time. I squeezed his thin shoulder and gently called his name, but still getting no response I left. Straightening to my full height outside the entrance I paused for a moment, wondering if I ought to return and press him further as to his meaning; but, several flakes of snow settling just at that moment amid the folds of my cloak, I decided that I must go forward without more delay. Ulnoth had made it plain that he did not want my company.

By the end of what I calculated to be another hour, and when I judged that Cederwell Manor must soon be coming into view, it was snowing with a gentle persistence that might not in itself have boded ill, but for a freshening wind blowing in from the sea. Every moment the smell of salt and fish grew stronger, and I knew that I must be very close by now to the Severn estuary. The land on the left-hand side of the track, which had originally fallen steeply away, was levelling out with each succeeding furlong of ground I covered, while on my right, the cliffs now soared above me. This was partly due to the fact that the track, which followed the high ground all the way from Bristol, was descending towards the shore. Thick brakes of scrub had begun to replace the wind-bitten trees.

Then, in front of me, I saw the outhouses and barn of the manor, above which rose the chimneys of the house itself, nestling back against the face of the towering cliff behind it. Turning my head I noted, some hundred yards or so to the left and standing well clear of the homestead, a round tower, three, or maybe four, storeys high.

And on the path ahead of me walked a solitary figure who, although his back was towards me, was immediately recognisable.

Chapter Five

I lengthened my stride.

'God be with you, Brother Simeon,' I called. 'I think we are bound for the same destination.'

The friar slowed to a halt and turned to face me. For a moment puzzlement deepened the lines between his brows.

'We've met somewhere before,' he said, then the frown cleared. 'Bristol. That was it. You and your mother were at the High Cross. Afterwards, she provided me with an excellent meal.'

'My mother-in-law,' I corrected. I had by now caught up with him and we continued to walk together. 'You've been summoned to Cederwell Manor.'

His head came round sharply. 'And how do you know that?'

'Four days ago, quite by chance, I met two men who were searching for you on the orders of their mistress, Lady Cederwell. She had urgent need of you, they said. A miller and his wife, who'd kindly let me eat with them, directed them south, to Woodspring Priory.'

Simeon nodded. His steps were beginning to flag and he leaned heavily on his staff as though he could barely keep himself upright. He looked even frailer than he had done in Bristol, his face gaunter, his body thinner, his black Dominican robe and cloak more travel-stained and tattered. Only his eyes burned with the same fanatical zeal, the driving force which gave him the will-power to carry on with his mission.

'I have indeed come from that direction. The men you speak of did not find me until I was nearing my destination, and I told them that first I had to fulfil my promise to Abbot Hunt of Saint Augustine's Abbey in Bristol, to preach to the prior and his canons.' He added darkly, 'It seems that morals have grown lax amongst the brothers, and it needed someone to warn them afresh of the terrors of hellfire and eternal damnation; of the peril to their immortal souls if they continued with their sinful ways; to remind them that, under secular law, such malpractices would condemn them to the fire.'

'But what of Lady Cederwell?' I prompted.

'I said that I would be with her as soon as possible. As you say, her need of me seemed to be so great that one of her messengers offered to take me up and carry me to Cederwell there and then. But, "God's work will not be hurried," I told him. "It must proceed at His pace and in His good time. I shall come to your mistress on my own two feet when He wills that I shall do so, but not before, even if it means that Lady Cederwell must wait a week or so." However, with the Almighty's help, my words had such a powerful effect upon the monks of Woodspring that I was able to leave them after only three days, and I set out before first light this morning in the certain knowledge that Father Prior would have no more trouble with them. I have been walking steadily ever since, stopping for neither meat nor drink.'

In that case, I reflected, it was small wonder that he appeared to be in the last stages of exhaustion, for he had now been nearly eight hours on the road without food or rest. He must have passed Lynom Hall only a short while before I quit it, and for most of the way been less than a half-mile ahead of me. I could have caught up with him sooner had he tired more quickly or had I not stopped to speak to Ulnoth. I was sorry, for even his company would have been a welcome relief from the tedium of a winter journey, when there were so few fellow travellers to be met with.

I offered him my arm, saying, 'We can at least walk the last half-furlong together.'

But he spurned my proffered support.

'God will provide all the strength I need, Chapman. When that fails me, I shall know the time has come to prepare for death.'

His words made me remember Ulnoth.

'Do you recall passing a boulder house, some mile and a half back, just after you turned westwards from the Woodspring track?'

Friar Simeon shook his head. 'I look neither to left nor right when I am walking, but keep my eyes fixed on the road ahead, towards that place where God has called me next. Why do you ask? What significance does this boulder house have? Is there a lost soul there who is in need of my ministrations?'

'No, no!' I exclaimed hastily as the friar paused, ready to retrace his steps if necessary.

As we descended the last few yards to Cederwell Manor,
I explained as well as I could my connection with Ulnoth
and what he had said to me during our second brief meeting
this afternoon. But Friar Simeon made nothing of it, merely
hunching his thin shoulders.

'We are all of us concerned with thoughts of death,
Chapman. Or we ought to be if we are wise. For the one
thing we can be sure of from the cradle onwards is that we
shall die, and we must see to it that we are always in a state
of spiritual grace, ready to meet our Maker.'

Threading our way between two or three of the
outbuildings, we found ourselves at last in full view of
Cederwell Manor. This was of somewhat curious
construction, with what I later discovered to be the great
hall and, behind it, the servants' quarters, built at an angle
to the entrance passage and kitchens. The barn stood opposite
the main porch on the other side of a wide courtyard and a
fish pond, and beyond that the land stretched, empty and
desolate, towards the estuary. Only a few feet of ground
separated the back of the house from the lee of the cliff which
rose, steep and barren, behind it. A strange, remote spot,
even, I guessed, in summer; a place in which there was plenty
of time to brood on real or imagined wrongs and ills.

A little earlier it had stopped snowing, but suddenly it
began again, more heavily than before, falling in sudden
flurries from an iron-grey sky. The wind, too, had
strengthened so that the air was a mass of dancing, whirling
flakes, biting and stinging every exposed part of the body
until the skin burned under their touch. Hurriedly I led the
way round to the back of the house where, against the angled

wall, a flight of stone steps led up to a narrow, slate-tiled gallery and two doors which opened into the second storey. But it was the ground-floor room, whose shutters opened on to the cliff face and now stood wide in order to let out the steam and smells of cooking, which focused my attention. I rapped on one of the shutters as I passed the window, entering the door alongside and finding myself in the main passage which ran the whole length of the house. An archway immediately to my left led into the kitchen.

At first glance this seemed to be full of women, all arguing vehemently with one another. A stout body, whose shiny red face and greasy apron proclaimed her to be the cook, was standing, arms akimbo, confronting a younger, slenderer woman dressed in an unadorned grey woollen gown and a plain linen hood, yet whose general demeanour suggested that she was not one of the servants. As I made my appearance, the latter stamped a foot in frustration.

'When my sister-in-law is absent, you should take your orders from *me*,' she cried. '*I* am next in command!'

'You! You're a nobody!' the cook retorted indignantly. 'A nothing! You're here on sufferance, through the master's bounty! I'm not obliged to do anything you tell me! Isn't that so, Mistress Talke?'

Thus appealed to, a third woman, probably as old as the cook but taller and of a sparer build, wearing a large bunch of household keys at her waist, raised her own voice to make herself heard above the others'.

'You're both wrong. *I* am the housekeeper and *I* am in charge when my lady is not here.' Her handsome, sallow-skinned features creased into an expression of contempt. 'And

61

at every other time,' she added; a remark which her companions, now united against her, were too angry to heed.

'No one's in charge in my kitchen except me!' proclaimed the cook, picking up and brandishing a spoon.

The younger woman exclaimed, 'You're not family, Phillipa Talke, much as we know you'd like to be!'

'And what does that mean, my fine madam?' the housekeeper demanded, rounding on her furiously. Without however waiting for a reply, she continued, 'Martha Grindcobb is right. You have no place here but as a dependant of my lady. It would be as well if you remembered that.'

The younger woman let out a high-pitched scream and thumped the kitchen table, making all the pots and pans standing on it rattle.

'My husband is my lady's brother! Perhaps it would also be as well if *you* remembered *that*!'

I felt Brother Simeon, who had followed me into the kitchen and was now pressed close against my shoulder, flinch at the sudden crescendo of noise. The next moment he pushed me aside and, striding forward, quelled the cacophony with a single word.

'Silence!'

He had not raised his voice, but his naturally penetrating tone commanded their immediate attention. All three women turned slowly in his direction, their quarrel momentarily forgotten, in mutual astonishment. The housekeeper's mouth flew open to demand an explanation of this intrusion, but when she saw the friar's habit and tonsured head her protestation faltered. The younger woman, however, she whom I understood to be the sister-by-marriage of Lady Cederwell, was not so reticent.

'And who might you be, Brother?'

'I am Friar Simeon,' he announced majestically, drawing himself up to his impressive height, the blue eyes flashing with the promise of hellfire and brimstone for anyone who was foolhardy enough to challenge his authority. 'I have been sent for by Lady Cederwell. Where is she?'

The housekeeper, recovering her nerve a little, said, 'My lady's in her private chapel in the tower, fasting and praying, where she has been since daybreak.' Her glance went past the friar to me. 'Who is this you've brought with you?'

I took my pack from my back, dropping it on to the kitchen table, and spoke cheerfully in an attempt to lighten the general atmosphere.

'Oh, I'm nothing to do with Brother Simeon. We met by chance on the road and just happened to arrive together. I'm a chapman, trying to make some extra money in this bleak mid-winter.'

A little kitchen-maid, whom I had not previously noticed, crept from the corner where she had been quietly observing the antics of her elders, her eyes round with anticipation of possible, unlooked-for delights.

'Got any pretty ribbons, Chapman?' she asked in a husky whisper.

'I may have one or two,' I answered, 'that will suit a pretty girl like you.'

She giggled, then self-consciously put up a hand to touch her face which was afflicted with the weeping pustules of youth.

'Go on with you!' She giggled again.

Brother Simeon rapped his knuckles on the table.

'Enough of this!' he exclaimed harshly. 'Things temporal are of no importance when God's work is waiting to be done. As for you, my child—' he glared fiercely at the little kitchen-maid '– you would do well to contemplate the state of your immortal soul rather than consider ways of adorning your body.' He turned to the housekeeper. 'You may send to inform Lady Cederwell that I am here.'

Phillipa Talke hesitated, unwilling to disoblige a holy man, but even more afraid of defying her mistress's orders.

'You must seek her out for yourself, Father,' she answered, but with a hint of apology in her voice. 'When Lady Cederwell is at her devotions no one is allowed to disturb her. Anyone who did so would be severely punished. You, however, would suffer no such fate.'

Friar Simeon inclined his head.

'Your mistress sounds as if she is a woman after my own heart. What a truly fortunate lot yours must be—' he included all those present, except myself, in a comprehensive sweep of his arm '– to be in the employ of such a one.' He did not appear to notice the lack of enthusiasm and almost audible murmur of disagreement which his statement provoked, but continued, 'Where may I find your mistress?'

The youngest of the women, if you discounted the kitchen-maid, which it was easy enough to do, now stepped forward, determined to establish her superiority over the others.

'I,' she announced grandly, 'am Adela Empryngham, the wife of Lady Cederwell's brother. Of course it goes without saying that *I* should not be punished were I to show you the way, but,' she added hurriedly, 'it is snowing again and I suffer from delicate health, so you will understand, Brother, why I cannot accompany you. You will find Jeanette in the tower which you may have noticed as you arrived on manor lands. It stands clear of the outbuildings, south-west by about the length of a furrow.'

I thought her estimate of the distance over-generous, but was willing to concede that my own first glimpse of the tower had been a cursory one, and it might well be further off than I had imagined. I had no time to pursue the thought, however, for at that moment there was an interruption. A man who could only be Sir Hugh Cederwell strode into the kitchen.

He had seen, I guessed, some forty or more summers, a handsome, florid man with brown eyes and an abundance of dark brown hair which clustered in thick waves and curls across the nape of his neck and around his ears, but which was starting to thin a little on the crown. He was heavily built, barrel-chested, but not short of stature due to long, tapering flanks and a surprising length of leg from knee to ankle. The whole effect was one of power but with a curious top-heaviness. His voice, when he spoke, was deep and resonant.

'What is going on here? Why all the noise? Where's Lady Cederwell?' He caught sight of the friar and myself. 'Who are these people?'

It was my companion who answered, silencing the women with an upraised hand.

'I am Brother Simeon of the Dominican Order, and I have been summoned here by your wife, for what reason I have yet to discover. I demand to be allowed to speak to her forthwith.'

The knight's forehead puckered. 'Brother Simeon? The same friar who has been preaching hell and damnation in these parts for the past two weeks?' When Simeon nodded, I thought I saw a sudden apprehension flicker at the back of the dark brown eyes, but it was too momentary for me to be certain. Sir Hugh gave a blustering laugh and continued, 'I might have guessed that my wife would wish to meet a man with such a pious reputation. She is a very devout woman.'

The last words were spoken with what could have been a sneer. The friar certainly chose to interpret it as such, and his eyes sparked with fury.

'Never mock at the godly, Sir Hugh! It would be as well for you if all the females of your household were to follow the example of your lady. Our acquaintance has been brief, but they seem to me to be a pack of gibbering fools, concerned only with the material things of this world; with which one of them is of greater earthly importance than her sisters.' He rounded with such ferocity on the women that they drew back from him, huddling together in a frightened little group. 'You stupid creatures! As Our Lord reminds us in the Holy Scriptures, your soul may be required of any one of you this very night! What will it matter then, when the pit of hell yawns at your feet, who is in charge in this kitchen? What will it profit you?'

Sir Hugh interrupted without compunction. 'Are you sure Lady Cederwell sent for you, Brother? I have no knowledge of her doing so. Does she know you? Have you met?'

The friar's lips thinned until they were almost invisible and he sucked in a rasping breath.

'No, she knows me only by reputation, but that is

sufficient. Do you dare to suggest that I am lying? I, Simeon?'
His thin chest swelled. 'However, I have a witness. The pedlar
here can vouch for the veracity of my words. Tell him,
Chapman!'

So I told Sir Hugh of my meeting with the two men at the
mill, and confirmed that they had indeed been searching for
the friar on the orders of Lady Cederwell. The knight looked
grim.

'Can you describe them to me?'

I did my best, which proved to be good enough, for both
he and Mistress Talke said in unison, 'Jude and Nicholas.'
Sir Hugh added bitterly, 'Of course! Her own men, brought
with her from Campden.'

Adela Empryngham nodded in confirmation. 'My father-
in-law's people were always noted for their loyalty to him.
Once he was dead, they transferred that loyalty to Jeanette
and Gerard.'

Sir Hugh snorted derisively. 'I should take care how you
link Jeanette's and Gerard's names, my dear Adela. I doubt
that either Jude or Nicholas feel much loyalty towards a
bastard.'

The silence which followed this last remark was broken
by a snigger from the cook, Martha Grindcobb. Mistress
Empryngham coloured painfully, her bosom heaving with
anger and indignation.

'I always knew it was a mistake for us to come here with
Jeanette,' she shrilled breathlessly, as soon as she could trust
herself to speak. 'I've always known how you regard us; as
poor dependants, with every penny grudged that's spent on
our food and clothing. Many and many a time I have told

Gerard that he should leave here and stand on his own two feet, so that we should not have to be beholden to you.'

Sir Hugh lifted his lip.

'And what did Master Gerard say in reply?'

Again the colour suffused Adela Empryngham's face.

'He won't go,' she mumbled. Then she added with greater spirit, 'He feels it necessary to remain with his sister . . .'

'His half-sister!' Sir Hugh cut in, but she ignored him.

'. . . knowing how unhappy she is.'

Sir Hugh laughed, but there was no mirth in the sound.

'Jeanette has always been unhappy and always will be. She is as God made her, and He made her, seemingly, to be one of the most miserable of His creatures.' He shrugged. 'How can it be otherwise when she spends three-quarters of her waking life upon her knees and the other quarter sniffing out the wrongdoings, real or imagined, of her fellows? However, I am delighted to know, Adela, that you at least have enough sense to see that Gerard would be best away from here, instead of battening on my goodwill. There's plenty of honest work to be had if he looks for it. Persuade him to return to the Cotswolds. Sheep country, where wealth abounds. There are any number of rich sheepmen who would offer him employment.'

Friar Simeon intervened.

'Am I to be kept waiting here all day? I wish to be conducted to Lady Cederwell immediately.'

Sir Hugh answered indifferently, repeating what we had already been told, 'You will find her in the old Saxon tower, which you can see well enough if you cross the courtyard and go out by the little gate. It stands some way distant from the manor, on the mudflats of the estuary, and is her own domain. She has made it hers in the five and a half years since she first came here, turning the uppermost storey into a chapel, even though there is one here, in the house.' He went on, as if struck by a sudden thought, 'Our chaplain is sick at the moment. He has been for more than a week and is therefore unable to carry out his duties at present. Perhaps that's why my wife has sent for you, Friar. She is in constant fear for her immortal soul. She must confess her sins and be granted absolution every day or she cannot sleep at night.'

'A truly godly woman,' breathed Simeon. 'A shining example to us all. Her like is to be treasured, Sir Hugh, not held up to ridicule. Now, with your leave, I shall go to her and discover what it is she wants of me.'

His tone implied that he would do so with or without our reluctant host's permission, and I was not surprised to see Sir Hugh's grimace of resignation.

'You must do as you wish, Brother. I will call one of the men to show you the way.'

'There is no need to trouble anyone.' The friar drew his cloak more tightly about his emaciated frame. 'I can follow your directions well enough.'

'I'll come with you,' I volunteered. 'In this weather the ground can be treacherous. This time, you might be glad of my arm in support.'

Simeon made no response as he turned and left the kitchen, but as he did not positively say me nay, I dropped my pack by the table and followed him, also wrapping myself in my cloak.

It was beginning by now to grow dark. The early January

dusk was closing in, the sky black and louring, showing few rifts of light in the low-scudding clouds. It was still snowing, faster than it had been and rapidly covering the ground with a carpet of white. Simeon and I crossed the courtyard, skirting the fish pond and making for the barn and attendant outhouses which formed the southern boundary of the manor. Between the laundry and the dairy was a narrow gate, set into the short stretch of wall which connected the two buildings. It was not yet locked and swung outwards on its hinges at the first touch of the friar's hand.

The open country beyond it was also covered in snow, but I could feel the tough, coarse grasses, which are to be found in coastal regions, crunch beneath our feet. The cries of the seagulls, as they wheeled inland, scavenging for food, sounded mournfully in our ears. Even Friar Simeon shivered a little as we made our way towards the tower, but whether from cold or from a sense of the desolation of the place I was unable to guess.

Mistress Empryngham had been right: the tower stood clear of the manor by very nearly the length of a furrow. As we approached, I could see that it was in a state of disrepair, some of the stones chipped and crumbling. Efforts had been made, however, particularly about the first and second storeys, to renew the mortar and render the building sound enough for habitation. Facing us was a door, and as we drew close, I saw that it was slightly ajar, a drift of snow already covering the floor immediately inside it.

I turned my head and glanced questioningly at the friar, but his steady pace did not falter. He strode ahead of me, pushed the door wide and entered the tower.

Chapter Six

It was dark inside. What daylight there was, apart from that admitted by the open door, filtered through four slits in the circular wall. It was just possible, however, to make out the shape of a small table standing in the middle of the room, on which was placed a tinder-box and a horn lantern. By the time I had used the one to light the candle inside the other, Friar Simeon was seething with impatience.

'Why are you so slow?' he complained. 'Get on with it! Get on with it!' He walked to the foot of the staircase, winding its way upwards into the gloom, and shouted, 'Lady Cederwell! Are you there?'

When he received no reply, I reminded him, 'Sir Hugh said that the chapel was on the uppermost floor of the tower. She cannot hear you. You may as well save your breath.' I closed the lantern and raised it above my head. 'Let me go first. These steps are narrow and badly worn.'

We proceeded cautiously, with the friar hanging on to my cloak, while I directed him, as far as I was able, where to place his feet. A flight of some two dozen stairs brought us to the second storey and another circular room almost as empty and as cold as the one immediately below it. The lantern's pale rays showed us a stool, a slightly larger table than the one downstairs, on which were scattered two or three well-thumbed folios, and a bench alongside it. That was all. There was nothing here, not a single wall hanging nor even any rushes on the floor, to relieve the general austerity.

'Lady Cederwell!' Simeon shouted yet again. And again there was no answer.

'She's either praying or has fallen asleep at her devotions,' I suggested. 'If, as the housekeeper told us, she has been here since daybreak, I should fancy the latter.'

Simeon made no response and, without this time waiting for me to lead the way, started up the stairs to the final storey. I hurried after him, once more holding the lantern high, afraid that he might lose his footing.

Lady Cederwell was not to be found there, either.

This third room was slightly less bleak than the others, largely because of a pair of ornate silver candlesticks which stood one at each end of a makeshift altar, the metal gleaming richly in the light from the lantern. Two scented wax candles had burned down almost to nothing, the flame of one still guttering feebly in the draught, while a faint spiral of black smoke rising from the stump of the second showed that it had not long gone out. A prie-dieu, made of rosewood, was placed against another part of the circular wall, and above it hung one of the ugliest crucifixes I have ever seen. Made of ebony and ivory, the black cross, at least three feet in height, supported the pale, contorted body of the crucified Christ writhing in all the agony of a Roman execution. I could almost feel the excruciating pain of dislocating joints as the body began to sag, and the swelling of the tongue in the Palestinian heat. The crown of thorns, too, was like a row of jagged spikes across the forehead, piercing the tender flesh, but there was no wound in the side of this figure. The victim was not yet dead: he still suffered. Again, there was nothing here of serenity or comfort.

Friar Simeon gave the crucifix no more than a passing glance and a brief genuflection before continuing to look around him.

'Well, my lady's not here,' he said. 'We must go back to the house and hope to find that she has returned there before us.'

'Wait!' I exclaimed. 'There are more stairs. They must lead up to the look-out platform.'

'Lady Cederwell won't be out of doors in such weather as this,' my companion protested. 'You'll be wasting your time, Chapman, if you go up there. Come, let's be off.'

'It won't take long,' I encouraged him, 'and we shall have the satisfaction of knowing that we have searched everywhere possible.'

Grumbling under his breath, the friar followed me up the steps, pointing out sourly, when we discovered that there was no one on the roof of the tower, that he had been right. Ignoring his sudden bad temper, I ventured warily over to the parapet which surrounded the platform and, raising my lantern, leaned between the battlements, looking out towards the estuary. The snow flurries had eased, and a fleeting break in the clouds enabled me, just for a moment, to see something, or someone, lying sprawled below me on the frozen earth. I called Brother Simeon over.

'What do you make of that?' I asked in a voice which was not quite steady. 'Down there! Surely it's a body.'

But that pallid shaft of light, a last echo of the short winter's day, had disappeared beneath the darkening pall of sky, and it was difficult now to make out any part of that storm-tossed landscape.

'You're talking nonsense,' the friar said sharply. 'We should have seen anyone lying on the ground as we approached. The light had not completely vanished.'

'No, no,' I answered impatiently, catching at his skinny wrist with my free hand and shaking it. 'Here, we are standing on the opposite side of the tower to the door and the track from the house. Whatever it is down there . . . whoever it is, was completely hidden from our view.'

'I still say that you're imagining things,' the friar insisted. He shivered. 'Understandably, perhaps. This is not a spot which encourages congenial thoughts.'

I wondered if Simeon had ever entertained a congenial thought in the whole of his life, but I was too anxious to investigate further to pursue the idea. I made for the stairs.

Some ten minutes later, after I had nearly slipped twice on the worn treads and Simeon had only saved himself from a nasty fall by grabbing at a notch of stone which stood proud of the wall, we emerged from the tower into the snowy darkness. Without wasting any further words in argument, I groped my way around the outside of the building until I judged myself to be roughly on the opposite side to the doorway. I was about to raise my lantern higher when I tripped over something lying in my path and went sprawling.

'What's happened? What are you doing?' Simeon

The Wicked Winter

demanded querulously from behind me. He had, however, stopped short several paces away and so avoided a similar accident. 'What is it? What have you found?'

I made no answer but picked myself up off my hands and knees, my first action being to discover what damage had been done to the lantern when I dropped it. By some miracle it had landed on its base and remained upright, the candle still burning brightly inside it.

'What have you found?' Friar Simeon repeated. His voice was shriller than before.

'I don't know yet.'

I crouched beside the object and once more held the lantern high. Even in that dim light, and without touching it, I knew it was a body; a woman's body. Several long strands of hair had been shaken loose from the plain lawn hood and veil which normally confined them. She was lying prone, the head turned away from me, the splayed hands seeming to claw at the earth in a kind of final desperation. I crossed myself, then put out a hand and felt the shoulder nearest me, but the flesh beneath the clothes was unyielding. That stiffening which afflicts the dead within a few hours of the soul's passing had already taken hold, hurried on no doubt by the icy weather.

Simeon had come to kneel on the other side of the body, his eyes two great pools of blackness in his haggard face.

'You were right,' he whispered. 'Who . . . who is it?'

'I don't know for certain,' I answered grimly. 'But I should guess it to be Lady Cederwell.' I lifted my head and looked at the sheer wall of the tower beside me. 'She must have been leaning over the battlements for some reason, lost her balance and fallen.' I rose awkwardly to my feet, still feeling a little bruised from my own tumble. 'We have to go back to the house and inform Sir Hugh.'

Simeon did not move at once, but stayed kneeling. Then he, too, made the sign of the cross and started to intone the prayer for the dying. 'Go forth, O Christian soul, out of this world, in the name of God the Father Almighty, who created thee, in the name of Jesus Christ, the Son of the living God, who suffered for thee, in the name of the Holy Ghost, who sanctified thee . . .'

'She's gone, Brother,' I interrupted forcefully. 'She's been dead for many hours. You can do nothing now.' I helped him to his feet. Just for a moment, I thought he was going to faint. He staggered and fell heavily against me, so that I had to support him with my free arm, but he recovered quickly, pushing me away almost angrily, ashamed of his momentary weakness.

'Lead on, Chapman,' he said in a husky whisper. 'Let us do what has to be done. The sooner this unhappy business is resolved the better.'

The turmoil of the past hour had subsided, to be succeeded by an abnormal calm. The house was suddenly quiet, the silence broken only by the rustle of women's skirts and the low rumbling of muttered conversations as members of the household forgathered either in the kitchen or the great hall, according to their rank. The body of Lady Cederwell, her identity confirmed by her husband, had been carried home and now lay on the bed in her chamber, still locked into its unnatural pose. No laying out could be done, and therefore no proper mourning begun, until the rigor had passed.

Both Simeon and I had been offered shelter for the night which we had thankfully accepted, for the nearest habitation, the boulder house, was at least half an hour's walk distant.

'We'll leave early tomorrow morning,' the friar muttered, as we warmed our chilled bones at the kitchen fire. 'We must not intrude upon a house of grief.'

I said nothing, but in my private opinion there was precious little of that commodity on display in the wake of Lady Cederwell's tragic fall. Only two people had so far shed any tears in my presence, my lady's half-brother, who had been summoned in from the stables when Simeon and I first returned with our terrible news, and her personal maid, Audrey Lambspringe, cousin, as I recalled, to young Bet at Lynom Hall. The housekeeper, Phillipa Talke, the sister-by-marriage, Mistress Empryngham, and, above all, Sir Hugh himself, were either remarkably adept at hiding their sorrow or were indeed as unaffected by the calamity as they appeared to be.

There seemed no doubt in anyone's mind that Lady Cederwell's death had been accidental.

'She would often clamber on to the parapet,' Sir Hugh had confirmed in answer to a question from Simeon. He had shrugged and spread wide his hands. 'I've warned her – we've all warned her – of the danger, but she refused to listen. She would only reply that by doing so she could get still nearer to God. It was why she liked the tower, why she spent so much of her time there, why she set up a private chapel of her own in the topmost storey.'

He had gone on to explain that the tower was an ancient

Saxon dwelling, built by one Eadred Eadrichsson, who had fought for King Harold at Senlac.

'My forebear, Sir Guy de Sourdeval, was granted the property five months later when Eadred was dispossessed, as recognition by King William for his valour in that same battle.'

A poor recompense, I thought, this blighted tract of land on the edge of nowhere. Sir Guy de Sourdeval had evidently been of little importance; probably an impoverished knight who had followed in the wake of his overlord to see what modest pickings could be gleaned in a conquered country, if Duke William should prove successful. And in the 400 years since, I judged, little had altered. The name of Sir Guy's descendants, together with that of the house which he had built, had been mangled by the English tongue into Cederwell, but other than that no great change had taken place. No increase in fame and fortune had accrued to the family, no dynastic marriages had been contracted, no resounding feats of arms had been performed. And Sir Hugh, like those before him and in common with so many others of his kind, was content to live out his days on the periphery of events, the sole and sufficient source of his pride being his Norman ancestry.

Friar Simeon and I continued warming ourselves at the kitchen fire while Martha Grindcobb and the little maid, whose name I had learned was Jennifer Tonge, started to prepare the evening meal.

'It'll be late. It's already well past four o'clock, but that can't be helped, I suppose,' the cook observed, before suddenly recollecting herself and raising one corner of her apron to wipe away a non-existent tear. 'Poor lady! Poor lady!' Her voice rose sharply. 'Watch that broth, you stupid girl! It's boiling over!'

There was a loud hissing sound as the liquid ran down the sides of the pot and extinguished some of the flames. A cloud of steam rose towards the blackened ceiling where it hung, bringing tears to the eyes, until it found its escape route through the smoke-duct in the outside wall. I smote Friar Simeon on the back as his narrow chest heaved with a paroxysm of coughing, and Martha Grindcobb flung wide both window shutters just as Phillipa Talke entered the kitchen.

The housekeeper paused in the doorway, her long nose wrinkling in disgust.

'What a smell!' she exclaimed. She glanced at the shrinking figure of Jennifer Tonge, then at the fire, now beginning to burn up again, and rightly interpreted the situation. She shrugged helplessly. 'Why don't you keep a better watch on that child, Martha? You know she's next to useless.' Ignoring both the cook's sullen rejoinder and Jennifer's sniffling, she turned to Simeon. 'Brother, Sir Hugh requests that you will join him and the rest of the family in the great hall for supper. He would like to question you more closely about your discovery of Lady Cederwell's body.'

'Why?' the friar demanded angrily. 'Does he think that I have been guilty of concealing information from him?'

The housekeeper looked shocked. 'Of course not. It's just the natural wish of a grieving husband to glean all the facts he possibly can in order to reassure himself that . . . that . . .'

Mistress Talke hesitated before continuing, 'To reassure himself that . . .' Again she faltered, reluctant to state openly what had plainly not yet crossed Simeon's mind.

'What are you talking about? Reassure himself about what?' the friar asked with growing irritation. I could see that our unhappy find had shaken him more than he cared to admit, so I rose from my stool and went to stand behind him, gently pressing his shoulders for comfort.

'Sir Hugh,' I told him, 'is afraid in case it might prove that his lady took her own life. Anything you can tell him which will set his fears to rest on that score will, I fancy, be welcome.'

'Why should it be thought that Lady Cederwell would do such a thing?' Simeon demanded angrily. But I saw his hand go to the plain wooden cross which he wore on a leather thong around his neck. 'She had sent for me, requesting me to visit her here as soon as I could. Would she have done so had she intended herself a mischief?'

Neither the housekeeper nor I made any reply, but both of us were able to envisage a despair which might have been assuaged by talking to so holy a man, but which had not, in the end, been able to tolerate the delay of his arrival. The friar, I guessed, although I could not see his face, must be following the same train of thought, but guilt would prevent him from accepting such an intolerable conclusion.

At last, I said quietly, 'There is no reason to think that Lady Cederwell's death was other than a tragic accident. Sir Hugh himself has told us that she often used to stand on the parapet in order to get closer to heaven. From even the little that I have heard tell of the lady, I suspect she was not one to be deterred by icy weather when she felt the need to communicate with God.'

Phillipa Talke nodded vigorously. 'That is so. I have no doubt at all, Brother, that she simply slipped and fell, and you need have none, either. Come with me to Sir Hugh and tell him that. It is all he wants to hear to be at peace.'

Jennifer Tonge, who had been stirring the broth but also listening to the conversation with wide-eyed fascination, suddenly giggled nervously and said, 'She died unshriven.'

The housekeeper rounded on the unfortunate child, dealing her a box on the ear which felled her to the ground.

'There never was a whiter soul than your mistress, and don't you forget it! Always on her knees, morning, noon and night.' I heard the note of contempt, hurriedly suppressed. 'Her passage through Purgatory to the heavenly gates is as certain as the fact that I'll box your other ear if you open your mouth once more while I'm in this kitchen. Now, Brother.' Mistress Talke turned back to the friar. 'Will you accompany me?'

But Simeon did not immediately rise from his seat.

'I should prefer it if the chapman came with me. It was, after all, he who discovered the body. It was his persistence in searching for Lady Cederwell which resulted in our finding her.'

The housekeeper looked properly shocked at his demand, and I moved to one side and knelt down by the friar's stool, where he could see me.

'Brother, Sir Hugh has invited you to sup with him and his family. That is right and proper, but he cannot ask a mere pedlar to sit down with him. I must eat supper in the kitchen with the servants.'

Simeon curled his lip. 'Then I shall eat here with you.' He addressed Phillipa Talke, his chin jutting arrogantly, 'Inform Sir Hugh that I shall willingly tell him all I can after the meal, provided that Roger Chapman is allowed to be present.' He waved an imperious hand, 'Hurry along, woman! I have spoken.'

'Why, Brother?' I asked, when an outraged Phillipa Talke had left the kitchen. 'Why do you need me with you? You're quite able to relate events as they happened. I know nothing that you don't know.'

'You are merely an excuse,' he said, indicating with a gesture of one hand his dislike of my proximity, and that I should return to sit on my own stool. 'I have no wish to sup with Lady Cederwell's bastard half-brother, nor with that shrewish wife of his.'

I realised that any notion I had had that the recent tragedy might have softened Friar Simeon was misconceived. With a grimace at Martha Grindcobb I went back to my seat, giving the still weeping Jenny a quick hug on the way while the cook's attention was momentarily diverted.

As the preparations for supper went on around me, I sat staring into the flames of the fire, lost in thought. Although I had no reason to suspect that Lady Cederwell's death was other than it seemed, an accident, three questions nagged at the back of my mind, causing me faint unease. Firstly, what had caused the precipitate return to Lynom Hall of the groom, Hamon? Secondly, why had Ulnoth repeatedly uttered the word 'death', a word which had proved to be so strangely prophetic? And thirdly, what was the true reason for the friar's urgent summons to Cederwell Manor by its châtelaine? But no answers were forthcoming, and in the end I decided that they were merely three separate incidents which had no bearing one upon the other.

Supper, in the kitchen at least, consisted of beef broth with cheese and oatcakes. The friar and I, together with the cook and Jenny Tonge, were joined by the two young men whom I had already encountered at the mill, introduced by Martha as brothers, Jude and Nicholas Capsgrave. (Other servants and manor tenants, I was informed, lived in the dozen or so huts and cottages which straggled north-westward, towards the higher reaches of the estuary.) The housekeeper did not reappear, and the absence of Lady Cederwell's personal maid, Audrey Lambspringe, was explained by her being so affected by her mistress's death that she was laid down upon her pallet in the women's dormitory. Sir Hugh, Gerard and Adela Empryngham and whoever else might be supping with them, were served at their table in the great hall by the remaining members of the household, two young girls, one called Edith, the other Ethelwynne. Saxon names seemed to be commonplace among the members of this isolated community.

Just as we had finished eating, Simeon sparingly, myself shamefully gorging until I could eat no more, a short, rotund man, with thinning grey hair and slightly protuberant blue eyes, bustled into the kitchen, introducing himself as Tostig the steward and requesting yet again that Simeon should come to Sir Hugh. The friar rose and beckoned me to do the same.

'Roger Chapman will accompany me,' he said.

The steward, although plainly annoyed by my companion's insistence on this condition, shrugged and capitulated.

'Very well, but you must delay no longer. Sir Hugh has already been more than patient, considering the tragic circumstances of this day.'

We followed him out of the kitchen, past pantry, buttery and counting-house, turned left down another, shorter stone-flagged passage just inside the main porch, and entered the great hall. I had no opportunity then to look about me, merely noting that the room had a central hearth beneath a hole in the smoke-blackened rafters, and that the rushes covering the floor were stale, littered with bones and emitting a strong odour of dog piss. The family had finished their meal, but were still seated at the high table on the dais at the far end of the hall. As we approached, I recognised Sir Hugh, Adela and her husband, Gerard Empryngham, whom I had seen earlier when he was summoned in from the stables, but not the other young man who sat with them. It was not difficult, however, to guess that he was the son of the house, for he had the same curling brown hair, dark eyes and heavy build as his father, although he was perhaps an inch or so taller. Maurice, I remembered Dame Judith had called him.

Simeon halted some few feet from the dais and consequently Sir Hugh was forced to rise from his place at table and come down to us. That he was none too pleased was obvious, but just as he opened his mouth, presumably to voice his annoyance, there was an interruption. After a commotion in the passage outside, the door behind us was flung violently open and Ursula Lynom, her cloak wet with snow, rushed into the hall. Oblivious to everyone else, she seized Sir Hugh's hand.

'I had to come!' she exclaimed. 'When you did not send to me with the news of Jeanette's death, I could wait no longer!'

Chapter Seven

There was a momentary silence, broken only by one of the hounds snuffling amongst the rushes to retrieve a half-concealed bone. Then Sir Hugh gave an uncertain smile, at the same time releasing his hand from Mistress Lynom's hold.

'Ursula! What . . . What are you doing here? Travelling in the dark and . . . and in such vile weather!'

Mistress Lynom looked disconcerted and took a step backwards. Beyond the open door, I could see the two grooms, Hamon and Jasper, who had ridden with her.

'I have been waiting since early this afternoon,' she said reproachfully, 'for you to send me word of Jeanette's unhappy accident. When Hamon returned and informed me of what had occurred, I naturally assumed that as your oldest and . . . that as your oldest friend, you would wish to let me know what had happened.'

Maurice Cederwell, Gerard and Adela Empryngham had by now descended from the dais and were ranged behind Sir Hugh, expressions of perplexity on all their faces. Sir Hugh himself looked very pale, although this, I conceded, might be due to the flickering torchlight. The hall was not well lit, being poorly supplied with wall cressets, and the candles in the candelabra of latten tin, which was suspended from one of the rafters, had burned low in their sockets. The fire, too, needed replenishing.

'How could I possibly send to tell you of Jeanette's death, when I did not know of it myself until an hour or more ago? What in God's name are you talking of, Ursula?'

It seemed to me, standing on the edge of the group, that Sir Hugh, with both voice and eyes, was desperately trying to convey a warning to Mistress Lynom. She also became aware of it and gave a high, forced laugh.

'How very foolish of me.' She pressed a hand to her breast as if to calm the beating of her heart. 'It was just . . . that I had sent my man, Hamon, here—' she turned towards the door, beckoning Hamon to show himself ' – to Cederwell with a present of buttons that I bought from a chapman who called at Lynom this morning. But on the way, Hamon met with . . . someone who told him that Jeanette was dead.'

Gerard Empryngham stepped forward. 'Who could have known such a thing?' he demanded of her. 'As Hugh says, it is not two hours since my sister's body was discovered. It cannot be much longer since the accident happened.'

I could not let this pass without argument and said respectfully, 'That is not so, Master Empryngham, under your sufferance. The rigor affecting Lady Cederwell's body, even allowing for the coldness of the weather, is sufficiently advanced to mean that she must have died well before noon.' I found myself the focus of all eyes, some haughty, some angry at my unasked-for interference, some disbelieving. 'Have you never noticed,' I continued undeterred, 'that the stiffening of a body, starting in the face, neck and jaw and gradually spreading to all other parts, does not take hold until several hours after death? But in the case of my lady, her shoulders and arms were already rigid when we found her. Therefore she must have fallen from the tower much earlier in the day.'

'You seem to know a great deal about dead bodies,' Adela Empryngham remarked suspiciously.

I smiled at her. 'I know as much as the next man who has eyes in his head. Death is all around us.'

'What the pedlar says is true,' Maurice Cederwell put in, speaking for the first time since Simeon and I had entered the hall. 'But it's something no one thinks about in the normal way, when the laying out of a body is completed before the rigor commences.'

'This is all beside the point,' Gerard said impatiently. 'The fact is that no one here knew of Jeanette's death until less than two hours since, yet Mistress Lynom says that her groom told her of it early this afternoon. How is this possible?'

Sir Hugh looked annoyed at this assumption of authority by one he plainly regarded as no more than a poor relation, but was too anxious himself to hear the answer to administer a reproof. So he merely frowned angrily at Gerard before bending an inquiring gaze upon his unexpected guest. The lady, however, seemed confused and unable to reply, turning instead to Hamon who stood, uncomfortably shifting from one foot to the other, just inside the doorway.

Friar Simeon prodded me in the ribs.

'Did you not tell me, Chapman, that some hermit had

been babbling to you of Lady Cederwell's death? Ulnoth, I think you said his name is.'

'He did not speak of death in connection with Lady Cederwell,' I amended hurriedly, 'but only in a general way.'

I silently cursed the friar for his untimely intervention, for I was afraid that because of it, we should have difficulty now in learning the truth. And I was right. Hamon, like a drowning man clutching at a straw, seized upon this fortuitous explanation of his strange pre-knowledge.

'I, too, met with Ulnoth,' he confirmed eagerly, 'who informed me that Lady Cederwell was dead, and I rode straight home with the news. You recall, Mistress, that that was what I said.'

Ursula Lynom pressed a hand to her forehead. 'Of course,' she agreed. 'It's just that . . . I had forgotten it in my distress.' She smiled tremulously at Sir Hugh. 'My dear friend, forgive me for intruding at such an unseemly moment, before you have even had time to come to terms with your grief. What must you think of me?'

He returned the smile warmly. 'There is nothing to forgive. For heaven's sake, what am I thinking of? You must be chilled to the bone. Come to the fire.' He turned to the steward. 'Get someone to bring wine for Mistress Lynom, and broth if there's any left. And her horses must be safely stabled. They must be rubbed down and fed. Tell Jude and Nicholas to look to it and also to see her men safely billeted for the night.' At Ursula's slight murmur of protest, he added, 'You cannot possibly return to Lynom Hall in this weather. It's snowing hard. Tomorrow, I shall ride back with you. Tostig! Request Mistress Talke to prepare the guest bedchamber.'

The steward bowed and withdrew through a second door near the dais; a door I had not previously noticed. From the blast of cold air accompanying his exit, I guessed that it must open into a triangular courtyard which, by my calculations, had to lie between the great hall and the rest of the house. In the meantime, Mistress Lynom allowed herself to be relieved of her cloak and installed in the one armchair the great hall boasted, placed close to the fire by Sir Hugh himself. I saw the resentful, almost malevolent glance that Gerard Empryngham gave them, and wondered how well the real relationship between the pair was known at Cederwell.

'Tell me, then, exactly what has happened,' Ursula Lynom entreated, a little breathlessly I thought, and twisting her hands together in her lap.

Sir Hugh explained as briefly as he could the circumstances of his wife's death, adding, 'But I do not understand how the hermit could have known.'

Hamon said quickly, 'He rambles abroad looking for food. Maybe, this morning, he followed the track down through the scrubland leading to the foreshore and the tower and . . . and saw Lady Cederwell's body lying on the ground. He is a simple soul. It must have frightened him and he ran away.'

'Yes. Yes, that would doubtless be it,' Sir Hugh agreed with relief. He turned back to Ursula Lynom. 'Brother Simeon here was about to answer some questions concerning his discovery of . . . of . . .' He seemed unable to complete the sentence.

'I have heard of the friar,' Ursula said, raising her head

and peering at Simeon. 'His sermons have been the talk of the district for a week or more. But who is this young man with him? Surely, you're the chapman who was at Lynom this morning?'

'I am, Mistress.' I smiled my most ingratiating smile. 'I had the honour to wait upon you and Dame Judith, and you were both kind enough to give me your custom.'

'The buttons.' She turned back to Sir Hugh. 'The buttons which Hamon was sent to deliver but which you have not yet received, I purchased from this man.' It seemed to me that she was still extremely ill at ease, talking at random, afraid to be silent. 'I took the liberty of buying them for you, Hugh, not knowing that the pedlar intended to come on to Cederwell. I didn't think you'd mind. Nor Jeanette. We're such old friends, and the buttons are silver, inlaid with mother-of-pearl. Just the sort of thing you like.'

'Thank you, my dear. You're very kind.' But his words were accompanied by an almost imperceptible shake of the head, a warning to her to be silent. 'Now, Brother, a moment of your time, if you please. Tell us again the circumstances of how you found . . . Lady Cederwell's body.'

'It was Roger Chapman's persistence which was really responsible for the discovery,' the friar insisted, urging me forward.

So I told the assembled company what I could, but in spite of Sir Hugh's close interrogation, there was nothing new to be added. At some point, one of the maids arrived with a tray bearing a glass of wine and a bowl of broth which Mistress Lynom gratefully accepted, but there were no other interruptions. Everyone listened carefully to what I had to say, and to the muttered corroboration throughout from Simeon.

When the final question had been asked and I had given my answer, there was a pause. Sir Hugh stood staring abstractedly into the fire lost in thought, while the rest of us maintained a respectful silence. At last, however, he roused himself, shook his head as though to clear it of unhappy thoughts and turned to Adela, speaking of more practical matters.

'Will you please supply Mistress Lynom with a nightshift and whatever else she might need. Ursula!' He addressed his guest once more. 'When you have been provided for, will you honour me with your company, here in the hall? It's a sad business, and I feel in want of congenial company.'

Maurice Cederwell snorted with laughter and gave an ironic bow.

'Thank you, Father. You make it only too plain what you think of your usual nightly companions.'

Sir Hugh shrugged, not bothering to contest the accusation. It was Mistress Lynom's turn to send a swift, upward glance of warning, but he either did not notice or chose to ignore it. In fact he compounded his offence by adding, 'I am sure the rest of you will wish to retire early to be alone with your grief. Phillipa and the maids will lay out the body sometime before morning, when they can do so without . . . inflicting any damage. Tomorrow, we must hope that Father Godyer will be able to rise from his sickbed and say the offices for the dead. Has anyone thought to inform him of what has happened?'

It seemed that no one had. The steward was summoned

once again and given instructions not only to enlighten the chaplain, but also to see Friar Simeon and myself safely bestowed in some warm corner for the night. Tostig bowed and signalled for us to follow him, but before we could do so, Gerard Empryngham again stepped forward. He spoke loudly and clearly in a voice taut with anger.

'I wish to say that I am not deceived. I know what I know, and although I can prove nothing at this moment, I refuse to keep silent for much longer. We may have had different mothers, but Jeanette was still my sister. The ties of blood are strong.' And he rushed out of the hall.

Adela prepared to go after him, but first she laid a placatory hand on Sir Hugh's sleeve.

'You mustn't take too much notice of Gerard. He's very upset. He was fond of Jeanette from her babyhood onward. He never resented the fact that she was younger and legitimately born.'

Sir Hugh shook off her hand.

'My dear Adela, I am uninterested in your husband's posturings. He will enjoy playing the grief-stricken brother for a week or two, but I should warn you that I am unwilling to go on supporting the pair of you, now that Jeanette is dead. I've had enough of being bled white just because she believed it her Christian duty to provide for her bastard half-brother and his wife.'

Instead of taking offence at these words, as I had expected, Adela smiled and raised her chin.

'You will be doing us both a favour, Hugh. As you are very well aware, I have long maintained that Gerard should get away from here and stand on his own two feet. We should never have left Gloucestershire and come south with Jeanette when you and she were married. He understands sheep, as does everyone who grows up in that part of the country. He would have done better to have sunk his pride and found employment as a shepherd, however poor the wage, rather than live on charity in a house where it was begrudged him. You need not fear that we shall remain to plague you for very long after the funeral. Only until the weather improves, if that is not asking too much.'

She swung on her heel and marched out of the room, head held high, leaving Sir Hugh looking somewhat shamefaced. Simeon and I followed in her wake with Tostig, just as Phillipa Talke arrived to conduct Mistress Lynom to the guest bedchamber.

As I had surmised, there was indeed a triangular courtyard between the great hall and the main part of the building, the well being sunk in the middle of it. It was bitterly cold and snowing steadily as we crossed to a door on the opposite side, causing us both to huddle deeper into our cloaks. We re-entered the house by a passage which led into the main one and separated buttery from pantry, the pantry lying next door to the kitchen.

'You'll be warm enough in here,' Tostig said, opening the kitchen door and ushering us through. 'Or there's a storeroom beyond, with plenty of empty sacks to use as bedding and full ones to protect you from the draughts.' He was plainly anxious to be gone about more important business. Nevertheless, his conscience suddenly smote him at using a holy man in so offhand a manner. 'I must apologise, Brother, but the men-servants' dormitory is no fit place for

one of your calling, especially not tonight with the addition
of Mistress Lynom's two grooms. You understand.'

'I understand that profanity and lewdness make up the
general run of conversation when men are alone together,'
Simeon replied austerely, 'and I deplore it. More, I condemn
it outright!' He glanced around the now empty kitchen, where
the smells of the afternoon's cooking still clung, and at the
pile of dirty dishes cluttering the table. 'I shall be happy to
sleep here with my friend, the chapman. We have both known
worse billets, I'm certain.'

'Far, far worse,' I agreed feelingly, noting that the fire
still smouldered on the hearth and that there was a pair of
stout bellows handy.

The steward's glance indicated that my opinion was of no
concern to him, but reassured about the friar, he hurried away.
I seized the bellows, reignited the glowing embers and threw
on some logs from a basket which stood nearby. A comfortable
blaze soon gave both light and warmth to the room.

'We shall be cosy enough, as Master Steward says,' I
remarked, removing my cloak and sitting down.

It was too early to sleep, but I was bone-weary after the
day's events and stretched out among the rushes to ease my
aching limbs. My mind, however, was in turmoil as,
obviously, was Friar Simeon's. Exhausted as he must have
been, he could not settle, but prowled around the kitchen,
idly picking up one thing after another and then putting them
down again, without even realising what he was doing. I
indicated one of the stools we had occupied earlier.

'Come and tell me what's preying on your mind, Brother.
It would be better to talk about it, whatever it is.'

He agreed reluctantly but did not immediately sit down, scuffing the rushes with a sandalled foot. His toes, I noticed, were covered with painful-looking chilblains.

'Well?' I encouraged him after a moment or two had passed in silence.

'Why did Lady Cederwell send for me?' he asked at length. 'Why was her message so urgent?' And without expecting an answer he went on, 'There is something wrong in this house!' His narrow chest began to swell and his eyes to flash. 'There is the scent of adultery, can you not smell it? Did you not notice the way Sir Hugh and that Mistress Lynom looked at one another? The way she clung to his hand when she first came in?' Knowing too much, I judged it wisest to say nothing and waited for the friar to continue. 'Adultery,' he repeated. 'And it was against this evil that Lady Cederwell needed my help.' He smote his forehead with a clenched fist. 'I failed her!'

'You know nothing for certain,' I pointed out. 'It might just have been that she had a desire to hear one of your sermons. They have been spoken of everywhere I have been in the past two weeks. Your fame has gone before you.'

He slowly shook his head, sinking on to the stool and scratching at his chilblains as the heat began to irritate them.

'No, I don't believe that and neither do you, any more than you believe that Mistress Lynom's groom met your hermit, Ulnoth, on his way here.' He took a deep breath and admitted, not without difficulty, 'I made a mistake in revealing what you'd told me. I should have held my tongue.'

'It . . . was unfortunate,' I agreed, but diffidently. Simeon was not a man who could lightly be taken to task. 'Yet if you

97

don't believe Hamon's story, what is the truth?'

Simeon's expression grew grimmer. 'I think that when he arrived, he saw Lady Cederwell's body lying on the ground. I think it probable that he also saw something or perhaps someone else which sent him chasing back to his mistress instead of rousing the household here and telling them what had happened.'

I moved an inch or two further away from the fire.

'But if,' I objected, 'Hamon was searching for Sir Hugh, as I have good cause to believe that he was, in order to present him with the buttons, he should have approached the house, not wandered down towards the estuary. And furthermore, the body was hidden from view unless you went around to the far side of the tower.'

Simeon's jaw hardened. 'All the same,' he protested obstinately, 'and for whatever reason, he walked to the tower instead of coming straight to the house.'

I stared up into the blackened rafters overhead.

'I'm inclined to agree with you, Brother, although we've not a shred of evidence, and it would therefore be most imprudent for us to make any accusations. Between ourselves, however, I should guess that the groom might have seen someone as he neared the house, and followed him.'

Simeon nodded. 'You say "him" and I think you speak truly. It could only have been Sir Hugh, or why otherwise would he have pursued him, rather than keep his course?'

This interesting conversation was abruptly brought to a close by the arrival of Martha Grindcobb and Jenny Tonge. The former was none too pleased to see us already ensconced for the night.

'Some of us still have work to do,' she remarked, crossing to the table and the pile of dirty dishes. 'Jenny, see if there's enough water in the barrel for washing this lot. If not, go to the courtyard and draw some from the well.'

I sprang to my feet. 'Let me go! The child can't go out in this weather.'

Martha Grindcobb shrugged. 'Please yourself. She has to when you're not by. As it happens there's sufficient in the barrel for our present needs, but if you're willing, you could bring up a couple of pailfuls for the morning. Do you know where the well is?'

'In the inner courtyard. We passed it as we crossed from the hall.' And I made for the main kitchen door.

'No need to go that way,' Jenny piped up. She indicated the kitchen storeroom. 'There's a door leads directly into the courtyard from there.'

The storeroom was piled high with sacks of winter supplies; joints of salted meat hung from hooks in the ceiling. A second door in an adjoining wall opened into the courtyard. I pulled up the hood of my cloak, turned the key in the well-oiled lock, stepped outside and, within a very few minutes, had raised a pail of water. This, thanks to the well's stout wooden cover which I had first removed, had not frozen over. As I was about to return with the bucket to the kitchen, a door which I had not previously noticed, but which stood side by side with that of the storeroom, opened and Gerard Empryngham looked out, a lighted candle in his hand.

'Who's that?' he demanded, startled by the sight of my tall, cloaked figure.

I pushed back my hood and stepped forward so that the

candlelight played full on my face.

'It's the chapman, Master. I'm fetching water for the cook to refill her barrel. I'll be out again in a moment to draw a second.'

He grunted. 'Very well. But don't forget to replace the well cover when you've finished.'

I reassured him on that point and returned to the kitchen. Martha and Jenny were waiting for a cauldron of water to heat on the fire, and Simeon was still scratching at his chilblains. I told them of my encounter with Gerard, and Martha Grindcobb nodded.

'It's his bedchamber, his and Mistress Empryngham's,' she sniggered. '*He* don't care for it at all, I can tell you, for it's really no more than another storeroom, between the big one and the men-servants' sleeping quarters. He's always considered that he's deserving of something better; one of the bigger, upstairs chambers. But the master has other ideas of what's suitable for a penniless bastard brother and his serving-wench wife.'

With one brawny arm, she lifted the cauldron off the fire and poured some of its now seething contents into a wooden bowl, while I emptied the fresh water into the barrel and went back for a second pailful. This time there was no interruption, although I heard voices raised behind the closed door of the Emp*ryng*hams' bedchamber, but was unable to distinguish anything of what they were saying. It was snowing too hard to eavesdrop, and I hastened back to the warmth of the kitchen.

Chapter Eight

As I re-entered the kitchen with my burden, I saw that a young man had joined us, still wearing boots and cloak, both garments liberally caked with snow. He was arguing vehemently with Martha Grindcobb about the necessity of providing him with food.

'You'll have to make do with bread and cheese,' she was complaining loudly. 'I can't be expected to start cooking again at this time of the evening.'

'It's barely past the hour of Compline!' he protested indignantly. 'I'm cold and hungry. I'll not be fobbed off with bread and cheese.'

The cook snorted, plunged her arms once more into her bowl of hot water and continued to wash the dishes.

'*You'll* not be fobbed off! And who do you think you are?' she demanded sourly, but answering her own question went on, 'Sir Hugh's rent and debt collector, that's who! No one of any great importance, whatever you might think!'

The young man smoothed back the pale, fair hair which hung to his shoulders. The grey eyes glittered angrily.

'I've been on the road for three whole days and have ridden all the way from Woodspring since dinner time, weighed down by two saddle-bags full of money. I've done *my* job, so why can't you do yours?'

Martha Grindcobb withdrew her arms, red to the elbows, from the bowl and stood with hands on hips, regardless of the water dripping steadily down her skirt.

'Because I'm busy. Because I'm having to do a task that should normally be done by Edith and Ethelwynne. But they've decided to indulge in a fit of the vapours and are no good to man nor beast. That's one thing I'll say for you, Jenny,' she added grudgingly, turning to the little kitchen-maid who was silently drying the dishes, 'you don't let your feelings get the better of you. If you have any, that is.'

The young man had by now removed his boots and cloak, but paused in the act of shaking them free of snow to glance inquiringly at the cook.

'Why should the girls be having the vapours? What's happened to upset them?'

We all stared at him for a moment, then Martha Grindcobb shrugged and said, 'Of course, you don't know.'

'Know what?' As I passed him to empty my pail of water into the barrel, the young man followed my progress with his eyes. 'And who's this?'

'This is Roger Chapman and this, Friar Simeon. Both are spending the night here.' The cook resumed her labours. 'This is Sir Hugh's rent and debt collector, Fulk Disney.'

The youth drew himself up to his full height, so that the crown of his head came just above my shoulder level.

'Fulk D'Isigny!' he hissed. 'My forebears came with the Conqueror from France.'

I held out my hand. 'Master Disney, I'm pleased to make your acquaintance.'

My gesture of friendship was pointedly ignored. '*D'Isigny!*' he breathed again.

'Bless you, my son,' Simeon intoned, giving the sign of the cross, but he continued to stare solemnly into the heart of the fire, detached from the proceedings of us lesser mortals.

'What has happened?' Fulk Disney repeated impatiently.

'The mistress has slipped and fallen to her death from the tower,' Jenny Tonge put in, unable to remain silent any longer, and received a damp box on the ear for her pains.

'You speak when you're spoken to, my girl,' Martha Grindcobb told her, before enlarging on the subject to the horrified Fulk.

To do her justice, the cook was brief and to the point, not wasting her breath, as so many women are inclined to do, on fruitless speculation and patently false emotion. But there was only one aspect of the tragedy that interested Master Disney.

'What of Maurice? How is he bearing up? I must go to him at once – to tender my condolences,' he added swiftly.

But I saw Simeon's gaze rest briefly on the young man's face before returning to the fire. I reflected that our holy man was not as divorced from what was going on around him as he would have us believe. He was as capable of leaping to conclusions, either rightly or wrongly, as I was myself. I looked at Martha Grindcobb but, apart from a slight thinning of the lips, her face gave nothing away. Jenny Tonge's was equally expressionless, but I judged her too young and innocent to be possessed of such thoughts as Simeon and I were sharing, and I suddenly felt ashamed. Nevertheless, as soon as Fulk had quit the kitchen, all idea of eating temporarily forgotten, I went to sit beside the friar, dragging my stool as close as possible to his.

The two women being once again absorbed in their task, anxious to finish it as quickly as they could, Simeon turned his head and muttered wrathfully, 'Small wonder that poor dead creature wished for my guidance and advice. This house is a dung heap of iniquity! Adultery and the ancient vice of the Greeks! My presence was needed to cleanse this Augean stable!'

I choked back a laugh at the thought of Simeon in the guise of Hercules, but then realised that his moral strength was probably just as great as the physical prowess of the ancient hero.

'We mustn't allow ourselves to be misled,' I whispered in return, 'or make false assumptions without proof. All Fulk Disney has so far done is to express a natural concern for his master's son, who has just lost his mother.'

'His stepmother,' Simeon replied tartly, 'and one, moreover, young enough to be his sister. I noted very little sign of grief in Maurice Cederwell.'

'All the same,' I urged, 'let's curb our imaginations. We are allowing them to run riot with nothing more to spur them on than a single, unguarded sentiment. Why should Fulk Disney not be worried for someone who is obviously his friend?'

The friar sent me a glance of ill-concealed contempt before hunching his shoulders, turning his back pointedly in my direction and sinking once more into his reverie. Resigning myself to the fact that I had for the moment forfeited his respect, I shifted my stool a little distance from both him and the fire, intent on finding out as much as I could from Martha Grindcobb. But before I had had time to utter more than a pleasantry or two, there was an interruption. We heard the door in the adjacent storeroom rattle open and then slam shut. Seconds later, Adela Empryngham made a tempestuous entrance into the kitchen.

'I'll not share a bed with Gerard any more tonight!' she announced to anyone who cared to listen. 'I've talked to him until I'm blue in the face, but he'll not see reason. We should leave here and go home to Gloucestershire now that Jeanette is dead. What can we possibly hope for if we stay, except humiliation and ultimate defeat? For Hugh doesn't want us here and will turn us out as soon as he can. He's already made that plain. But Gerard refuses to budge and talks wildly of retribution and other such nonsense, as he did earlier, in the hall.' She burst into noisy sobbing.

Martha Grindcobb left her dishes and placed a brawny arm about Adela's shoulders.

'Come to the fire, my dear, and warm yourself. Get up, Chapman, and let a lady sit down.'

I duly gave up my stool to Mistress Empryngham and sat on the floor among the rushes, while Jenny was sent running to the buttery for a stoup of ale. The recent animosity I had witnessed between the cook and her late mistress's sister-in-law seemed to have evaporated in their mutual condemnation of men.

'There's no doing anything with them when they're in that sort of mood,' Martha commiserated. 'I know. I've had two husbands and both as stubborn as mules when the fit was on 'em. Don't you worry, my dear. I'll make you up a spare pallet in the women's dormitory. Master Gerard'll be more likely to see reason in the morning. Jenny,' she added, as the child reappeared with a cup carefully cradled between both hands, 'you'll have to finish the dishes on your own. I'm away to settle Mistress Empryngham for the night. She's sleeping in with us, and perhaps she can talk some sense into the rest of the girls, for one of them'll have to assist Mistress Talke with laying out the body. All our nerves are a-jangle, and no wonder after the happenings of this day.'

When Adela Empryngham had drunk her ale, she and the cook left the kitchen together and calm was restored. While Jenny washed what was left of the dirty pots and pans, I dried them for her. She gave me a timid smile but said nothing, for which I was grateful as I tried to marshal my thoughts into some sort of order. But I realised yet again how very tired I was, and my mind reeled under the impact of all that had occurred since I had left the boulder house that morning; the visit to Lynom Hall, the subsequent two-mile walk to Cederwell, revisiting Ulnoth on the way, my encounter with Friar Simeon, the finding of Lady Cederwell's body and everything which had taken place subsequently. I was suddenly desperate for sleep, and as soon as I had finished my chore, I gathered up my belongings and retreated to a shadowed corner of the kitchen where the wall ovens still gave out some heat. I wrapped myself in my cloak, stretched my length on the floor and pillowed my head on my pack, keeping my cudgel close at hand. I was only vaguely aware of Simeon following my example and settling himself within a few feet of me, saying his prayers and shifting around for a while in the straw, searching for a comfortable position. After that, I was oblivious to everything and everyone around me, and knew nothing more until next morning.

I was suddenly wide awake, refreshed after my long, deep, dreamless sleep and at once aware of a strange, almost unearthly light creeping through the cracks in the shutters. The only sound in the kitchen was made by Brother Simeon's snoring, and as I rose to my feet, I could see that he was lying on his back, spittle dribbling from one corner of his gaping mouth down into his straggling beard. The night's growth of stubble adorned my own chin, and I reckoned that the sooner I got the fire rekindled, the sooner I should have hot water in which to shave. I trod softly across the kitchen and picked up the bellows, thrusting them into the remains of last night's fire, working them hard.

The room was freezing cold and I was shivering in spite of being fully dressed. I thought at first that the fire would have to be swept away and relaid, but at last a spark caught and then a stick began to crackle. I threw on extra logs from the basket and was rewarded by a sudden blaze. Satisfied that it would now burn well, I went into the main passageway, walked the length of the house to the front door, drew back the bolts and opened it. A remarkable sight met my gaze. Every undulation, every contour of ground had vanished under a thick pall of snow. It lay inches deep in drifts of pure, dazzling white, stained here and there with shadows the colour of bilberry juice. I felt again the insensate longing of youth to stamp on it; experienced the same destructive

107

urge to mar that pristine freshness, because such unadulterated beauty was more than the heart and eye could stand.

It had stopped snowing, but the watery sunlight was without warmth and the cold was intense. Blowing on my fingers, I returned to the kitchen where the sight of the fire crackling on the hearth was more than welcome. I filled one of the smaller cauldrons with water from the barrel and hung it from a trivet-hook to heat. The friar was still asleep, but began to rouse a little as I tramped about in my usual clumsy fashion. By the time I had unearthed the razor and a bar of soap from my pack, he was sitting up, sneezing violently.

'Bless you, in the name of the Father, the Son and the Holy Spirit,' I said, grinning.

'Where . . .? Where am I?' he demanded, wiping his nose on one of his sleeves. 'Ah! Yes. I remember. Well, I suppose there's nothing more for either of us to do here, Chapman. When we've broken our fast, we'd best be on our way.'

'Without first cleansing the Augean stable?' I asked, surprised.

Simeon clambered stiffly to his feet.

'Don't mock!' he ordered. 'The gentle lamb who brought me here is dead. Let the rest of them stew in their filth. God will exact His payment on the Day of Judgement, when they are all cast down into the Pit! He needs me elsewhere! My preaching mission is as yet only half accomplished.'

'I'm afraid neither you nor I will be going anywhere today,' I answered cheerfully, ladling some of the hot water into a bowl and proceeding to lather my chin. 'Several inches of snow have fallen during the night. Depending on how quickly it melts, and whether or not there is more to come, we might be snowed up here for days.'

He stared at me in horror, then rushed to throw open two of the shutters. A frame of thin, oiled parchment obscured his immediate view, but once, with my assistance, this had been removed, he was able to see for himself the heaviness of the fall. The narrow gully between the back of the house and the sheer cliff which rose behind it was, I reckoned, almost a foot deep in snow.

'It's worse here than in other places,' I said, 'but that's only to be expected. Nevertheless, it's bad and the tracks will be impassable. We may both heartily thank God that we're in a safe billet and not holed up in some barn or byre. At least we're assured of warmth and food, four solid walls and a roof above our heads. Sir Hugh may not welcome our presence, but the laws of hospitality won't allow him to turn us out in such weather. Nor,' I added, struck by a sudden thought, 'Mistress Lynom and her grooms.' I chuckled. 'He'll not be pleased by all these extra mouths to feed.'

Simeon made no reply, but edged closer to the fire, holding out his hands to the flames. He appeared even more bedraggled than he had done the day before. His sparse hair and beard were unkempt, a faint fuzz of down covering his tonsure. His robe was mired almost to his knees and I noticed a great rent in the hem. The winter pallor of his skin was more pronounced and his shoulders drooped, but no amount of discomfort or fatigue could quench the fiery fanaticism of his eyes.

'Do you know,' he cried accusingly, as though it were

somehow my fault, 'that last night, for the first time in my life, I failed to awaken to say the Matins office? Sir Hugh told us that there is a chapel somewhere in the house. I must find it at once and confess my sin of omission. It must also be nearly the hour of Prime.'

I realised that I, too, had slept so soundly after the rigours of the day that for once I had broken the old habit of waking in the small hours of the morning. I kept quiet, however. Brother Simeon knew nothing of my past, and I had no wish to be taken to task over what he would undoubtedly regard as my backsliding. So I merely advised him to wait until one of the servants could guide him to the chapel, rather than go blundering about a house of mourning. That, anyhow, was the excuse I gave, but it had occurred to me that Mistress Lynom might well have passed the night elsewhere than in the guest room.

'Someone is bound to come in a moment,' I assured him.

The words had hardly left my mouth when I heard much shrieking and squealing outside. I hastily pulled on my boots and went to discover the cause, although I could guess it. Martha Grindcobb, Jenny Tonge and the two other girls, Edith and Ethelwynne, were trying to negotiate the snow-covered steps which led down from the covered gallery and the female servants' quarters. Behind them, her red-rimmed eyes still heavy with sleep, trailed the young woman I had seen briefly the previous evening, Lady Cederwell's personal maid, Audrey Lambspringe. Their skirts were already soaked for several inches above the hems.

Stretching up, I caught the cook around her ample waist and managed to swing her into my arms. Her weight almost winded me, and I staggered a little as I struggled the foot or so to the open passage door and deposited her inside. After that, the other women presented no problem, but I was glad, all the same, to see Jude and Nicholas Capsgrave emerge from their ground-floor dormitory behind the great hall. It took them half a minute or more to wade through the snow drifts, which nearly reached the top of their boots, but when they had done so they helped Edith and Ethelwynne to descend the last few steps, leaving Audrey Lambspringe to me.

She was like a little bag of bones in my arms, as delicate and brittle as the tame sparrows I used to trap between my hands as a boy, and then release. The blue eyes gazing up at me had the same wide, terrified stare, and when I put her down, she darted away just as swiftly. The kitchen was filled with a babel of voices as everyone, including Ursula Lynom's two grooms who had by now joined us, exclaimed in wonder at the night's fall of snow, and Martha Grindcobb tried to press me to her bosom in gratitude for finding the fire already lit and water boiling. The noise was only quelled by the arrival of the housekeeper and steward.

'Silence, all of you!' Mistress Talke commanded. 'Have you no sense of decency? Do you think that this laughter and chatter is seemly with your mistress lying dead upstairs?'

There was a general shuffling of feet and everyone looked uncomfortable. It was true, I think, that they had momentarily forgotten the fact in the excitement of the snow, and I sympathised with them. There is still something today, at my advanced age, which drives everything else from my mind when I see those sparkling white wastes outside my door.

'Has the body been laid out yet?' the cook wanted to know, but Phillipa Talke shook her head.

'The upper part has lost its stiffness, but not the lower limbs. I have spoken to Father Godyer who informs me that it will take well over a day from the time Lady Cederwell died.'

The mention of the chaplain recalled Martha to a sense of her duties.

'I must take some food to the poor man. But it's little he's been able to fancy these past few days. How is he, Mistress Talke? Does he seem any better?'

'A little perhaps,' the housekeeper conceded. 'He's always suffered in his head, it's nothing new. These rheums pass in the end. Now, I think it high time we all got on with our work. We have a guest in the house. Mistress Lynom, Sir Hugh informs me, will break her fast with him in the great hall.'

She swept out of the kitchen, her household keys jangling at her belt, and I wondered if it were my imagination that she appeared even grander and more important than she had done the day before. But when she was out of earshot, Martha Grindcobb sniggered.

'Poor fool,' she said to no one in particular. 'Can't she see what's going on under her nose? Has been going on for years? Doesn't she realise that the master has never looked at her except as his housekeeper? Doesn't she know that Mistress Lynom is more to him than just an old friend?'

No one seemed disposed to argue with her, or even show any particular interest in her words. Familiarity with the situation had bred indifference. The gossip was stale except to an outsider like me, and when Brother Simeon had been led away by Tostig to be conducted to the chapel, I sidled up to the cook where she was frying dried, salted fish in a skillet.

'Sir Hugh's very partial to herring,' she told me, and then, lowering her voice, added, 'I'll cook you a couple as well, if you like.'

I accepted with alacrity. I evidently stood high in her favour at present, so I took advantage of the moment and asked her to explain her words concerning Mistress Talke and Sir Hugh. She was only too willing.

'The poor gowk thinks he's in love with her, although what encouragement the master's ever given her to believe so, no one knows but she. I've seen no sign of it, nor anyone else that I can discover.' Martha broke off for a moment to upbraid the girl, Edith, for not stirring the gruel vigorously enough, then returned to the subject in hand. 'There's few in these parts that don't know he's besotted with Mistress Lynom and always has been. I reckon she'll be the third Lady Cederwell within the year.'

I nodded. 'I, too, heard a rumour before I got here that Sir Hugh and Mistress Lynom were more to each other than simply friends.' I added that I knew him to have been at Lynom Hall the previous morning and repeated what Dame Judith had said.

'There you are then!' Martha tipped the herrings on to a plate and sent Ethelwynne running to the storeroom for two more. 'The world and his wife knows it for the truth, all but Phillipa Talke who's got this maggot in her head that she's his secret fancy.' Martha heaved a sigh. 'She'll learn better soon.'

Adela Empryngham entered the kitchen, having just struggled down the stairs from the women's dormitory, where she had spent the night. She had obviously benefited from the fact that Jude and Nicholas Capsgrave had been out clearing the steps of snow, for the hems of her gown and cloak were barely wet.

She grimaced at Martha Grindcobb. 'I'd best go and make peace with Gerard, I suppose, and try to hammer some sense into his thick skull. There's one thing, as long as this snow lies, there's no moving anywhere. I shall pray that it doesn't last beyond poor Jeanette's funeral.'

She disappeared into the storeroom and, a few moments later, we heard her open the door which led into the triangular courtyard. Ethelwynne returned with the herrings and Martha dropped them into the skillet.

'Nice plump ones,' she said. 'You'll enjoy these, Master Chapman.'

A blood-curdling scream rent the air. For a second no one moved, everyone staring at everyone else in wild surmise. Another scream however sent us all pell-mell in the direction of the sound, following in the steps of Mistress Empryngham. As we pushed and jostled with each other to get through the courtyard doorway, we saw her standing by the well, hands pressed against her cheeks, her mouth open and emitting a high-pitched wail. Something, two things rather, stuck up out of the well, stiff and frozen solid.

It took me a moment, as I think it did the others, to realise that it was a pair of naked legs.

Chapter Nine

Even now, I can clearly recall the sudden desire I had to laugh, so finely in this life is the line drawn between tragedy and comedy. But there was, for a brief moment, something very amusing about those seven or eight inches of leg pointing skywards above the low parapet of the well.

'Who . . .? Who is it?' quavered the voice of Martha Grindcobb behind me.

'Who *was* it, you mean,' Brother Simeon corrected in sepulchral tones. 'No creature could survive outdoors in his nightshirt in this weather.'

This bald statement of fact brought me up short, and any desire I had to laugh evaporated.

Adela Empryngham said between sobs, 'It's . . . It's G-Gerard! I recognise . . . his . . . his feet.'

Edith and Ethelwynne gave way once again to hysterics, and I was conscious of a small, cold hand tucking itself into one of mine. Glancing round, I saw Audrey Lambspringe, her face chalk-white, standing beside me. I closed my fingers over hers and squeezed them reassuringly.

By this time Tostig and Mistress Talke had appeared in the storeroom to discover the cause of the commotion. The steward immediately sent Jenny Tonge to the stables to fetch Jude and Nicholas Capsgrave, but before she could return with the grooms, Mistress Lynom's two men had arrived on the scene. Releasing Audrey's hand, I went forward to assist them in removing Gerard from the well.

It was a difficult business. The body was stiff; moreover, some part of it was wedged tightly between the stonework of the walls, and up to the waist it was below the level of the water which had frozen solid to a depth of several inches. The ice had to be broken before any attempt could be made to free the corpse, and Jude Capsgrave was dispatched to find a long-handled mallet while his brother joined us in peering into the depths of the well.

'Sweet Virgin,' he breathed, awe-struck. 'How did this happen? What fool left the cover off?'

My heart gave a sickening jolt. Surely I had replaced the lid after fetching that second pail of water for Martha last night! Surely I had! I thought desperately, trying to recollect my actions. I had drawn up the bucket, tipped its contents into my pail, listening all the while to those raised voices behind the door of Gerard and Adela's chamber, and then . . . And then? Had I bent down and picked up the heavy wooden cover, replacing it on top of the well? Or had I forgotten it, my mind elsewhere as I vainly attempted to make out a phrase or even a word of the Emprynghams' quarrel? I tried to conjure up the feel of the handle against my palm, the lid's weight dragging at my arm as I lifted it, but I could not. Had my mother's often repeated warning at last come true; that my insatiable curiosity would one day prove to be the death of me or some other poor creature?

I was not the only person wondering if blame for the tragedy lay at my door. Raising my head, I encountered the reproachful and horrified gaze of both Martha Grindcobb and Brother Simeon. Even Jenny Tonge was staring at me in wide-eyed speculation. I hastily looked away again and concentrated on the matter in hand. Jude Capsgrave came back with the mallet, Sir Hugh and Mistress Lynom, together with Maurice Cederwell, in his wake.

Sir Hugh immediately took charge of the operation. Under his guidance, although without receiving anything in the way of practical help from him, Jude broke the encasing ice and then the five of us – the two brothers, Jasper, Hamon and myself – lifted out the stiff and frozen body, laying it reverently upon the coarse, grey woollen blanket which Phillipa Talke had sent for in the meantime. It was indeed Gerard Empryngham, or all that remained of him, eyes and mouth wide open in horror at his fate. He was naked except for his nightshift, or if he had been wearing a nightcap, it had fallen off and was now somewhere in the icy depths of the water.

'Well, here is another corpse we shall be unable to lay out for some time,' commented Sir Hugh. 'Carry him to his chamber and lay him upon his bed.' If he felt any grief at the death of his brother-in-law he concealed it admirably. 'Then all assemble in the great hall so that we may decide how this unfortunate accident could have happened. Breakfast must wait. Adela, my dear, cease that noise. Weeping and wailing can do no good either to Gerard or to yourself and is unpleasant listening for the rest of us. I give you all ten minutes to compose yourselves, but no more. Mistress Talke, have a word with those stupid girls.' And he glanced darkly at Edith and Ethelwynne before offering his arm to Ursula Lynom and escorting her back into the house.

Sir Hugh was seated in the centre of the long table on the dais, his guest behind him and Hamon and Jasper standing behind her chair. The rest of us were ranged in front of them, so that the general impression was that of a courtroom, judges aloft, accused below. And I was the chief suspect, the finger being pointed at me by both the friar and the cook, with Jenny Tonge in reluctant support. Adela tearfully explained how a quarrel with her husband had led her to seek sanctuary in the women's dormitory the previous evening, in the hope that a good night's sleep would bring Gerard to his senses, and the others attested to her presence.

'You are all aware that Gerard walked in his sleep from time to time,' she added, bursting into noisy sobs once more.

There was a murmur of assent from the regular inhabitants of Cederwell Manor, and Maurice, who was standing a little apart from the rest of us, one arm laid about Fulk Disney's shoulders, said, 'It was one of the reasons, my dear Adela, why it was thought better you and he should have a room downstairs. Isn't that so, Father?' And as Sir Hugh nodded curtly Maurice went on, 'Moreover, we know that Gerard was deeply distressed by his sister's death. Isn't it likely that such disturbance of mind caused him to walk? And if the cover wasn't on the well, it would be easy enough in those circumstances for him to fall headlong into it. The shock of the icy water alone might be sufficient to kill him.'

This was the cue for everyone to turn and look at me.

The time had come to defend myself.

'I am sure,' I protested, 'that I replaced the lid.'

'Quite sure?' asked Sir Hugh, peering accusingly at me.

Honesty compelled me to admit, 'I'm almost certain that I did.'

The knight shook his head sadly. '"Almost" is not good enough, Chapman. However,' his countenance lightened, 'no blame can be attached to you. You are a stranger to this house and its people. It was an oversight which normally would have had no worse consequence than a few inches of ice to be broken up before water could be drawn from the well this morning. You were not to know that Master Empryngham was prone to walk in his sleep. I therefore exonerate you of any guilt for his death. It is just another blow delivered by Fate to this unhappy household and one which, in some sort, may be said to be an unfortunate result of the first.'

As Sir Hugh rose to his feet, thus declaring the investigation to be satisfactorily concluded, he permitted himself the bleakest of smiles, but my feeling was that he could barely contain his mood of elation. And indeed, what was there in either death to dismay him? Within twenty-four hours he had been rid of an uncongenial wife and her unwanted half-brother; two accidents which, as he had pointed out, could plausibly be linked one to the other. But although, following Sir Hugh's example, no one showed me anything but the utmost sympathy at having been the unwitting cause of Gerard Empryngham's death, I remained unconvinced in my own mind that I was. True, I still could not recall replacing the well-cover, but neither could I remember not doing so. And until that happened, I refused to accept responsibility, and said as much to Brother Simeon.

'You must learn to live with the results of your actions, both of omission and commission,' he told me austerely, while we ate our delayed breakfast of herring and black bread in a corner of the kitchen. 'To seek to deny them is a sin in the eyes of God.'

I made no reply, busy watching the bustle of activity all around us as Martha and the maids tried to blot out the horrors of yesterday evening and this morning by throwing themselves wholeheartedly into their work. The family and Mistress Lynom had to be waited upon in the great hall, and there was Adela to be fussed over and cosseted in the women's quarters, where she was laid down upon one of the beds. Also, the first numbed silence was gradually giving way to gossip and speculation about the future now that the mistress and her brother were no more. I was content to remain thus, warm, well fed and unnoticed, for a while, but the friar was growing restless again, getting up and going first to the back door and then to the front, staring out across that unending white wasteland of snow.

'It's no good, Brother,' I said when he eventually rejoined me, 'the tracks are impassable today, and maybe for many days to come.' Adopting something of his own sententious tone when speaking to me earlier, I added, 'You would do well to reconcile yourself to the fact. Nothing you can do will alter things. The weather is not at your command.'

He looked down at where I still lolled on the kitchen floor, my back propped against the wall, my long legs stretched out in front of me. His eyes narrowed in disapproval.

'This idleness may suit you, Chapman, but I have God's

work to do. My mission to the people of this region cannot brook such delay.'

'Then ask God to send you better conditions,' I answered flippantly, and heard his sharp intake of breath.

'That may be impiously meant, but it is precisely what I shall do. I am going now to find the chapel.' He bent down and gazed fiercely into my eyes. 'For the sake of your immortal soul, my friend, you would do well to remember that God is not mocked!' With which parting shot, he quit the kitchen, passing Phillipa Talke on the way.

'Do you want either of the girls to help you lay out the mistress?' Martha Grindcobb asked, but the housekeeper shook her head.

'No, not yet. The stiffness is still present in parts of the body. We must wait a while longer. It seems,' she added, 'that Mistress Lynom and those two men of hers will have, perforce, to remain here until the snow melts sufficiently to allow them home again. I must find out if there's enough clean linen in the linen press. If not, one of the men will have to dig his way through to the cottages and fetch the laundress up to the house. How is everything here?'

The cook smiled, pleased to be able to confirm that in her domain all was very well indeed, in spite of the extra mouths to feed.

'We shan't starve,' she answered briskly, 'even with appetites like his to satisfy!' And she nodded in my direction.

Phillipa Talke glanced sourly at me. 'Make sure he earns his keep,' she recommended. 'You can surely find some work for a great lout like him to do!'

I noted for the first time since she entered the kitchen

how drawn the housekeeper was looking. Her eyes were heavy as though she had slept badly, and in spite of her sharp words she appeared preoccupied, hurrying off without waiting to see that her advice was followed. Martha Grindcobb merely winked at me and returned to ordering the kitchen-maids about. I settled myself more comfortably and closed my eyes.

It had been my experience that the stiffness which seized bodies a few hours after death lasted for roughly a day. It began in the head and neck, spread to all other parts, then passed off in much the same sequence. Therefore, by my reckoning Lady Cederwell had not died until at least the middle of the previous morning, perhaps even later. I should be interested to discover when the rigor began to loosen its hold. In the meanwhile, having assured myself that Martha indeed had no employment for me, I disposed myself for sleep.

Even when young, I had the ability to cat-nap during the day and awake refreshed, but rarely, if ever, did I dream anything but the most arrant nonsense during these brief spells of unconsciousness. Those half-visions which sometimes disturbed my slumbers were for the long stretches of the night, for the depths of darkness when the soul can be on the verge of severance from the body, for that time when past misdeeds or too hearty a supper can lie heavily on the mind and stomach. Yet that morning, almost as soon as I closed my eyes, I was standing in the small, triangular courtyard created by the odd angle of the great hall to the rest of the house at Cederwell Manor. It was snowing as I paused by the well, and behind the closed shutters at my back, voices were raised in angry recrimination. With those slow, deliberate movements that endow any dream with its trance-like quality, I drew up the bucket, unhooked it, emptied its contents into the pail on the ground beside me and hung it once again on its peg, having first locked the spindle into position so that the rope would not uncoil. Then, stooping to my right, I picked up the heavy wooden lid and replaced it on top of the well. I clearly felt the rough wood of the handle against my palm and the sudden, small, sharp stab of pain . . .

I awoke with a resounding snort that made Martha Grindcobb and the kitchen-maids turn their heads in my direction. Edith began to giggle.

'That was a short sleep, lad,' the cook said. 'It's barely five minutes since you shut your eyes.'

'I . . . I had a bad dream,' I answered, which was only half a lie.

I raised my right hand, examining it carefully, and it took no more than a second to find what I was looking for, a tiny splinter embedded in the soft flesh at the base of the thumb. I now knew that I *had* replaced the cover on the well the previous evening, although it would be almost impossible to convince anyone else of that fact. The tiny sliver of wood could have been acquired anywhere at any time; when I removed the lid for example. A dream would carry no weight in my defence; it could easily be dismissed as a lie or a fabrication of my imagination, occasioned by the anxiety to prove myself innocent of Gerard Empryngham's death. Nevertheless, I was absolutely certain that I was not responsible.

I closed my eyes again, but now I was only feigning sleep.

My mind was as busy as one of those caged squirrels which fine ladies keep for their amusement, turning over all the implications of my discovery. If I had replaced the lid, then someone else had deliberately removed it. But why would anyone wish to do so? There had been no call for more water to be drawn last night; my second pailful had filled the indoor barrel to the brim. Furthermore, no one had come into the kitchen after Martha and Jenny Tonge had quit it on their way to bed. They had left by the back door and mounted the outside staircase to the covered gallery and the women's dormitory at its end. And shortly after their departure, I had heard the housekeeper come bustling along the main passageway to lock the back entrance with an important rattle of her keys.

All the same, when I thought about the situation more closely, I had to assume that one of the women, probably Martha Grindcobb, on account of her superior position, must have possession of a key which would allow her and the others access to the house ready for their duties each morning. There was, too, a door leading from the great hall into that inner courtyard, although no one could have entered the storeroom because it was locked from the inside. But then, there would be no need to enter the storeroom if the object was to murder Gerard Empryngham . . .

My eyes shot open as I silently put into words the suspicion which had been hovering at the edges of my mind ever since I had seen those two feet protruding from the well earlier this morning. And if Gerard had been murdered, why not his half-sister also? I realised now that Brother Simeon and I had both been toying with the notion when we had talked together the previous evening, but had each dismissed it through lack of evidence and the belief that we were letting our imaginations run away with us. Yet why had Lady Cederwell sent so urgently for the friar, if it were not to enlist his aid against the adultery of her husband and the perhaps even greater sin of her stepson, both offences rank in the eyes of the Church, and therefore in her own?

This theory pointed the finger of suspicion at Sir Hugh himself, his son, Maurice, and at Fulk Disney; for Brother Simeon's reputation had gone before him, and his determination to root out immorality wherever he found it had become a byword throughout the surrounding villages. The news would certainly have spread as far as Cederwell, and the knowledge that Jeanette had invited him to the manor must have rung alarm bells in more than one head.

But there were others in the house who might have persuaded themselves that they would benefit from its mistress's death. Phillipa Talke, if Martha's gossip were true, either remained in ignorance of Sir Hugh's liaison with Mistress Lynom or refused to believe in it, and hoped to marry him herself one day. Adela Empryngham loathed her position as poor relation and the contempt shown to her and Gerard by her brother-in-law and many of his servants. Maybe she had at last come to the end of her tether. If Jeanette were to die, to have a fatal accident, then Sir Hugh would certainly turn Gerard out, and he and Adela would be able to return to their original home.

And there might well be others whose motives were more obscure. I could not think, from what I had so far learned of her, that Lady Cederwell had been a greatly loved châtelaine.

Audrey Lambspringe, it was true, seemed to have held her mistress in some affection, but no one else, apart from her brother, had shown any outward sign of grief. And now Gerard himself was dead, the victim of yet another seeming accident . . . Slowly, I drew up my legs and folded my arms around them, my chin resting on my knees.

I was suddenly aware of Martha Grindcobb talking. 'And we'll have pears in wine syrup and a sweet cheese tart. With Mistress Lynom stopping, I'll have to be on my mettle. They say that cook of hers is a wonder.' She sniffed. 'We'll see about that. She won't out-wonder me!'

Ursula Lynom! I had forgotten her, but why should not she or one of her household have had a hand in Jeanette Cederwell's death? That groom of hers, Hamon, had come riding back to the hall in an almighty hurry. Perhaps he had not just discovered the body, as Simeon and I had surmised, or seen someone else bending over it, but seized an opportunity fortuitously presented to him, and carried out what he knew to be his mistress's wishes . . .

I reined in my galloping thoughts. This was going altogether too fast. I could see that Mistress Lynom might wish Jeanette Cederwell out of the way, but why her brother? And then I remembered Gerard's barely concealed threat, made in the great hall yesterday evening. 'I wish to say that I am not deceived. I know what I know, and although I can prove nothing at this moment, I refuse to keep silent for much longer.' Ursula Lynom had been present, and surely Hamon had been there as well.

'You're very quiet, my lad,' the cook said as she bustled past me, shouting several orders at once to the harassed

kitchen-maids. She was plainly in her element with a houseful
of people to cater for, and I suspected that her talents were
not normally given much chance for display.

I got to my feet. 'Do you need me for anything?'

Martha paused, considering. 'You could take up some
broth to Father Godyer,' she said. 'To the best of my
recollection, he's had no breakfast. What with one thing and
another and all the upset, I've quite overlooked him yet
again.' She ladled some stew from the pot simmering over
the fire into a bowl, stuck a wooden spoon in it, placed it on
a tray and handed the whole to me.

Following her directions, I made my way to the front of
the house and mounted the narrow, twisting staircase which
led to the upper storey. At the top, I turned left and walked
past the solar, two bedchambers and the chapel – where I
had a brief glimpse through the open door of Brother Simeon,
still on his knees before the altar – to a small, dark room
which managed to be stuffy and yet icy cold at one and the
same time. An elderly man, teeth chattering, was huddled
under inadequate bedclothes, sneezing violently every now
and then and blowing his nose into a soiled piece of linen.

'Father Godyer,' I said, 'I've brought you breakfast.'

He sat up, peering suspiciously at me from red-rimmed,
watery eyes.

'Who – who are you?' he quavered; and when I had
enlightened him and explained my part in all the tragic events
of the last two days, he shook his head in disbelief. 'That
such terrible things should happen under this roof! It doesn't
seem possible.'

'You've heard about Master Empryngham?' I asked.

The chaplain nodded. 'The friar, Brother Simeon, looked in on me before he went next door to pray. He told me what had occurred.' I placed the tray on his knees and he took a spoonful of broth, only to choke on it as the tears coursed down his emaciated cheeks. He pushed the bowl away. 'I can't eat it. I can't eat anything. I'm too upset. Gerard, I don't care so much about him, although I know that's a terrible thing to say, and God will rightly punish me for it. But Jeanette! My lady! She was one of God's chosen from her earliest years. When she was little, I used to think that she would enter the Church and become a nun, but somehow it never happened.' He wiped his face with the back of his hand.

I seated myself on the edge of his bed. 'You've known Lady Cederwell a long time then, Father?'

'Since childhood. And Gerard. I came here with them from Gloucestershire when my Jeanette married Sir Hugh. His own chaplain had just died and it seemed providential, because otherwise I should have been out of a place.'

Gently I pushed the bowl of broth back towards him and offered him the handle of the spoon.

'You must eat something,' I coaxed, 'to keep up your strength. And while you do, you can tell me all about Lady Cederwell. *Your* Jeanette.'

Chapter Ten

The chaplain flushed slightly.

'Did I call her that? Yes, yes, so I did. And if I'm honest, it's as a daughter, a real daughter, that I've always thought of her. I've never had any family of my own, you see.' He picked up the spoon and began to drink the broth, already feeling a little happier simply by talking about what was obviously a subject dear to his heart. 'I had no brothers or sisters and my father died before I was born. My mother survived for only a short time after I entered the priesthood. Nor did I have any other kinsfolk in my village.'

'Where was that?' I asked as he paused to swallow another mouthful.

'Amongst the Cotswold hills. Sheep,' he added succinctly.

I nodded. I knew what he meant. The best wool in England, in the whole of western Europe, is still spun today from the fleeces of Cotswold sheep. It has brought great riches to our region.

'Go on,' I urged him.

'When I was twenty-four years of age, I went to be chaplain to Lady Cederwell's father, Master Walter Empryngham, near the village of Chipping Campden. (He was a sheep farmer, one of the wealthiest in the district.) That same year – it was the year that the present king's father, the Duke of York, was named Protector when poor King Henry went mad – Jeanette was born. Mistress Empryngham died of milk fever about six weeks later. Jeanette was her only child, and Master Walter's only legitimate child. Because of that, everyone expected him, after a suitable period, to marry again, but he never did. He remained faithful to his lady's memory.'

'Gerard was Master Empryngham's bastard son?'

The priest grunted assent, scraping the last of the broth from the bowl. 'He was four years old when his half-sister was born, and I was told that he'd lived in his father's household since the age of one, a twelvemonth before Master Walter got wed. The mother, by all accounts, was a daughter of one of the local cottars, a respectable man who'd have nothing more to do with her once she got herself pregnant, nor with her son. She also died in childbirth – it's a chancy business for women, poor souls—' I thought silently of Lillis '– so Master Walter decided to take responsibility for the boy and had him raised, as I say, in his household.'

'What sort of status did Gerard enjoy?'

The chaplain shrugged, blowing his nose again in his piece of linen and plumping up his pillows so that he could lean back more comfortably against them.

'It was rather a strange position thinking about it now, although it didn't particularly strike me so then. Sometimes Master Walter treated him like a son, and at others as one of the underlings.' Father Godyer pursed his thin lips judiciously. 'I suppose the best way to describe Gerard's treatment by Master Walter, as by everyone else, was as a highly privileged servant who mostly got away with things, but occasionally was forcibly reminded of his place.'

'In other words, the sort of treatment that is bound, sooner or later, to breed bitterness and resentment.'

When he had finished sneezing, the chaplain nodded.

'I think the lad did feel in some sort aggrieved, but he was wise enough not to show it openly. He liked the perquisites attendant on his position as an Empryngham – albeit a left-handed one – too much to risk offending Master Walter. And to give Master Walter his due, he did have a genuine affection for the lad.'

I grimaced. 'So you had a father who was fond of his son, and a son who was fond of what his father could give him. Am I right?'

It was the chaplain's turn to draw down the corners of his mouth. 'I'm afraid so. But it was you, yourself, who suggested that Gerard had small cause to be grateful. Dogs which are fondled one minute and kicked the next never grow into loving animals. Moreover, bastard children are always in an unenviable position, particularly those who are both male and older than the heir. But – and here is the contradictory element in the story – Gerard worshipped his little half-sister. Not,' he added with a sentimental sigh, 'that it was surprising. Jeanette was a sweet and pretty child who grew into an even sweeter and lovely young girl.' There was a long pause before Father Godyer went on, almost inaudibly, 'Too sweet and lovely for her own good.'

I waited, but when he seemed disinclined to continue, I prompted, 'Why do you say that?' He made no answer, so I changed the subject, asking, 'Was she always inclined to the religious life?'

This obtained an immediate response. 'From her earliest years she was extremely spiritual, and was never happier than on her knees, either in church or at her prie-dieu.' The chaplain must have seen something in my face, for his own immediately assumed a sour, closed expression. 'You find that strange, Chapman?'

'Somewhat,' I admitted. 'Children should surely have their fair share of naughtiness and of mischief-making.'

'Why? There are those people on this earth who are born to be better than the rest of us, to do God's work, and we should thank the Virgin and all the saints for them.' The rheumy eyes grew dreamy. 'Jeanette's own favourite saint was Alphege. She dedicated her chapel in the Saxon tower to him.'

I felt this to be appropriate. Aelfheah, to give him his Saxon and not his Norman name, had been Archbishop of Canterbury under King Ethelred Unraed, and had suffered martyrdom at the hands of the invading Danes; an uncompromising man who had led a bleak life, and met an even bleaker death unflinchingly, secure in the righteousness of his faith. And not for the first time, I knew a pang of envy for such certainty, but as usual I kept these thoughts to myself. I have always had one sort of courage, but not the kind to suffer the tortures of the damned for what I believe in. But there again, I have never been absolutely sure what that is.

'How did Master Empryngham get along with his daughter?' I inquired.

Father Godyer was shaken by a spasm of coughing. When

it subsided, he said, 'He had little to do with her, being a girl. He passed her over to the women of the household and left her upbringing in their charge. Such masculine affection as there was in her life came from Gerard and from me.' He hastened to add, 'I was her confessor, her spiritual adviser, you understand. Whatever paternal feelings I had for her were . . . were in that capacity.'

I removed the tray from his knees and placed it on the floor beside the bed.

'Naturally. Did Master Empryngham show no interest in her at all?'

The chaplain screwed up his face. 'She was his child. His heir. He was careful to ensure that she had everything in life which should rightfully be hers, but he found her extreme piety difficult to fathom.' He flung up a hand, the back covered in a tracery of fine blue veins. 'You must not run away with the idea that Master Walter was not a devoted son of Holy Church, but there are those people who find saintliness hard to cope with.'

I restrained myself from agreeing too vehemently, letting him ramble on in the hope that he would eventually return to that point in his discourse which had so intrigued me: why he thought that Jeanette Empryngham had been too sweet and lovely for her own good. At the age of sixteen, it appeared, she had declared her intention of never marrying. She would be no bride but the bride of Christ.

'What happened,' I asked, 'to make her change her mind?'

The chaplain's face darkened and his bloodless lips set in a hard, thin line. For a moment, I thought my curiosity was

133

about to be thwarted a second time, but then he said baldly, 'She was raped.'

Even I was shocked into silence. At last I said, 'Who was the villain?'

'One of her father's shepherds. I can't recall his name, if I ever knew it. Jeanette used, on occasions, to walk up to the pastures when the flocks were out to graze. She loved the hills. This fellow must have lusted after her in his heart for some while until, one day, he could no longer control himself.'

'No one was with her?'

'It was her father's land. Why should she fear for her safety? The shepherds were her friends.'

'What happened to the man?'

'He ran away. What else could he do? He must have been terrified by the consequences of his crime, once he had slaked his desire and come to his senses. Of course, Master Walter raised the hue and cry. Every able-bodied man for miles around went after the blackguard, but sad to say, he cheated the gallows. He was found after two days. He had been set upon and killed by outlaws, who left his body to rot in a ditch. Justice had been done, but the damage he had wrought could not be undone.'

'Yet, surely,' I urged, 'Lady Cederwell's decision to enter a convent could only have been reinforced by what had happened to her. Who prevented this, and why? Was it her father's doing?'

The chaplain shook his head. 'No, no! Just the opposite. Master Walter now saw it as the only solution for Jeanette. Who, after all, would want to marry spoiled goods?'

'So?'

'It was the girl herself who refused to take the veil. She saw her presence as defiling any sisterhood that she might enter, and therefore renounced all intention of becoming a nun. Master Walter was furious. He began to see her as a permanent burden upon his resources, the spinster daughter always at home. Moreover, the effect of her ordeal upon Jeanette was to make her spend even more time praying and fasting, locked away long hours together from all those around her, until, I am sorry to say, most of the household lost patience with her. In the end, there were only Gerard and myself to whom she could turn for sympathy and understanding.'

The miserable little room had grown so icy cold, that I was beginning to shiver. I was too intrigued by the chaplain's story, however, to return just yet to the warmth of the kitchen. Instead, I picked up his rusty black cassock, which had been thrown down on top of a chest when he took to his bed, and wrapped myself in it. Father Godyer raised no objection.

'But Master Empryngham's fears obviously proved to be ill founded,' I said. 'Someone did offer for his daughter's hand. When and how did Sir Hugh happen to meet her?'

'About a year later, he was in the neighbourhood of Gloucester, visiting a cousin.' (I recollected that Dame Judith had told me as much.) 'And from there, he rode north with his kinsman to visit a mutual friend who lived near Chipping Campden. This friend, in his turn, was a friend of Master Walter, and so Sir Hugh and my lady met. It was within a month of their first encounter that my master suddenly died, falling down in some kind of fit while he was at supper one afternoon, and from which he never recovered. He lingered for a couple of days, but we all knew he'd been touched by death. He knew it himself, and in his dying hours laid two commands upon Jeanette. The first was to take care of Gerard, even though he was, by now, married and in his twenty-first year, and the second was to accept Sir Hugh's offer of marriage, should he make one.'

'Master Empryngham was fairly certain, then, that Sir Hugh wanted to marry her?'

'Oh yes! We all were. She was sixteen, young enough to be his daughter – indeed, we discovered later that he had a son of almost the same age – and I think that was the attraction for him. That and her money, especially when her father died and she inherited everything he had.'

I smiled. 'You're a cynic, Father.'

He hotly refuted the accusation. 'I am a realist. There is a world of difference.'

'Perhaps,' I acknowledged, unwilling to offend him. 'Pray continue. I don't need to ask if Lady Cederwell did as she was bidden.'

The chaplain was racked by yet another spasm of coughing. Then he went on, 'It was her father's dying wish, when he stood on the very brink of eternity. How could she refuse to obey? I suspect, too, that she did not know what else to do. She was at a loss. She knew nothing of sheep-farming, and would have been at the mercy of her bailiff. Furthermore, she had no interest in the raising and welfare of sheep. So she accepted Sir Hugh's proposal with the one proviso that Gerard and his wife came south with her to Cederwell Manor, and were housed and cared for by her future husband.'

'Sir Hugh agreed?'

'Mmm ... yes, but not readily. He was reluctant to have two more mouths to feed. He is not a generous man, as you might have gathered. But yes, he did agree. He had no choice if he wanted to marry her, for she would not have consented otherwise. Nor, I suppose, did he wish to be seen as a man who would ignore a father's dying request.'

'And why do you think he wanted to marry her? Was it only the fact that she was a wealthy heiress?'

The chaplain thought about this for a moment or two, giving several loud trumpet blasts into his handkerchief while he did so. At last he said, 'I confess I think that to have been his main consideration. She was also very young and pretty. But I believe, too, that he was intrigued by her – her – er – circumstances. Like many men, he felt sure that Jeanette must have done something to encourage her attacker; that she must have led him on. He thought that, secretly, she was hot-blooded and promiscuous, and what would have been a deterrent to many of his fellows, fascinated Sir Hugh.'

'But this was not the case?'

'Far from it. Indeed ...' Father Godyer hesitated, a little uncomfortable and carefully picking his words. 'It is possible that Jeanette was in ... in one respect, not a ... a satisfactory wife to him.' He took a deep breath and speech flowed more freely. 'But having once taken her marriage vows, she was prepared to be a good and faithful helpmate.'

'And, in return, expected the same loyalty from Sir Hugh?'

The chaplain spread his thin arms. 'With her strong religious beliefs, she would expect no other. She was a child who knew nothing of the world.'

'Had never wanted to know,' I suggested. 'How soon did things begin to go wrong between them?'

Father Godyer gave a gusty sigh. 'They were never really right, and if my assumptions about Sir Hugh are correct, how could they have been? But they rubbed along tolerably for a couple of years – until Mistress Lynom's husband died. Everyone on the manor, except Jeanette, suspected, or maybe even knew for certain, that his relationship with the lady was more than simple friendship. But once Anthony Lynom was dead and buried, neither made much attempt at concealment. It became apparent even to my mistress that they were lovers.'

'This shocked her?'

'Deeply. Not because she was jealous.' The chaplain gave a wry, shrewd smile. 'I think Sir Hugh might have made an effort to end the affair if that had been my lady's reason. No, no, but because it was a mortal sin. Because it was an affront to God for her husband to imperil his soul in such a manner. Many a time, she has implored me to speak to him; to beg him to see the error of his ways, but alas, Chapman, she appealed in vain. I may as well tell you, for you'll probably discover it for yourself, that I am morally a very weak man. My feet are made of clay. I could never risk upsetting Sir Hugh for fear of losing my place here. You can despise me if you like. I give you free leave.'

I laid one of my large hands over both his fragile ones as they lay clasped together on the shabby counterpane.

'I assure you that I have far too many frailties of my own to despise you for yours. But continue. Was this liaison between Sir Hugh and the Widow Lynom the reason why

Lady Cederwell sent for Friar Simeon?'

The chaplain nodded. 'When word of his being in the district reached us, Jeanette became very excited. His reputation had preceded him by many weeks, and we all knew his views on immorality and carnal vice. She told me that if the friar failed to convince Sir Hugh of the error of his ways, she would suggest that he threaten both him and Mistress Lynom with excommunication.'

I did not put such a course of action past Brother Simeon. To fanatics like himself and Lady Cederwell it would not matter that, if adultery were to be made an offence worthy of exile from the Church, there would be very few communicants left within it. Such people were prepared to take on all the world. But there was something else to which I needed an answer.

'What of Sir Hugh's son and Fulk Disney?' I asked.

A wary look entered Father Godyer's eyes. 'So? What of them?'

'They make no secret of the great friendship between them.'

'There have been great friendships between men throughout the ages. David and Jonathan. Damon and Pythias. Pylades and Orestes.'

'The second Edward and the Gascon, Piers Gaveston.'

The chaplain shot me a look through half-closed lids. 'I know nothing of that.'

Nor wish to know, I thought to myself. Adultery he could cope with, it was a common enough sin. But the vice of the ancient Greeks was unthinkable to a man of his timid nature, because, if once suspected, his calling would require him to root it out, bringing death in its train. But I did not doubt that Lady Cederwell would have known no such compunction.

Father Godyer also began to shiver. I urged him to lie down and cover himself with the blankets.

'You are still far from well. I'll see if I can procure a hot stone from the kitchen to put at your feet.' I moved closer and tucked the bedclothes around his shoulders.

He peered at me. 'Is that my cassock you're wearing?'

'Yes. I was so cold and this was on top of the chest. You watched me put it on and made no objection.'

'Oh, I don't object,' he assured me. 'You're welcome to it. I just couldn't see what it was, that's all. Keep it on if you like.'

I laughed. 'I'd meet with too many ribald remarks in the kitchen.' I unwound it and draped it across my arm. 'I'll take it with me, though. It'll do to wrap the hot stone in, unless one of the maids can find me some flannel.'

'You're very kind, my son. God bless you. Do you stay long on the manor?'

'Only until the tracks are passable. Will you remain as Sir Hugh's chaplain now that Lady Cederwell and her brother are dead?'

'If he wants me. Where else am I to go?' The pale blue eyes filled with tears. 'But it won't be the same. It won't be the same. I shall be very lonely.'

I patted his shoulder consolingly, then picked up the tray with the empty soup bowl on it and left the room. As I passed the open chapel door, Brother Simeon was just rising from his knees, so I stepped inside and made my obeisance to the crucifix above the altar. This was nothing like the one in the Saxon tower, being of silver and cedarwood, the face of the Christ peaceful, as though its owner were sleeping; a quiet, untroubled death, this, the crown of thorns resembling a halo rather than an instrument of torture. The wound in the side just showed above the loincloth, a faint dent in the silver. Cruelty and barbarism were absent; you could look at it and feel only a gentle sorrow.

The altar itself was draped with a cloth embroidered in jewel-bright colours, vivid reds and greens and blues with, here and there, the rich glow of amber. The walls were painted with pictures of the saints; Saint George with his raised lance, about to slay the dragon, Saint Cecilia, playing the harp, Saint Erasmus being fed by a raven. There was also a stained glass window depicting the Virgin with the Christ child on her lap. Both faces were serene and happy, giving no hint of future agony.

'You've been closeted a while with our friend, the chaplain,' Brother Simeon remarked as we eased our way down the narrow stairs. 'Did he have anything worthwhile to say? I thought him a poor dab of a man. Small wonder that Lady Cederwell could get no help from that quarter.'

'He admits it himself. His lack of courage, I mean. But the poor man is afraid for his place with Sir Hugh. He's not young any more.'

The friar snorted contemptuously, but contented himself with asking, 'Did you glean any information from him?'

'I'll tell you later,' I said as we were, at that moment, entering the kitchen.

Here, all was fuss and bustle as before. My request that

141

Father Godyer be given a heated stone for his feet met with scant favour, but eventually I was able to persuade Jenny Tonge to set one in the oven with the baking bread, until it was warmed right through. Then, swathing it in the cold cassock, I returned upstairs as I had promised. The chaplain was fast asleep, lying flat on his back, mouth open, loudly snoring. I lifted the covering bedclothes and slipped the stone under his feet.

As I again passed the chapel, it occurred to me that I had not said my prayers that morning. I went in and knelt before the altar, trying unsuccessfully to concentrate my thoughts on God. But Father Godyer's snores reverberated through the dividing wall, making this well-nigh impossible. As I raised my head and glanced around in desperation, I noticed what I had missed before, a confessional box in one corner, to the left of the window. I thought that perhaps God would not mind if I offered my devotions in its comparative peace and privacy, so I entered the penitent's cell and pulled the curtain closed behind me. But I had barely resumed my orisons when there was an interruption.

'In here,' said Sir Hugh's deep voice, and I heard the door close. 'No one will think of searching for us in the chapel.'

Chapter Eleven

I wish I could say that I had intended to disclose my presence immediately, but that they began to speak before I had sufficient time to do so. The truth, however, is that there was a long enough pause for me to have shown myself and I kept quiet, huddled silently in the musty gloom of the confessional box.

A second voice belonged, unsurprisingly, to Ursula Lynom. She sounded a little breathless, less self-assured than she had done the previous morning, and her words made it apparent that this was the first occasion since her arrival on which she and Sir Hugh had thought themselves sufficiently out of earshot of any other inhabitant of the manor. They had not after all – or so I guessed – dared to spend the night together.

'Hugh, you've no need to pretend with me. Hamon told me everything.' The tone was low, but perfectly audible.

'What do you mean by that, pray? What could Hamon possibly have to tell you?' The knight's voice was edged as much by irritation as by fear.

'He saw you bending over Jeanette's body outside the tower.'

There was a silence during which I scarcely dared to breathe. The pounding of my heart sounded so loudly in my ears that I was convinced one of them must hear it. I started to sweat in spite of the cold.

At last, Sir Hugh demanded harshly, 'What was Hamon doing at the tower?' I wondered if he had considered denying the accusation. If so, he had thought better of it.

'He came here on my instructions, to deliver some buttons to you; buttons that I'd bought from the chapman. I explained all this yesterevening.' She was impatient.

'I haven't forgotten.' Her lover was equally annoyed. 'But why was Hamon anywhere near the estuary? I should have expected him to look for me in the house.'

'He . . . He probably did.' Mistress Lynom's tone was guarded. 'He . . . saw you, and followed.'

I thought to myself, 'Simeon, you and I may congratulate ourselves on having approached so near to the truth.' But the next moment, I was not so certain.

'No.' Sir Hugh was confident. 'No one followed me from the house, I'm sure of that. You know as well as I do that once you leave the gate in the wall, the path lies across open country. I looked over my shoulder several times, but there was no one behind me. If your man was at the tower, he must have left the main track before he reached the manor and approached it by the path through the scrubland. And if that is so, he had to be there for his own purposes.' After a moment's hesitation, he added, 'Or yours.'

Another, longer silence succeeded his words, and although I could not see either the knight or Mistress Lynom through the worn velvet curtain, I could imagine them eyeing one another up, wary as a pair of cats.

Eventually, the woman asked, 'Why should he be there for any purpose of mine?' continuing, with a flash of inspiration, 'How can you be so sure that Hamon didn't follow you from the house? Tostig or one of the others might have told him where to find you. You could have reached the tower some time ahead of him and gone inside, looking for Jeanette.'

'No. I told no one where I was going and I didn't enter the tower. In heaven's name, Ursula! You must have questioned your man on this head?'

'I . . . No! Why should I? I . . . I was too upset. It was enough to know that Jeanette was dead and that he had seen you stooping over her body. If what he told me was true – and I have no cause to think him a liar – my first concern was to ensure his silence on the subject. For your sake, Hugh! For our future happiness! Oh, my dear! If, in a moment of desperation, you took the law into your own hands, are you afraid that I won't understand? You did it for me! For us!'

'Oh, no!' Sir Hugh's voice shook with growing apprehension. 'You don't plant the blame on me, Ursula, for something you planned. You sent your bravo to murder Jeanette; to throw her down from the tower. Do you think my memory's so short that I've already forgotten what your mood was yesterday morning, at Lynom Hall? All you could talk about was the possibility of some accident befalling her, which would set us free to marry. You even referred to her dangerous habit of standing on the edge of the parapet.'

'You were the one who mentioned that!' Mistress Lynom's

voice was low and rasping. '*You're* the one who's trying to plant the blame on *me*!'

'Nonsense! What was Hamon doing at the tower? Answer me that if you can!' The knight had worked himself into a temper, but whether in a righteous cause or simply to conceal the truth, I had no means of knowing. 'He most surely didn't follow me from the house, for I had no need to enter the tower to discover Jeanette. As I got near to it, I heard her moaning.'

The silence now was almost physically oppressive. I was frozen into immobility, my hands gripping the rungs of the penitent's stool so hard that their marks remained imprinted on my palms for a least half an hour afterwards.

'She was alive when you found her?' breathed Mistress Lynom.

'Yes. But she died almost immediately. Not, however, before she had time to utter the one word "Hamon".'

'I don't believe you!' The woman's voice trembled. With anger? With fear? I could not tell. A moment later, however, it strengthened as she flung her accusation. 'You left the body lying there! You pretended you didn't know Jeanette was dead! You waited for someone else to make the discovery and played the innocent. Would you have done that unless you yourself were guilty of the deed?' I heard the rustle of her gown as she paced to and fro. 'There would be no point to such an action, unless *you* killed her.'

'I stayed silent for you!' Sir Hugh exclaimed in exasperation. 'As soon as Jeanette uttered Hamon's name, I knew what must have happened; that you'd paid him to do it. He's a man who'd do anything for money. You waited all day for news of Jeanette's death to reach you, but there was a delay in finding her body and you became impatient. When you could contain yourself no longer, you rode to Cederwell for reassurance that all had gone as planned. It was very fortunate for you, my dear, that the friar mentioned Ulnoth the hermit, or you might have found it impossible to explain how your groom came by his news.'

'I came solely to discover how you were! As soon as Hamon told me what he'd seen, I guessed that you must have thrown Jeanette from the tower in a sudden fit of rage. I didn't blame you. No man could contain his patience for ever with such a creature! I just wanted to make sure that everything was well and that you weren't suspected.'

The pause this time was even more heavily charged with conflict than before. Each was accusing the other of having murdered Lady Cederwell. Was one of them a killer? Or, despite appearances, was neither responsible for her death? There were those who also might have wished for it; Phillipa Talke, Adela Empryngham, Fulk Disney, Maurice. Or could it truly have been the accident it was assumed to be?

'Do you seriously think me capable of doing away with my own wife,' Sir Hugh demanded in a tone of barely suppressed rage, 'however great the provocation?'

'For my sake, yes!' was the spirited reply. 'And for your sake, also. My dear, why can't you just admit it? I've already told you, you'll hear no word of blame from me, and you cannot believe that I would ever lay information against you! As for Hamon, he'll say nothing as long as I make it worth his while. And in a year or so's time, he won't find it easy to make an accusation without revealing his complicity in our silence.'

'Oh, I don't fear Hamon,' Sir Hugh replied furiously, his anger boiling up and bubbling over. 'He would never dare to accuse me of anything, for he'd only be putting his own neck in a noose. He'll be thankful to let it remain the "accident" that everyone thinks it. Ursula, why don't you confess that he was acting on your instructions? I shan't condemn you! I love you!'

'I take leave to doubt that.' Mistress Lynom's tone was icy. 'Any man who tries to shuffle off his guilt on to his woman is unworthy even to speak the name of love. I shall leave this house, sir, as soon as the roads are passable, and I trust that our paths may never cross again. Meantime, while I am forced to remain under your roof, you will do me the favour of having my meals sent to my chamber and of making no attempt to speak to, or even see, me. I bid you good-day!'

I heard the door open, protesting a little on its rusty hinges, and Sir Hugh exclaim anxiously, 'Ursula!' Then silence reigned. I waited for several minutes before daring to rise from my stool and peer outside, half expecting to find Sir Hugh still there, but the chapel was empty. I wondered if he had followed Mistress Lynom in an effort to make up the quarrel, although such a rift could not easily be repaired, or had simply let her go before busying himself about his own concerns. I bit one of my fingernails thoughtfully; then recollecting that I still had not offered up my morning prayers, I knelt down before the altar and, Father Godyer's snores having at last abated, was finally able to concentrate my mind on higher things.

I returned to the kitchen to find Martha Grindcobb in a state of high dudgeon over the request from Ursula Lynom that henceforth all her meals be served in her bedchamber.

'And the master upholding her commands as if she were already mistress of the manor!'

'And what exactly do you mean by that remark?' Phillipa Talke demanded sharply, as she emerged from the storeroom.

The cook, who had plainly forgotten her presence, jumped and looked agitatedly from one to the other of the kitchen-maids.

'Nothing, nothing,' she muttered, continuing to roll out her pastry, dipping her hand in the crock for more flour and making her own miniature snowstorm in the process.

The housekeeper set down the jar of oil she was carrying and faced Martha squarely.

'What do you mean?' she insisted.

Once again Martha glanced around the kitchen, seeking help, before suddenly deciding that it was time for a little plain speaking.

'I mean that the master'll marry Mistress Lynom as soon as it's decently possible. They've been lovers for years.'

'I don't believe it.'

The cook laid aside her rolling pin and sighed. 'Then you're the only person at Cederwell who doesn't. Ask anyone. Ask Edith or Ethelwynne here! Ask Jenny! Ask Tostig; if, that is, he can bring himself to utter an indiscretion. You poor, blind fool! Is it that you can't, or you won't, see what's been under your nose for all this time?'

I thought for a moment that the housekeeper was going to faint. She staggered a little and grasped at the edge of the table for support. Her face had gone grey and seemed to have collapsed from within. Her breathing came hard and short, but after a moment, she rallied.

'They're friends,' she said stoutly, 'everyone knows that. Old friends. But I've never heard there's more than that between them.'

'That's because you don't want to hear,' Martha Grindcobb retorted. 'You've shut your ears against any gossip that's run contrary to your own secret hopes and desires. Oh, don't bother to deny it! We all know you think Sir Hugh's in love with you, and no doubt he may even have led you on to believe it, when it suited him. With my lady constantly on her knees at prayer, and Mistress Lynom a couple of miles distant, he must sometimes have had to take comfort where he could find it. The master would think nothing of deceiving you in such a cause. After all, he's a man.' The cook broke off, her face suddenly full of concern. 'Are you feeling ill, Mistress Talke? I'm sorry to have been so blunt, but it's high time . . . Jenny! Edith! Quickly! She's going to swoon!'

But it was I who stepped forward and caught the housekeeper in my arms as she tottered and almost fell to the floor. I helped her to a stool while Jenny, as on the previous evening for Adela Empryngham, was sent to the buttery for a cup of ale. By the time she returned, however, Mistress Talke was beginning to recover.

'Leave me alone, all of you!' she commanded huskily, forcing herself to her feet and trying to control the shaking of her hands. She picked up the crock of oil, but some of it slopped over the rim and spilled on the flagstones.

'You should rest longer, Mistress,' I urged. 'You're not fit to resume your duties. Let me help you to your bed.'

150

'No!' she spat. 'If you so much as set foot in the dormitory, I might be accused by some people of letting you have your evil way with me.' She turned on Edith and Ethelwynne, who were giggling together in a corner, and seemed about to lash them with her tongue in much the same vein; but then, suddenly, all the spirit went out of her and she hurried from the kitchen without a backward glance.

'It was time someone opened her eyes,' Martha Grindcobb said defensively. 'Sir Hugh won't marry anyone but Mistress Lynom.'

Had I wished, I could have told her that even that marriage was now in jeopardy, but decided to keep my mouth shut for several reasons. Firstly I should have been forced to admit that I had deliberately eavesdropped on a conversation not meant for my ears; secondly, I was not at all sure that the couple would not eventually kiss and make up, sooner, perhaps, rather than later; and thirdly, I would have to have given the reasons for the quarrel, which would not only have raised the spectre of murder, where all was now thought to be accident, but also, by their very words, implicated both Sir Hugh and Mistress Lynom in Lady Cederwell's death. And in addition to these considerations, I was not convinced that their suspicions of one another were justified. All in all, therefore, it was much better, for the time being at least, that I stayed silent.

The housekeeper's reaction to Martha's home-truths had interested me. Phillipa Talke did not strike me as a woman who would normally faint, however disquieting the news she received. I suspected that she prided herself on her ability to take life's knocks without flinching. If Sir Hugh, for his

own selfish ends, had indeed allowed her to believe that he
might one day marry her, I should have expected the discovery
that she had been duped to have angered her to the point of
fury, prompting an outburst of temper and talk of revenge.
But she had almost swooned away, and left the kitchen like
a beaten woman. Suppose Phillipa Talke had killed Jeanette?
Suppose she had gone to the tower searching for her mistress
and discovered her on its roof, standing on the parapet's
edge, as was her custom? Suppose Phillipa had succumbed
to a momentary temptation to push her over, only to find out
later that she had committed murder, damned her immortal
soul, simply to clear the way for Sir Hugh to marry another
woman? Might she not then have fainted? Suppose . . .

I pulled my thoughts up short. Such a theory, however
plausible, did not tally with Sir Hugh's assertion that his
wife's dying word had been 'Hamon'. And thinking again of
Sir Hugh, was this a lie? Was he himself guilty of Lady
Cederwell's death? And was he, as Mistress Lynom said,
simply trying to shift the blame on to her and her servant?
But why should he do such a thing? Perhaps because he did
not want her to have any hold over him after they were
married. If he not only refused to confess his guilt but also
insisted on questioning her innocence, then, as his wife, she
could enjoy no unequal advantage. She was plainly a strong-
minded woman, used to ordering everything as she wished
and, above all, getting her own way. If she had any power to
wield over her husband, I had no doubt that she would use
it.

But could not this argument also apply to Mistress Lynom?
If she was the one who had arranged for Jeanette Cederwell's

death, then she, too, might not relish the thought of Sir Hugh being a party to the truth for the selfsame reason. If she continued to profess herself convinced of his guilt, she would achieve the same end . . .

'For heaven's sake, lad, move!' Martha Grindcobb gave me a great dig in the ribs with her elbow as she went past me on her way to the oven. 'You've been standing there for five minutes or more, just staring into vacancy like you were hagridden. If you've nothing better to do, you can go out to the woodpile and fetch in some more logs. Or take a spade and start moving the snow from the gallery stairs. It's fair dangerous as it is, going up and down to the dormitory. No good reason, when I think of it, that you shouldn't do both. Mistress Talke said I was to keep you busy.'

'I'll do both willingly,' I answered, and meant it. Fresh air would do me good and clear my head, which was beginning to ache from being mewed up indoors and too much thinking. I looked around me. 'Where's Brother Simeon?'

Martha opened the oven door to rake out the charred remains of the brushwood and twig fire, which had heated the clay bricks inside it. She then threw in a handful of flour to make sure that it was sufficiently hot and, satisfied, picked up her longhandled wooden shovel, putting in the pies and pastry coffins. When she had finished, she slammed the door shut, wiped her hands on her apron and turned to answer my question.

'He's gone up to the women's dormitory to visit Mistress Empryngham, pour soul, and offer spiritual guidance and comfort. Now, you'll find a spade in a corner of the storeroom, and there's a basket over there for carrying the wood. All in all, I think you'd better clear the snow away first, before someone has a nasty accident.'

I fastened my jerkin up to the throat and put on my cloak, pulling the hood's drawstring tight around my face to protect my head from the cold. I did not immediately go to pick up the spade and basket, however, being once more deep in thought. The mention of Adela Empryngham had jolted my memory, and I realised that, in the events of the past half-hour, I had almost forgotten that her husband had died.

If Lady Cederwell's death had indeed been murder, what bearing did the fact have on that of her brother? Maybe none. Even if Jeanette had been pushed from the tower, Gerard's death could still have been accidental. He was known by members of the household to walk in his sleep, and he had quarrelled with his wife, which had in all probability disturbed him. But for me, the question remained as to who had removed the cover from the well, and why. I was perfectly convinced in my own mind that I was not the culprit; so who would have gone outside on a bitterly cold night, in the middle of a snowstorm, to draw up water, especially when the barrel in the kitchen was full? No one, surely, of any sense, and therefore it had to be someone bent on mischief. Had that shadowy person then lured Master Empryngham out of doors on some pretext or another before pushing him, head first, down the well, secure in the knowledge that Gerard's sleepwalking would make it seem an accident? And whoever had last used the well would be blamed for forgetting to replace the cover. But why? For what purpose? What advantage could accrue to anyone by Gerard's murder? Sir

Hugh might rid himself of an unwanted drain on his resources, but he meant to do that in any case, as he had informed Adela only the previous evening. He had no need to resort to violence in order to free himself of his brother-in-law's presence.

'Are you going to stay there all day?' Martha's voice demanded wrathfully in my ear. 'Saints alive, I don't know what's come over you, for you've been mooning around this kitchen like a great calf, ever since you came down from seeing Father Godyer. Five minutes ago, you were going to clear those steps and fetch some wood. Now here you are, still standing around and nothing done! Get on with it, lad! Get on with it!'

I pulled myself together and, stooping, lightly kissed her cheek, which instantly mollified her. She began to giggle and blush like a young girl.

'I'm going,' I promised her, picking up the basket. 'I'm sorry. I've a lot on my mind.'

'You! What have you to think about, apart from where your next meal's coming from? Or which pretty girl you're going to bed down with next. Get away with you! You don't fool me!'

I grinned and went into the storeroom to collect the shovel. Thus armed, I let myself out of the back door and surveyed the steps leading up to the gallery. Much of the night's fall of snow had already been displaced by the traffic of the morning, but what was left was freezing over fast as the day grew steadily colder. The hill behind the house rose like a shadow, and above its crest, the clouds rode high and thin. Its slope was dotted with stunted trees and bushes, weirdly shaped now because of the snow, dwarfs and hobgoblins with outstretched hands.

I could not foresee Simeon and myself, or Mistress Lynom, escaping from Cederwell today, nor perhaps tomorrow, and I knew in my heart that, for the time being at least, I was content to remain. There was a mystery here, I could feel it in my bones. All was not as it seemed. God had brought me here for a purpose, and the weather was His means of keeping me here to do His work. Well, I thought cheerfully, as I began to shovel the bottom step clear of the frozen snow, I would do my best. The warmth began to tingle along my limbs as I hacked my way from tread to tread until the whole of the flight was clear.

Once at the top, I worked my way along the gallery, making a path between the piles of snow which had drifted over the balustrade during the night. There were two doors before the one at the end, which gave access to the female servants' dormitory, and the first of these was, in spite of the cold, standing slightly ajar, wide enough for me to be able to see inside. It was evidently the guest chamber, for Mistress Lynom was seated on the edge of the bed, her head buried in her hands, her whole body shaken by spasms of silent grief.

Chapter Twelve

For a brief moment, I was tempted to knock on the door and enter, but then came to my senses. There was no consolation I could offer, no course of action I could recommend without revealing that I knew more than I was supposed to know. Moreover, Mistress Lynom was a proud woman who would not take kindly to advice from a common pedlar. So I shovelled my way past the open door to the end of the gallery where, breathing hard, I rested on the handle of my spade.

I was now immediately outside the women's dormitory which, in its turn, was behind the upper half of the great hall's northern end. I was therefore at an angle to the main part of the house and in command of a wider, more extensive view of the approaches to Cederwell Manor than that afforded by the narrow passage between the kitchen and the hill. Over the snowladen roofs of the outbuildings, I could see the ground ascending towards the path by which I had so recently travelled. Yesterday in fact. Could it really be so short a time ago?

Earlier, there had been a little needle-sharp sunlight which had turned everything white and gold. But now the clouds had gathered again, their underbellies pregnant with further snow, except for one solitary, broken banner of iridescent light high above the trees. Everything seemed frozen into immobility, and over all there was a sense of eerie desolation, of a lost land, an enchanted, fairy world of silence, where nothing stirred . . .

A faint movement, somewhere away to my right, caught the tail of my eye and made me turn my head quickly. All was quiet, yet I was sure that I had not been mistaken; and in confirmation of my suspicion, three or four dark patches of scrubland which bordered the track showed where the undergrowth had been shaken free of snow. I waited, forcing myself to stand perfectly still, peering with narrowed eyes across the line of single-storey buildings – smithy, barn, pigsty, byre – towards the rising ground. Someone was there, watching, and I felt the hairs lift on the nape of my neck. Whoever it was must be aware of having attracted my attention and would not break cover until I was gone. Deliberately I resumed my work, although there was nothing much left to do. It was time to go down and collect the logs.

The door to the women's dormitory opened and Simeon emerged, looking stern and grave. In the room behind him, I could hear Adela Empryngham's muffled sobs.

'Your words of comfort have fallen on stony ground then, Brother,' I remarked.

'I was not there to give comfort,' he answered severely, 'but to point out the error of her ways. Had Mistress Empryngham not quarrelled with her husband, had she not flounced out and left him on his own, he might not now be lying stiff and cold upon his bed.'

I raised my eyebrows and pulled down the corners of my mouth.

'Dear me! Not, I imagine, what the poor soul wanted to hear. Martha Grindcobb thinks that you're condoling with the widow.'

The friar snorted. 'It is not my office to tell people what they want to hear, but to show them the truth, to help them recognise their sins.' He added, 'I'm glad to see that you've been put to work at last!' and nodded at the cleared pathway of bare boards between the banked-up piles of snow. Then he raised his head and stared glumly at the sky. 'What do you make of the weather?'

'I think it's going to snow again, tonight if not before. No good your looking like that, Brother. God's will be done. Besides, you can help me achieve His purpose as well here as on the road.'

'What do you mean by that?'

I lowered my voice. 'I've a deal of importance to tell you.' Then, in my normal tone, I went on, 'But first, I must fetch some more logs for Mistress Grindcobb. I've a basket at the bottom of the steps . . .'

My words trailed away into silence. As I spoke, I had half turned to face Brother Simeon, my glance straying across his shoulder to the distant prospect beyond.

'What is it?' he demanded, also turning. 'What have you seen?'

'A little while ago,' I answered slowly, 'I thought I detected a movement in the scrubland, as though someone were hiding there. And I'm sure I saw something again, just now. Yes, look! Over there! That dark patch to the right of the oak! The snow has been shaken from the bushes!'

The friar's eyes followed the direction of my pointing finger, but after a moment he shook his head. 'There's no one there as far as I can tell.'

I sighed in exasperation. 'There is, but he's lying low. He can see us up here on the gallery. We can't see him because he's hidden from our view by the undergrowth, but we can guess where he's been by the way that the snow has been disturbed.'

Simeon, however, preferred to put his own, more optimistic interpretation on the facts.

'It may simply mean that the thaw is setting in.' His eyes brightened at the prospect.

'No,' I said. 'Don't delude yourself, Brother. At present, the snow on the ground is freezing hard. I've had to chip it piece by piece from the steps and the gallery boards. If it gets even slightly warmer, we shall have another heavy fall. You've only to look at those clouds to know that. No, there's someone out there, I'm certain of it.'

'What fool would be scrambling about amongst dense undergrowth in this weather?' Simeon's tone was scathing. 'You're the one who's deluding himself, Chapman. We've enough tragedies under this roof without imagining trouble where none exists.'

I saw that he was unwilling to be convinced, and we walked along the gallery and descended the stairs in silence. As we passed the guest chamber I noticed that the door had been shut, which was hardly surprising. Mistress Lynom could not have remained ignorant of our presence. I wondered if she had overheard any part of our conversation; but if she had, I did not feel that she could have learned very much from it. Even had she listened that long, she would probably share Simeon's scepticism of my assertion that someone was watching the manor.

'I shall go and warm myself at the fire,' the friar announced as we reached the bottom step. 'You can tell me whatever it is you have to say when you return with the logs. Bring plenty of them and be quick about it.'

On this parting shot, he scuffed his way through the snow choking the narrow channel between hill and kitchen and disappeared inside the back door with a whisk of his rusty black habit. I grinned to myself as I propped the shovel against the outside wall and stooped to pick up the basket: Friar Simeon was not always as unworldly as he liked to seem. Then, with a silent curse, I realised that I had not inquired of Martha the whereabouts of the woodpile. I was just going indoors for her instructions when I was saved the trouble by the appearance of Fulk Disney. Booted and cloaked, he rounded the western corner of the house, his thin face red and raw with cold, a drop of moisture suspended from the end of his long, pinched nose. He did not look to be in the best of humours.

'Master Disney, well met!' I exclaimed cheerfully. 'Where can I find the woodpile?'

At the sound of my voice, he jumped in alarm. His eyes had been firmly fixed on the ground and the five or six inches of snow which reached well above his ankles. I wondered why, in such conditions, he had been out walking.

'D'Isigny,' he snapped. 'How many more times do I have to tell you?'

'Ah, yes,' I murmured. 'Your ancestors came over with the Conqueror. You must forgive a mere Saxon peasant. Can Your Honour direct me to the woodpile?'

For a moment he glared as though he would like to hit me, but thought better of it once he had weighed up my size. He jerked his thumb backwards over his shoulder.

'You'll find wood stored in an empty stall in the stables.' I thanked him politely and would have pushed my way past, but he stopped me with a hand on my arm. 'What is that friar saying about me and Maurice?' he demanded fiercely.

I hedged. 'What is there to say?'

'Why was he brought here? Surely he must know why Lady Cederwell sent for him?'

'How can he? She was dead before his arrival.'

'But her messengers, Jude and Nicholas Capsgrave, they must have given him some idea of what she wanted from him.'

'If they did, he has not confided in me. And now, if you'll excuse me, Master Disney, I must fetch in the wood, or Martha Grindcobb will be wondering what has become of me.'

He snatched his hand from my arm.

'Don't get uppity with me, Chapman, or I'll have you turned out into the snow. And for the last time, I am called D'Isigny!'

'Do you have that much ascendancy over Sir Hugh, *Monsieur D'Isigny*?' I asked with heavy emphasis on his name. 'Or is your influence all with Maurice?'

His face was suffused with colour.

'I've warned you, Chapman, watch your step. I'm not a

person to cross in this household. I make a bad enemy.'

'I'm sure we all do that,' I answered levelly, 'especially Brother Simeon.'

He stared at me for a moment, the grey eyes full of anger and dislike, the blood draining from his face and leaving it pale where before it had been bright red.

'You can prove nothing,' he muttered at last. 'Sir Hugh will ensure that no charges are ever brought against his son, now that that woman is dead.'

He elbowed me to one side and entered the house. I gazed after him thoughtfully.

It was surprisingly warm inside the stables. Much of the snow had been cleared from around the building, presumably by the grooms, and the doors fast shut to keep out the cold. Within, straw had been piled high in every occupied stall and braziers lit where they could do least harm, the glowing coals encased in narrow-barred, iron cages. The mingled scents of sweat and dung and leather filled the air, and the horses shifted and whinnied as they chomped the hay in their mangers. I recognised the big, white-stockinged black belonging to Sir Hugh which I had noted yesterday morning at the Hall, and also the chestnut mare with the pale mane and tail, owned by Mistress Lynom. There, too, were the cob and Jessamine, the raw-boned grey, presumably ridden here by Jasper and Hamon. The remaining occupants of the stalls I had not seen before, and must therefore be the property of the manor.

There were two further stalls at the end of the line, one containing firewood, stored for safekeeping out of the winter weather, and the other empty except for the grooms, Jude and Nicholas Capsgrave and their guests, Jasper and Hamon. The four men were huddled around a brazier, taking it in turns to drink from a black leather bottle and, judging by their long, sombre faces, discussing the gruesome discoveries of last night and this morning.

'God be with you, gentlemen,' I said.

I had unlatched and relatched the stable door so quietly, and they had been so absorbed in what they were saying, that no one had heard me enter. One of them yelped and Hamon, who was holding the bottle, spilled some of its contents on the floor, while the other two clutched wildly at each other as they all swung round to face me.

'Wh – who—' Jasper stuttered, then added on a gasp of relief, 'Oh, it's you, Chapman. God in heaven, what a start you gave us! What are you doing here, anyway?'

I held up my basket. 'I've been sent to get more firewood for the kitchen.'

One of the Capsgrave brothers relieved Hamon of the bottle and took a long draught of its contents, wiping his mouth afterwards on the back of his hand.

'I've seen you somewhere afore you came here,' he said, looking hard at me.

'I was at the valley mill when you arrived, searching for Friar Simeon.'

The younger of the pair nodded. 'So you were. I remember now. What were you doing there then?'

'Selling my wares, of course. Just as I was hoping to do at Cederwell, but so far there's been precious little chance. Which of you two is Jude and which Nicholas?'

164

'I'm Jude,' the older and thinner man said, adding, 'You came 'ere at a bad time, Chapman.'

'Couldn't 'ave bin worse,' concurred his brother.

I inquired, 'Did Lady Cederwell tell either of you why she needed to see the friar so badly?'

The brothers looked astonished.

'No,' said Nicholas, 'nor did we ask. It's our place to obey orders, not to query 'em.'

'Sir Hugh mentioned that you both came here with her from Campden; that you were both devotedly loyal to Lady Cederwell and her brother.'

Jude Capsgrave gave a short bark of laughter. ''E said that, did 'e? Well, I'm not surprised. 'E's never 'ad time fer any of the 'ousehold she brought down 'ere with 'er. But the truth is we weren't long in 'er service before 'er marriage. As for Master Gerard, neither of us 'ave ever thought much to 'im, and that's a fact. A poor creature, clinging to 'is sister's skirts and playin' at being the gentleman, when all the world knows 'im fer a bastard.'

'Knew,' corrected his brother.

'What? Oh, ar! Knew.' Jude shook his head incredulously. 'A bad business! A bad business!'

I agreed, and entered the other stall to begin filling my basket with wood.

Inevitably, the four of them followed to gather around the entrance and watch, for there are few things so pleasant in this world as to stand idle while someone else works. At last, however, Jasper, probably recollecting my assistance of the previous morning, came forward to help. Together, we sweated and strained to pack some of the biggest logs into the basket, straightening up when we had finished, both of us clasping our hands to our aching backs. I gave Jasper my heartfelt thanks, and he in his turn procured the leather bottle from Jude and passed it to me. I drank deeply.

'Has any one of you set foot outside the manor walls this morning?' I asked, wiping the neck of the bottle on my sleeve and returning it to Jasper.

They protested vigorously that they were not so foolhardy. They had all, at some time, visited the kitchen, and Nicholas Capsgrave admitted that he had been as far as the fish pond in order to feed the carp, a job not normally assigned to him, but which he had undertaken to save Jenny Tonge from getting her feet any wetter than they already were, after descending the gallery stairs from the dormitory.

'That was when I saw Fulk Disney going out by the gate in the wall. The snow were all churned up where 'e'd scuffed 'is way through it. But I don't know what errand 'e'd been sent on, nor what 'e were up to.'

'No good, that's fer certain,' opined his brother. 'And if 'e were gettin' 'is dainty feet wet in this weather, 'twas fer one person only. Though why Maurice'd be sending 'im abroad on a morning like this, I can't think.'

I asked innocently, 'Why should Fulk be dancing to Master Cederwell's tune? Surely it's Sir Hugh who pays the piper?'

I saw the brothers glance furtively at one another, as though they had said too much. Jude remarked with apparent irrelevance, 'You're very friendly with that friar; that Brother Simeon or whatever they calls 'im.'

'I heard him preach in Bristol and my mother-in-law gave

him dinner. Quite by chance I fell in with him on my way to the manor. That's all.'

Nevertheless, I could not deny to myself that I fully intended sharing such information as I acquired with Simeon, and so did not press my question. These men had their loyalties, and no doubt had heard of the friar's mission to stamp out immorality wherever he found it. It was far better for me not to seek confirmation of my suspicions than to bring the full wrath of the Church upon Fulk's and Maurice's heads. If I knew nothing to the contrary, I could acquit them in my own mind and presume them innocent. And I have often wondered in the secret places of my heart how we know for sure that the Church, that the Holy Father himself, is truly the mouthpiece of God. (There, I have set it down at last, but only because I know that these words will be read by no one but me until after I am dead. I did confess earlier to having courage of one kind, but not of another.)

'How did Lady Cederwell get on with her stepson?' I asked instead, adding a final log to my basket.

Once again the brothers looked at one another, then shrugged. At last Nicholas took it upon himself to answer.

'There weren't much love lost atween 'em, 'tis true. She were only a twelvemonth or so older than 'e is. An' she weren't easy to get on with. Always on 'er knees, always sermonisin'.'

'Did she—?' I hesitated, choosing my words. 'Did she object to Maurice's friendship with Fulk Disney?'

'Can't say nothin' to that,' Jude cut in tersely, attempting to nudge his brother in the ribs without me seeing. 'We're grooms. We're mostly in the stables. Don't take much

167

notice of what goes on indoors.'

'Why should she?' Nicholas demanded, staring straight into my eyes.

They still refused to trust me; but each, in his own way, had answered my question. I was content. Both Maurice and Fulk Disney could have wished Lady Cederwell dead before Brother Simeon arrived at the manor. But why either one of them would have wanted, or needed, to kill Gerard Empryngham was a mystery.

Hamon and Jasper had necessarily been silent bystanders during this exchange, quietly finishing the contents of the bottle between them. But now Hamon suddenly remarked, 'You ask a lot of questions, don't you, pedlar?'

There was a note of menace in his tone which made me glance sharply at him. But I gave a cheerful laugh and said as offhandedly as I could, 'I'm a naturally curious person.'

'They say curiosity killed the cat,' he answered.

'They also say that cats have nine lives. It's useless to threaten them.'

Hamon's eyes, grey with little flecks of brown in their depths, opened wide in innocent surprise.

'You mistake me! Why should I wish to threaten you, Master Chapman? Whatever gives you that idea?'

I picked up the basket of wood. 'I must get back to the kitchen. I shall no doubt see you all there at dinnertime.' And I took my departure without replying to Hamon's question.

Once outside the stable door, I found it already snowing again. Delicate, feathery flakes brushed my cheeks and settled across my shoulders, but this fall would not last long, for a little grudging sunshine was finding its way through the rent in the clouds, gilding the surface of the fish pond. I could see the black hole where Nicholas had broken the ice to feed the fish, and, on the opposite side, I could see a man's tracks leading to the gate in the wall, where Fulk Disney had kicked up the snow in front of him as he walked. On a sudden impulse, I set down the basket of wood and followed in his footsteps.

The gate had been used this morning, for the key still stood in the lock and it had not been properly fastened. I had only to push the iron-studded, wooden panels very gently for it to open without my having to lift the latch. Any resistance offered by the piled-up snow on the other side had already been overcome, and the gate swung back into an arc of cleared ground. And the footprints continued, running straight as an arrow homing into the gold, towards the door in the Saxon tower.

Why had Fulk gone there? Had he been looking for something? And, if so, who had sent him? Maurice Cederwell seemed the likeliest answer to that last question, and yet one could never be certain of anything. My instinct was to investigate at once, but I knew that if I did not return soon with the logs, Martha Grindcobb would be sending someone to find me. Reluctantly, I retraced my steps.

'And about time!' was the cook's greeting as I entered the kitchen. 'The friar here said you were going for the wood when he left you, and that was before *he* went off on his travels again. What's the matter with the pair of you? Why can't you both be happy to sit in the warm instead of wandering about in the cold?'

I made no reply, merely emptying the logs into the bigger basket which stood behind the door and then going to squat on the floor in the further corner, beside Brother Simeon.

'Well?' he asked, whisking aside the hem of his torn black habit. 'What do you have to tell me?'

For the next ten minutes, while Martha and the kitchen-maids bustled around us, I recounted the conversation I had overheard earlier that morning between Mistress Lynom and Sir Hugh. When I had finished, he drew in a long, hissing breath.

'So,' he said at last, 'they stand condemned out of their own mouths that one of them is a murderer.'

I shook my head. 'No, Brother. Neither admitted to the crime. But that they are lovers is certain. We can guess that Lady Cederwell wished to speak to you on the subject; to ask for your advice; to beg you to put the fear of God into Sir Hugh, enough at any rate to scare him into ending the affair. She was afraid for his immortal soul.'

'As well she might be.' The friar's face was grey with anger.

'But there's more,' I continued, and told him of my encounter with Fulk Disney and my conviction that he had visited the tower this morning.

'I should like to know why he was there,' I added. 'What was he up to? After dinner, before it gets dark and the snow sets in again, I intend visiting the tower myself. I shall probably be no wiser when I leave than when I got there, but you never know. I might find something.'

Chapter Thirteen

Dinner had been eaten. Pigeon pasties, served with dried peas and parsnips, and saffron and honey coffins had all been consumed with hearty appetites despite the recent bereavements and quarrels. Mistress Lynom's tray was brought down from her room with each platter wiped clean, Sir Hugh and his son, dining in state in the great hall, had also returned empty dishes, and even Adela Empryngham had consumed every morsel sent up to her in the women's dormitory. As for the rest of us – Tostig Steward, Fulk Disney and Phillipa Talke in a small room adjacent to the pantry, the Capsgrave brothers and their uninvited guests in the stables, Father Godyer in his bedchamber and everyone else in the kitchen – we had all managed to fill our bellies, if not to capacity then at least enough to blunt the edge of hunger. Martha Grindcobb apologised for there not being more.

'But you know how it is in the depths of winter, it's not wise to deplete your stores too much.'

What she meant of course was that Sir Hugh was on the niggardly side, and resented having to dispense hospitality with too lavish a hand. But there had been sufficient to feed everyone and now, with noon just past and the day as bright

171

as it was likely to get, I decided that it was time to visit the tower. I looked round to ask Simeon if he wished to accompany me, but he was already snoring, his back supported by a barrel of dried fish, his hands clasped together on his stomach. I got to my feet, pulled on my boots, which had been drying by the fire since my return to the kitchen, picked up my cloak and headed for the door.

'And where are you off to again?' Martha demanded as I passed her. She was busy scraping the coating of beeswax from a fresh batch of preserved eggs which one of the maids had just fetched for her from the storeroom. 'You're only just dryshod. What's the point of going outside to get wet all over again? It's still snowing.'

'Not heavily, not yet,' I pleaded. 'I can't stay cooped up indoors all day. These great legs of mine need to keep on the move.'

She sniffed. 'Don't give me that tale! You're off to the stables, I'll be bound, playing fivestones with Jude and Nicholas and those two ne'er-do-wells of Mistress Lynom's. Or Mary-on-the-Wall, or some other game of chance.'

She rolled a little of the beeswax into a pellet, popped it in her mouth and started to chew, a habit I've noticed amongst many people who like to exercise their jaws between meals. After a while, they will spit the beeswax out, lodging it wherever is handy; under the edge of a table, on the rung of a stool, or even on the rim of a cooking-pot. A filthy habit my mother always called it; but if it gives pleasure, where's the harm?

I did not enlighten Martha as to my destination, merely grinning amiably and allowing her to think what she pleased.

I suspected that she probably would not approve of my going to the tower. I was a guest in the house, there on sufferance because of the weather, and it did not behove me to go snooping around in what was not really my concern. So I put on my cloak, pulled up its hood and stepped into the main passageway. As I did so, Fulk Disney emerged from the steward's room, wiping his mouth on his sleeve, removing the final traces of his recent meal. He froze when he saw me, fixing me with another of his sullen and resentful stares.

'Where are you going, Chapman?' he demanded. 'You're very busy, running here, there and everywhere.'

'These long limbs of mine need constant exercise.' I offered him the same explanation I had given Martha Grindcobb, but he was less easily convinced.

'I've warned you, don't go poking your nose into affairs which are none of your business. You'd do well to heed what I say.'

'I'll try to keep your words in mind,' I assured him, and for the second time that day, let myself out of the back door.

The snow had eased a little, but a wind was blowing and the driven flakes were now as fine as dust. The hill rose bleak and bare beneath a threatening sky filled with dark and racing clouds. It was growing colder, and under the eaves, where a noonday thaw had only just begun, drops of water were already turning to splinters of ice. A few yards to my right were the gallery steps, and on a sudden impulse I mounted them to knock gently on the door of the women's dormitory. A tearful voice bade me enter. I paused on the threshold, letting my eyes grow accustomed to the gloom.

'Mistress Empryngham,' I asked hesitantly, 'may I come in?'

'Who – who's that?'

'Roger Chapman. We met yesterday.'

'What do you want?' She sounded suspicious.

I advanced a pace into the room. She was lying, propped up on her elbows, on one of a row of wooden cots ranged against the opposite wall. A large oaken chest at the far end of the chamber provided, I guessed, storage for the women's meagre possessions, and on a small table to my left, just inside the door, were a couple of candle-holders, some tallow candles and a tinder-box. Apart from these things the place was bare, without even a scattering of rushes on the floor. Sir Hugh Cederwell, as I might have expected, was not a man who set great store by the comfort of his servants.

'Mistress Empryngham,' I said, 'forgive me, but I've just come to see how you do.'

'How do you expect me to do,' she answered tartly, 'with my husband dead? Thanks to you,' she added.

I was startled. Because I was completely convinced in my own mind that I had replaced the lid on the well, I had forgotten that I had not been exonerated by others. I went and stood at the bottom of her cot.

'No, no!' I protested. 'I am certain that I'm not to blame. I'm sure I didn't leave the well uncovered.'

'How else could the accident have happened? No other person has owned up to being in the courtyard.'

'No one but yourself, when you quit your bedchamber and came to find Martha Grindcobb in the kitchen.' I spoke with urgency. This had not occurred to me before. 'Mistress

174

Empryngham, you must have passed close to the well after I had returned indoors. Think, I beg of you! Can you recall if the lid was on, or lying on the ground?'

She stared at me as though I were a fool. 'Good heavens, man! I was upset. It was snowing. Do you seriously think I would notice a thing like that?' She must have seen my disappointment and made a little gesture of reconciliation. 'Don't look so downcast. It wasn't your fault that Gerard walked in his sleep or that I left him to his own devices. No, the friar has shown me where the blame really lies.'

'Brother Simeon is sometimes too harsh in his judgements,' I consoled her, and was rewarded by a wintry smile. 'He expects too much of us ordinary mortals. Has – that is to say, did Master Empryngham always sleep-walk?'

She nodded dully. 'Since early childhood. It was a well-known fact amongst members of his father's household. Once, at least so Gerard said, a door was accidentally left unlocked and he wandered out of the house and away across the pastures. One of the shepherds, who was up late tending a sick ewe, saw him and took him home. The servant who had left the door open was severely punished.'

The story jogged my memory.

'I spoke to Father Godyer this morning. He told me of Lady Cederwell's . . . of her ordeal at the hands of one of her father's shepherds.'

Adela Empryngham curled her lip. 'Father Godyer is an old gossip who can't keep his mouth shut. Nevertheless, what he says is true.' She sighed gustily. 'Poor Jeanette, I think the experience turned her brain. She was always pious, but afterwards she was ten times worse than she had been before.' Adela lowered her voice. 'I believe it made her a little mad.'

'I understand that she refused to take the veil as she had intended because she thought it would bring disgrace on any Order that she entered.'

Adela laughed. 'She was a simpleton! As if any convent would have refused a postulant with the sort of dowry her father could have given her! But everyone who told her so was scorned for their evil minds. Jeanette believed that anyone who consecrated a life to God's service was purer than the driven snow, whereas I know and you know, Chapman, that all the religious houses of this land are avaricious and vice-ridden.'

I resisted the temptation to cavil at this sweeping statement, afraid I might antagonise Mistress Empryngham and prevent any further confidences.

'Your sister-in-law,' I ventured, 'or so it seems to me, was greatly disturbed by the – er – by the sins of the flesh.'

'Obsessed,' was the succinct rejoinder. 'But hardly surprising I suppose, after what she had suffered. Not that I think her entirely blameless.' There was a pause. I waited expectantly as Adela Empryngham continued, 'Raymond Shepherd was a well enough looking man and I daresay that Jeanette, maybe in all innocence, had led him on. He probably mistook her friendliness for encouragement. She wouldn't have been the first well-born girl to fancy copulating with one of her father's churls. But whatever the truth of the matter, he didn't deserve the fate that befell him.'

'It would have been a worse one if he'd been caught,' I pointed out. 'He would have ended his life on the end of a rope, most likely without benefit of trial.'

Adela shrugged. 'Perhaps you're right. Gerard would certainly have strung him up from the nearest tree if he'd had half a chance. But having your head split open by robbers, your body despoiled and flung in a ditch, is that much better?'

I was unable to answer that question, and could only pray that neither alternative would be my fate. I remarked instead, 'Your husband and Lady Cederwell were very attached to one another.'

The face in front of me was suddenly transformed into a vicious mask of loathing.

'There was something unnatural about it,' Mistress Empryngham said, and I realised for the first time how much she had hated her sister-in-law. Enough to contrive her death? Perhaps. But would she also have wanted to be rid of her husband? That, however, could have been a genuine mishap. On the other hand, Adela could have removed the lid from the well as she passed through the courtyard and left the result to chance. Who could say?

'I must be going,' I said, feeling that I should take my departure before she gave vent to her spleen and uttered words that she might later regret.

She made no effort to detain me, but I felt her eyes on me as I moved towards the door. As I was about to step outside, she called, 'Chapman!' I turned and she raised herself higher on her elbows. 'I loved my husband, you know.' Tears trickled slowly down her cheeks.

I nodded mutely, raised a hand in farewell and went.

The footprints of the morning had now almost disappeared

beneath a second fall of snow, although it seemed to me that there was a third set of tracks mingling with mine and Fulk Disney's. Once beyond the gate, I suddenly felt vulnerable and exposed in that desolate landscape, where the silence was unbroken by even the call of a bird. There was no other sign of life; the pigs which normally feed off the seaweed and fish refuse of saltings and marshland had been driven into their sties by the local swineherd in order to keep them safe from the cold. Here and there a few blades of marram grass had forced their way into daylight and air, but most tufts remained hidden by the snowy blanket.

As I approached the tower I glanced to my left, and was able to discern that other path, mentioned by Sir Hugh when talking to Mistress Lynom that morning, which led through the scrubland to join the main track. I hesitated, wondering whether to explore its length or no, but the extreme cold, now nipping at my toes and fingers, decided me against it for the moment. I pushed open the door and went inside.

Everything there was much as I remembered it from the day before. A little more light filtered through the four slits in the circular wall, but revealed nothing new. The lantern and tinder-box still stood on the table in the centre of the room, where I had conscientiously replaced them the previous evening, after Simeon and I had returned from the house with Jude and Nicholas Capsgrave, who had carried the stretcher. In order to make doubly sure, however, that there was no change of any sort, I prowled around for several minutes, but all was just the same. I mounted the narrow, well-worn stairs to the second storey, keeping one hand pressed against the outer wall for support.

There was nothing here either which immediately suggested any further visit since my own and Simeon's yesterday. Yet on closer inspection, I fancied that the folios which lay on the table had been slightly disturbed. I tried to recollect exactly how they had been placed, and it seemed to me that they had not been so widely scattered. I inspected them more closely. There were four, two bound in yellow silk with golden tassels, another covered with violet silk and fastened by a silver-gilt clasp, while the fourth one had a red velvet binding ornamented with two rows of small copper studs. But the material of each was frayed and badly rubbed, the metal tarnished, the tassels unravelling. Inside, the parchment had yellowed and occasionally cracked, but the careful scripts were still as clear as the day they were penned and the illustrations glowed like jewels.

The titles were unsurprising for someone of Lady Cederwell's tastes; the *Scale of Perfection*, the *Cloud of Unknowing*, *La Forteresse de Foi*, the *Imitatio Christi*. I wondered how she had come by them, but it was obvious that she had gloried in their possession and read them often. I turned the pages slowly, as I instinctively felt Fulk Disney must have done, searching for anything concealed between the leaves, but what I was looking for I had no idea. My eyes fell on some words in the *Scale of Perfection*. 'It needeth not to run to Rome or Jerusalem to seek Christ, but to turn thine thoughts into thine own soul where He is hid . . .' They were true when they were written, they are true today, and they will be true tomorrow and ever after.

I discovered nothing of any moment, and once the folios had been gone through there was no other place of concealment. Nevertheless I peered under the stool, the table, the bench, but saw only a dusty floor. I even examined the window slits, but nothing was hidden in any of them. It was no more than I had expected. I proceeded up the spiralling staircase to the chapel.

Here, at first sight, all was as orderly as in the lower two chambers, but I recognised almost at once that things were not as they should be. The great crucifix above the prie-dieu hung a little askew, the kneeling-desk itself had been shifted so that it now stood at a slight angle to the wall, and the silver candlesticks had been moved nearer to the centre of the altar, whose embroidered cloth had been hurriedly replaced inside out. I stared around me wondering if Fulk Disney had been successful in his quest or, as was equally possible, had satisfied himself that there was nothing there to find.

I began my own search, then stopped, feeling foolish. What was I looking for? More importantly, what would Fulk have been looking for? And had he found it, whatever it was? The answer to the second question was probably no. I recalled how sour-faced he had been, how out of humour, when I encountered him at the back of the house this morning. But that did not enlighten me as to his object. It could be nothing bulky or he would hardly have removed an altar cloth, peered behind the crucifix and, as I felt sure he had done, hunted through the pages of books. Something easily concealed then, and flat . . . A piece of paper, what else? But what could it contain? Why, a list of charges which Jeanette Cederwell had prepared against her husband and his mistress, ready to hand to Brother Simeon when he at last arrived; and quite possibly accusations, also, about her stepson and

Fulk Disney. I drew a deep breath, feeling certain that I had stumbled on the truth. Yet did it exist at all, this written indictment, outside the fevered imaginings of Maurice and Fulk? Did they know something which I did not? Had Lady Cederwell forewarned her stepson and husband of what she intended to do?

Another question arose. If Maurice or his father knew for a fact of the paper's existence, why were they so anxious to get hold of it now that Jeanette was dead? Answer, because the inclemency of the weather had detained the friar within the confines of the manor; and if one of the servants found the letter by chance before he left and handed it to him, there was little doubt that Simeon would use it to do them harm. Sir Hugh probably had nothing to fear unless he were suspected of killing his wife, but Fulk and Maurice would stand accused on a far more serious charge, and one which carried a stringent penalty.

I began my hunt. I felt convinced that if there were such a paper, it must be hidden somewhere in the chapel. There was nowhere on the ground floor where it might be concealed, and I had looked in every possible place in the room immediately below. So offering up a short prayer to God for His forgiveness, I stripped the altar and examined the table beneath the cloth. But it was innocent of any drawer, a plain oaken board set on four stout legs, as Fulk Disney must already have discovered. It would have been a waste of time to search for a secret compartment as there was so obviously nowhere where it could be. I replaced the altar cloth, right side out, and the candlesticks before turning my attention to the prie-dieu.

A close scrutiny of this, however, failed to reveal anything extraordinary, which left the crucifix. I wondered what Father Godyer, that gentle, timid man, had thought of it when he had come here to celebrate Mass for Lady Cederwell in her private chapel. Had he found the contorted face and body of the ivory Christ as terrifying as I did myself? There was something deeply disturbing about it; a warning that only through immense suffering could men attain a state of grace and approach the throne of God. How could Jeanette Cederwell have gazed upon it every day of her life and not gone mad?

Fulk had obviously looked behind it, which was why it now hung askew. I followed his example, but there was nothing to be discovered except the smooth back of the ebony cross. Slowly I replaced the crucifix against the wall and stood back a pace, forcing myself to scan it up and down and trying to ignore the frisson of horror that it gave me. I decided that I could not leave it as it was; it offended my sense of symmetry. So I stepped forward again, clasping it around Our Saviour's knees and shifting it half an inch to the left, hoping against hope that my action would not loosen the rusty hook on which it was suspended and cause it to come crashing down to fell me beneath its formidable weight. It was then that I noticed a crack where the carved loincloth had begun to split away from the main block of ivory which formed the body. And tucked into that crack, barely noticeable even when standing very close, was a piece of paper. Only its edge was visible and it took some prising loose, particularly as I had used my knife that morning to pare my nails. But I managed to tease it free at last, spreading it out on top of the prie-dieu and casting my eyes over the neatly written script.

Whatever else had been neglected in Jeanette Cederwell's childhood, it had not been her education. She wrote as well as, presumably, she could read, and here, clearly stated, were the charges against her husband and stepson which Fulk Disney had been seeking. They might also suggest a motive for murder by one of the three. Or by Hamon at Mistress Lynom's instigation, for surely the lady could not have wished her adultery to become common knowledge. At present, whatever was suspected of her relationship with Sir Hugh by members of both households, it was nothing more than servants' gossip which could easily be refuted. But a formal accusation placed in the hands of the Church by a wronged wife was something altogether different and could prove dangerous.

Had Lady Cederwell warned her husband, I wondered, of her intention to commit her accusations to paper, ready for Brother Simeon's arrival? And had he, in his turn, warned his son? Sir Hugh had seemed to know nothing of her invitation to the friar when first we talked with him in the kitchen, but that could simply have been a wish to deceive us. Whether he knew of the paper or merely suspected its existence I could not begin to guess, but I was the finder and now had to decide what to do with it. Should I place it in Brother Simeon's keeping immediately or wait a while until I was more sure of my ground? I had no positive proof, either in the case of Jeanette or her brother, that murder had been committed, and even with the list of condemnations in my hand, I still felt uneasy. The friar, however, would have no such doubts and would set off as soon as the bad weather lifted to wreak havoc on all four lives.

Slowly I refolded the thin parchment sheet and pushed it into the leather pouch at my belt. I would take the rest of the day to think the matter over and, if necessary, sleep on it as well. The faces of Phillipa Talke and Adela Empryngham kept surfacing in my mind, and who knew what others among the Cederwell servants had borne a secret grudge against their mistress? I cast another look around the chapel, now restored to its original order, then started to descend the stairs.

I was standing on the second step of the worn and slippery flight when someone pushed me hard in the back, and I went plunging through the air to the floor below.

Chapter Fourteen

I swam up through the mists of unconsciousness to find Brother Simeon bending over me, his narrow features alive with concern.

'Chapman! What's happened? Are you all right?'

I sat up slowly, tentatively stretching each limb to make sure that no bones were broken. Satisfied on that score, I became aware of my throbbing head and the fact that I was feeling dizzy.

'Someone pushed me,' I said, 'from the top of the stairs.'

The friar nodded. 'I wondered if something untoward might have happened when I found you like this.' He added by way of explanation, 'When I awoke from my doze, you were missing, and Martha Grindcobb told me that you'd gone out, in her opinion to play at dice with the grooms in the stables. However, remembering your words of this morning, I made straight for the tower. As I approached, a man came out of the door, but when he saw me, he turned to his right and disappeared along the path through the scrubland.'

'Did you see who it was?' I demanded with an eagerness that once again made my head spin.

'Unfortunately, no. I was too far away, and whoever it

was had his hood pulled forward, concealing his face.' The friar helped me painfully to my feet. 'At first, I thought it must be you, then I realised the figure was too short of stature. Furthermore, your cloak is dun-coloured and his was reddish-brown. Here, sit down a while.' And he guided me to the stool by the table.

Into my mind sprang an instant picture of Fulk Disney as I had seen him that morning, wrapped in a thick, russet-hued woollen cloak. I must have uttered his name aloud, because Brother Simeon looked sharply at me and raised his eyebrows inquiringly.

I told him of my earlier encounter with Fulk and the conclusions I had drawn from it. 'I also met him in the passageway,' I added, 'just before I quit the house. He either had unfinished business of his own in the tower, or he suspected my destination and decided to follow me. Whichever it was, because I delayed in order to pay a visit to Mistress Empryngham, he arrived first; and when I did, finally, get here, he must have concealed his presence by keeping one floor ahead of me and watching me from the top of each flight of stairs. While I was in Lady Cederwell's chapel, he was on the steps leading to the look-out platform . . .' I broke off with a sudden cry, struck by the full import of what I had said. I fumbled in the pouch at my belt, unhooked it and shook it upside down, but as I had feared it was empty. The letter to Brother Simeon had gone.

I explained this to the friar and his manner underwent a change. Any compassion he had been feeling for me was replaced by exasperation.

'You had her list of accusations in your possession and

you allowed them to be stolen?' he thundered. 'You
incompetent dim-wit! You jackass! You fool!'

It needed all my strength of will not to retaliate in kind.

'How was I to know that there was anyone else in the
tower?' I protested. 'I had no sure idea of what I might find,
nor indeed if I should discover anything at all.' I added, in a
bid to regain his sympathy, 'A fall like that could have broken
my neck.'

'True,' he admitted, relenting a trifle. 'What saved you?'

'I don't know. I think I must have been aware, just a second
or two before I was pushed, that someone was behind me.
Perhaps I felt his breath on my cheek. But, for whatever
reason, I instinctively jumped sideways from the staircase in
the very instant that Fulk shoved me in the back.' Tenderly,
I fingered the bump which was swelling above my left eye.

Brother Simeon was silent for several moments, then
hunched his thin shoulders.

'I suppose you're not altogether to blame,' he said
grudgingly. 'But you had the evidence against Sir Hugh and
Maurice Cederwell in your hands and now it's gone. It's
what I call careless, Chapman. Very careless! Without it,
there is nothing I can do. The wicked will continue to flourish
and enjoy the fruits of their wrongdoing because there are no
charges I can now lay against them. Never having spoken to
Lady Cederwell, I have no means of proving why she asked
me to visit her here at the manor.'

'Not unless somebody else would be willing to testify
against them,' I agreed.

The friar curled his lip. 'Small chance of that. Morals are
lax everywhere nowadays. The sins of the flesh are no longer

187

regarded as important. King Edward's court sets the example for the rest of the country. Do you seriously suppose that any inhabitant of Cederwell Manor would jeopardise his or her position in order to bring allegations of adultery and worse against the master and his heir? But I tell you this, Chapman!' Brother Simeon's eyes glowed with zealous fire. 'Wherever God may call upon me to travel in the future, however far afield the journey may take me, I shall never forget Sir Hugh Cederwell and the saintly young life that he has destroyed. If I can do him a disservice in any way whatsoever, it shall be done.' I gave an involuntary shiver. Such malevolence was disturbing. Then I realised that he was looking at me. 'You could stand witness,' he suggested. 'You could swear to what you overheard this morning between Sir Hugh and Mistress Lynom.'

I carefully refrained from shaking my head, but my answer was still emphatic.

'No! I won't repeat things I was never intended to hear.'

'You're prepared to condone immorality, that's what you mean.' The friar was contemptuous. 'You're like so many of the young; evil doesn't disgust you as it should. Well, I suppose I ought to have known better than to ask. Can you walk now? You have a nasty swelling on your forehead. It's time you returned to the house and had it tended.'

I rose unsteadily to my feet. 'What do we say about what's happened?'

'What can we say?' was the acid retort. 'We have no evidence that Fulk Disney attacked you. He has only to deny his presence in the tower and he'll be believed. You may be certain that he'll have rid himself of Lady Cederwell's letter by this time. It's been torn up and scattered to the wind, lost amongst the snowdrifts.'

'Very well,' I concurred, 'I shall say that curiosity drove me to look around the place and that I fell down the stairs. You found me. It's the truth after all.'

He nodded, and we descended the final flight of stairs to let ourselves out into the open air. I glanced briefly along what was visible of the path through the scrubland, but knew that at present I was in no fit state to go exploring. With a sigh, I followed Friar Simeon as he made his way back towards the house.

'I don't know!' Martha Grindcobb scolded. 'A widower with a child did you say you are? More like a great boy who's never grown up!' She fussed around me, making a poultice of rue and borage mixed with honey which she applied to the lump over my eye, holding it in place with a long strip of linen wound about my head. Brother Simeon made little attempt to hide his mirth at the spectacle, and I was thankful that none of the kitchen-maids was present. The three of them, Martha told me, had been summoned by Phillipa Talke to assist with their mistress's laying-out. The body had finally lost all of its rigor and could be decently washed and clothed, ready for burial.

With this information and such knowledge as I possessed, I tried to work out the time of Lady Cederwell's death the preceding day, but my senses began to swim again and I almost keeled sideways off my stool.

'You'd best lie down, lad,' Martha ordered. She cast a disparaging glance around the kitchen. 'There's no comfort here. Give him a hand, Friar, and help him to the men's dormitory. There'll be spare cots until bedtime, and Roger can snatch an hour or two's rest before supper. I daresay,' she added to me, 'that you'll be black and blue all over by tomorrow morning, but that's your own fault. All the same, I'll give you a drink of lettuce juice to make you sleep. Why did you want to go poking around in that horrible old tower anyway? Tell me that if you can.'

Unfortunately I could make no answer without revealing far more than I was prepared to, and allowed her to reproach me with what she regarded as my childish escapade until Simeon and I were out of earshot. We emerged once again into the fresh air to find that it had stopped snowing, but was even colder than before. The sky was like lead, and although only an hour or so past noon, the thin winter daylight was already receding, leaving behind it a grey and ghostly stillness. The men's sleeping quarters were immediately beneath the women's dormitory at the back of the great hall, the shuttered window protected by the gallery's overhang and therefore making the room a little warmer than the more draughty upstairs chamber. Otherwise, it was almost a replica of the one above, with its row of wooden-framed cots, its solitary clothes chest and a table bearing candles and tinder-box.

The place was empty but for ourselves, and the friar thankfully let me drop on to the nearest cot, glad to be relieved of my weight. Then, having helped me remove my boots, he felt free to go.

'Stay there for a while,' he advised, 'and try to rest. If you're still awake at suppertime, I'll bring you a bowl of broth.'

'Don't bother,' I murmured drowsily, Martha Grindcobb's potion beginning to do its work. 'If I'm awake, I'll get up for some proper food.'

I heard him give a rare snort of laughter before I was engulfed in a black tide of unconsciousness. I spiralled down and down into those depths of sleep which is the nearest approach in this earthly life that we ever come to death. We see nothing, we hear nothing, we are nothing, while time drifts by, all unheeded, over our heads . . .

Something, some noise, was forcing me upwards again towards the light. It was penetrating my senses, making me toss from side to side in the narrow cot, forcing me to sit up, to listen. The sound was coming from above, a woman's voice, screaming with terror. My legs felt like leaden weights attached to my body, and for what seemed to be several minutes, but was probably only seconds, they refused to obey me. At last, however, I dragged myself to my feet and staggered to the dormitory door, to find on opening it that it was now almost dark. I must have slept for several hours and it was nearly evening.

The screaming had abated a little, but already other people were arriving on the scene. As I stood there still somewhat confused, Martha Grindcobb and Brother Simeon rushed out of the back door, closely followed, but at a safe distance, by the three kitchen-maids, all agog with the anticipation of some unnamed horror. Simultaneously, Mistress Lynom and Maurice Cederwell emerged from their bedchambers and appeared side-by-side on the balcony overhead. Moments later Tostig Steward and Phillipa Talke came out of the house, preceding by only a matter of seconds Sir Hugh himself, testily demanding to be told what was wrong. The noise had even penetrated as far as the stables, and distant voices raised in inquiry, coupled with the flicker of lamplight gilding the snow, heralded the advent of the grooms.

'What is it? What's going on?' Sir Hugh pushed his way through the rest of us, who were gathered together nervously at the foot of the steps, and mounted to the gallery. 'Ursula, what has happened? Are you all right?'

The lady, obviously touched by this concern for her safety, unbent a little towards him.

'The sound is coming from the women's dormitory. I think it must be your sister-in-law, Mistress Empryngham. There is no one else in there. But take care! You don't know yet the cause of her distress. There may be someone hidden inside the room.'

I saw Sir Hugh nod brusquely, then stride forward, at the same time calling on the rest of us men to support him. The friar clapped me on the shoulder, urging me ahead of him, but the Capsgrave brothers and Jasper had already overtaken us, climbing the snow-covered steps as fast as they were able without slipping and falling. There was as yet, I noted, no sign of Hamon.

On reaching the women's dormitory, all of us clustering around the open door, we could just make out the figure of Adela Empryngham seated on the side of her cot, whimpering and shivering. Mistress Lynom at once went forward to sit beside her, placing a comforting arm around her shoulders. Sir Hugh lit a candle and held it aloft, its guttering beam illuminating his sister-in-law's white, terrified features.

'There, there, my dear,' Mistress Lynom consoled her. 'Have you had a bad dream?'

The convulsive sobs lessened slightly and the bent head was raised as Adela considered this suggestion.

'I . . . Oh . . . Could it have been, do you think? I . . . I was sure that someone was standing in the doorway . . . I . . . I was certain.'

'You woke suddenly while you were still riding the night mare,' Mistress Lynom soothed her. 'There's no one here. Hold the candle higher, Hugh, and let her see for herself.'

The knight obliged, slowly spinning full circle on his heel to reveal that no one was hiding in any of the corners. This seemed to convince Adela that the incident had been nothing more than the figment of a dream, but she was still very frightened, and Mistress Lynom, taking charge, insisted that a truckle bed was set up immediately alongside her own in the guest chamber.

'She must share with me. After all that has happened today, we cannot leave her on her own again, and it will be a few hours yet before the other women go to their rest.'

Pressing a hand to my head to stop its buzzing, I stepped forward.

'Mistress Empryngham, this person you saw standing in the doorway, was it a man or a woman?'

She looked at me, confused and bewildered. 'I couldn't see. It was just a shadow.'

Maurice Cederwell, who was standing behind his father, demanded roughly, 'Who asked you to poke your nose in, Chapman? Adela herself agrees that it was all a dream.'

There was a murmur of assent from the others.

Nevertheless, I would have pursued my inquiries had it not been apparent that Mistress Empryngham was in no fit state to give any sensible answers to my questions. But as we all began to go our separate ways – Phillipa Talke to arrange for the setting up of the truckle bed in the guest bedchamber, Martha, Ethelwynne, Edith and Jenny Tonge to the kitchen to finish preparing supper, Tostig to oversee the laying of the table in the great hall and Sir Hugh to help his sister-in-law into the room next door – I touched Nicholas Capsgrave on the shoulder, just as he, his brother and Jasper were about to return to the stables.

'You were one of the first people up here with Sir Hugh.' He nodded. 'Was this closed or open?' And I indicated the dormitory door.

Nicholas hesitated, but Jude cut in, 'It was open.'

'You're sure of that?'

'I'm positive.'

'Thank you,' I said, but when I offered no explanation for my question, they shrugged and descended the steps.

'What was that about?' the friar wanted to know.

'Don't you see?' I whispered as we stood aside to allow Sir Hugh and Mistress Lynom, supporting Adela between them, to pass along the gallery to the neighbouring room. 'No one in her right mind would sleep with the door wide open in this weather.'

'So?' Simeon frowned.

'So if Mistress Empryngham had simply had a bad dream, the door would have been fast shut.' I was growing impatient at his paucity of understanding. 'Surely even you can see that!'

My companion bridled. 'There's no need for that tone of voice. You can't expect everyone to think of these things. We're not all interested in solving crimes.'

'Not if it means bringing the criminal to justice?'

'"Vengeance is mine, I will repay saith the Lord",' was his only answer.

I was about to remind him of his declared intention to do Sir Hugh a disservice if ever he got the chance, when my attention was distracted. Just ahead of us, Maurice Cederwell had reached his own bedchamber door and pushed it open. As he stepped across the threshold, from within the room I heard someone ask, 'Is everything quiet now?' It was a man's voice, a voice I recognised. The speaker, unless I was very much mistaken, was Fulk Disney.

I refused, in spite of Martha Grindcobb's chidings, to return to my cot in the men's dormitory. I was wide awake now, even if my body was aching all over, and in no mood for lying alone in the dark and the cold. I needed warmth and light, although I could have wished for more peace and quiet than was to be had in the kitchen in which to pursue my thoughts. Above all, however, I was ravenously hungry, for very little in those days ever impaired my appetite, and I was able to persuade Martha to find me some black bread and goat's milk cheese which I ate together with a handful of small spring leeks which had been dried and stored. (I subsequently noticed, throughout the evening, people kept their distance from me, or if by chance they got too close, they did not inhale too deeply.)

The friar, who had disappeared upstairs to the chapel to

celebrate Vespers, chided me on his return for not going with him.

'You are not as strict in your religious observance, Roger, as I could wish to see you. I trust you're not a prey to any of the heretical views which prevail in so many quarters nowadays. I have heard it said that even the Duke of Gloucester possesses a Lollard Bible.'

'He also has the *Imitatio Christi* of Thomas à Kempis,' I answered without thinking, and saw Simeon's eyebrows shoot up in surprise at my unguarded comment. Fortunately, at that precise moment, raised voices, one angry, the other tearful and protesting, were to be heard in the passageway outside. Moments later, Phillipa Talke appeared dragging Lady Cederwell's little maid by the arm, while over one of her own hung a cloak of thick, russet-dyed wool.

'What's the matter?' Martha Grindcobb snapped, annoyed by this rowdy intrusion into her domain.

'I've just caught Audrey coming out of the mistress's room carrying this!' the housekeeper said venomously, and held the cloak aloft. 'The little thief!' she added.

'I'm not a thief!' the girl denied fearfully, her eyes brimming with tears which trickled slowly down her face. 'The mistress promised it to me only three days ago. She said she'd never liked it. She said she had no need of it and that it was more blessed to give it to someone who had.'

Phillipa Talke brayed with laughter. 'Oh, did she indeed? A likely story! Where's your proof, eh? Did she write her wishes down? Or make them known to anybody else?'

Audrey Lambspringe wiped her face with the back of her hand, and then blew her nose in her fingers.

'She might've done.' Her tone was defiant. 'I don't know. But I do know that's what she told me.'

'Liar!' Mistress Talke accompanied the word with a vicious slap which sent the poor girl reeling.

Brother Simeon and I both got to our feet ready to intervene, but Martha Grindcobb was before us. She pushed between the two women, standing with arms akimbo.

'That'll do,' she warned the housekeeper. 'I'll have no brawling in my kitchen. And I won't have you taking your disappointment and bad temper out on the child, either.' She turned to Audrey. 'All the same, you shouldn't have removed the cloak from the mistress's room like that, especially not with her still lying there, cold. Mistress Talke'll have to report the matter to Sir Hugh, so you can tell him then what you've just told us. Depends whether or not he'll believe you.'

'Lady Cederwell *did* say I was to have the cloak, she *did*!' Audrey declared, the tears starting to flow once more. 'Mine's all worn and threadbare. She said it would keep me warm in the winter.'

'She wouldn't give a beautiful thing like this to you!' Mistress Talke was scathing. 'The master bought it for my lady from a rich merchant in Campden, or so she told me. Before they were married it was, and it must have cost him a pretty penny.' She fingered the rich wool covetously, then glanced at me. 'What do you think, Chapman? You must know the value of such material.'

'It certainly wouldn't have been cheap,' I replied, reluctant to be drawn into the argument. 'It's made of the best Cotswold wool by the look of it.'

Brother Simeon nodded, drawing down the corners of his

mouth in an expression of deepest disapproval.

'Wool of that sort would be worth twelve or thirteen marks the sack. Think what could be done for the glory of God and all His works with money like that. Lady Cederwell was quite right to despise the vanities of this world, but wrong in promising it to you, my child. She should have sold the cloak and given the money to the Church.'

Behind his back, Martha Grindcobb grimaced at me, rolling her eyes heavenwards and wrinkling up her nose. To Phillipa Talke and Audrey Lambspringe she said, 'You'd best go to the master at once and get this thing settled. We've enough troubles hanging over our heads as it is, without accusations of theft into the bargain.'

The housekeeper was only too ready. 'I intend to! I don't need your advice on what's right and proper, Mistress Grindcobb! Follow me, girl!'

She and Audrey left the kitchen as abruptly as they had entered it, the younger woman trailing behind the older. I watched them go, my gaze fixed on the russet cloak draped across Phillipa Talke's left arm. And a thought began to stir uneasily at the back of my mind.

Chapter Fifteen

It snowed again that evening, but I was unaware of it until I awoke the following day, having curled up after supper near the remains of the kitchen fire and slept without stirring until cock-crow. This long, deep, dreamless slumber was all that was needed in those far-off days to cure any ills from which I might be suffering; and in spite of a multitude of bruises and the swelling over one eye, I had lost both my headache and the feeling of lassitude which had bedevilled me after my fall. I was able to throw off my bandage and get to my feet with so few twinges of pain that what there were could easily be disregarded.

Simeon lay close to me, supine, one arm outflung among yesterday's rushes, and his black habit had wriggled its way up as far as his knees to reveal a pair of spindly legs. As usual he was snoring, his lower jaw slack as he breathed in the chilly air. Taking care not to disturb him, I repeated the ritual of the previous morning, blowing the fire into life with the bellows and setting water to heat. By the time I had finished shaving, Martha Grindcobb and the girls had descended from the dormitory and were able to inform me that although it had snowed during the early part of the night, it must have ceased some hours ago. The rising sun gave promise of a beautiful day.

While they started to prepare breakfast, I went to the back door to see for myself. It was a morning of heavy frost and everywhere there was brilliance and light, from the sparkle of rimed branches and roof-tops to the glitter of the ice-bound earth. The hill which rose behind the house was nothing but a shadow, lost in a veil of amber mist, and the sky was a bright, uninterrupted blue as far as the eye could see. I suspected it would not be long before the weather improved sufficiently to make it necessary for myself and Sir Hugh's other uninvited guests to leave. If we had more frost tonight, the snow would be compact enough by tomorrow to make travelling possible, if taken at a careful pace and with a decent quantity of rags wrapped about the feet.

I returned to the kitchen to find Edith and Ethelwynne yawning cavernously and grumbling about getting late to bed. I gathered from their conversation that they had been summoned by Mistress Talke at an advanced hour the preceding evening, to lay out Gerard Empryngham's corpse.

'How is Mistress Empryngham today?' I inquired. 'Has she recovered from her fright?'

Martha nodded, digging out salted herring from a barrel.

'She's sent word that she'll get up and be down in a minute or two, so you can judge for yourself. We in the dormitory were all a bit jumpy last night and dragged the clothes chest across the door. I don't know how Mistress Lynom and her guest fared. Not that we thought anyone really did try to get in, mind you! Mistress Empryngham just had a bad dream.'

The words had hardly left her mouth before Adela herself

appeared, intent on returning to her own bedchamber as
quickly as possible in order to array herself in widow's weeds.
She scarcely paused to listen to my hopes for her well-being,
but vanished into the storeroom and out through the door
which led into the triangular courtyard. When she came back,
she was dressed from top to toe in funereal black, and it
struck me that now she was over the first shock of her
husband's death, she was beginning to enjoy her role as his
grief-stricken relict.

'You saw him?' Martha Grindcobb asked in hushed and
reverent tones, as she threw oats and salt into a pan of hot
water.

Adela nodded and bowed her veiled head. 'Gerard looks
very peaceful. I must thank Mistress Talke. She has done
well.'

Ethelwynne and Edith looked at one another and grimaced.

'Why do we never get any thanks?' the former demanded
sulkily when Adela had gone in search of the housekeeper.
'It was us two as did all the work.'

She was advised by the cook to hold her tongue and get
on with her chores. 'And Chapman,' Martha added, 'see what
you can do to rouse the friar. It's high time he was up. I
never knew a man who could sleep so soundly!'

I shook Simeon awake and told him the welcome news
that our sojourn at Cederwell Manor was probably drawing
to an end.

'Although it's freezing at present, the sun is shining, and
I think it could warm up enough to begin a slight thaw by
midday. I doubt if it will snow again for a while.'

He was considerably cheered by this intelligence, and

having spat into the rushes and cleared his nose by blowing it vigorously into his sleeve, he went to the back door and glanced outside.

'You're right,' he said, returning to the fire and holding his hands to the blaze. 'There's a change in the wind's direction and the clouds have dispersed. We might even consider going today.' His eyes brightened at the prospect.

'You'd be foolish to make any sudden move,' Martha advised him. 'Wait a further night at least and see what happens. You don't want to be caught miles from anywhere in another snowstorm. You've more sense, I hope, Chapman?'

I nodded emphatically. I had my own reasons for not wishing to quit the manor yet awhile, and I had need of the friar. Over breakfast, therefore, I persuaded him to trespass a little longer on Sir Hugh's hospitality.

'Your appetite is so small that you can hardly be a drain on his resources, and so quiet about the place that he can barely be aware of your presence.'

'That is of no consideration to me,' Simeon replied austerely. 'My duty lies among sinners and the fallen, urging them to repentance of their wicked ways.'

'But they won't receive your message,' I pointed out, 'if you freeze to death by the wayside.'

This argument seemed to strike him more forcibly than the rest, and I finally secured his promise to remain at Cederwell for another twenty-four hours, when we might reasonably expect to see whether or not the thaw was set to last.

'I want you to come with me to explore the scrubland

path,' I said, lowering my voice and hoping that no one else could hear me above the clatter of pots and pans. 'We saw movement in that direction yesterday, amongst the undergrowth. There may be something there to find.'

Brother Simeon was scathing. 'If anyone was there, he'll be long gone. My own belief is that it was falling snow or branches moving in the wind.'

'Perhaps. But I should like to satisfy myself on that head.'

'Oh, very well,' he agreed crossly. 'But I think it a fool's errand. We shall find nothing, only get chilled to the marrow in the process. We'd best make a good breakfast in order to warm ourselves.'

Martha, catching just the last few words, cackled with mirth.

'You've no call, Brother, to fear that Roger won't stuff his belly with everything that's going.' She addressed me. 'Salted herring again and porridge this morning, lad, and I'll give you some of my oatcakes to fill up the corners.'

She was as good as her word, and in addition she heated some ale, ready mulled by the time the grooms arrived from the stables. I thought that Hamon and Jasper seemed out of spirits, restless and anxious to get home. No doubt they were feeling all the petty vexations of confinement in a house with which they were unfamiliar; the boredom of having nothing to do except groom and feed their own three horses. Moreover, the tragic circumstance of two deaths within two days was bound to engulf everyone in a sea of gloom. But, even so, Hamon appeared far more sullen and taciturn than his companion, and during the meal kept rising from his stool and going to stare through the open kitchen window, assessing conditions out of doors.

I watched him thoughtfully, a man accused by Sir Hugh of murdering his wife on the orders of Mistress Lynom, and by the dame of having witnessed the knight stooping over Lady Cederwell's body hours before her death was discovered by Brother Simeon and myself. My thoughts then strayed to two russet-coloured cloaks, one the property of Fulk Disney, the other belonging to the dead woman. In my mind's eye, I could clearly see the latter draped across Phillipa Talke's arm.

Breakfast had been served late that morning, with added delay in clearing the dirty dishes from the great hall, Father Godyer's bedchamber and the steward's room. By the time we had all finished, the sun was rising in the winter sky, and Martha was agitatedly protesting that it was but an hour or so to dinner. Not only would the food probably not be ready, but no one would be hungry enough to eat it if it were, making a mockery of all her labour.

'And the water barrel needs filling again and there's more wood to be fetched,' she wailed, causing the precipitate departure of the Capsgraves, together with Jasper and Hamon, before they could be pressed into service.

I therefore had no choice but to offer, much to the friar's undisguised relief. He was able to settle down again by the fire for another half-hour, before we ventured forth.

'It will be warmer later,' he told me.

Taking the big leather pail, I passed through the storeroom into the little triangular courtyard beyond. Once there, I could not prevent my eyes straying towards the closed door of the Emprynghams' bedchamber where lay Gerard's body, now decently washed and clothed, all signs of his violent end removed, his contorted features smoothed into a false mask of serenity, and doubtless a crucifix placed between his clasped hands. For a moment or two I stood there, giving my imagination full rein . . .

I heard the bolts of the storeroom door being stealthily withdrawn and saw the emergence of a dark, cloaked figure: a figure which first carefully removed the cover from the well before going to rap on the Emprynghams' door. After a while, this insistent knocking was answered by a sleepy Gerard, clad only in his nightshirt . . .

Here, the succession of pictures in my mind's eye faltered. What had happened next? How had Gerard been persuaded outside, unshod and without even a bedrobe around him as protection against the inclement weather? For this was absolutely necessary if his death was to look like a sleepwalking accident. I eyed the distance from the well to the doorway; two yards perhaps, but not much further. I therefore saw my cloaked figure step to one side as the door was opened, melting into the darkness. Still only half awake, Gerard took a step forward into the snow to find out who or what had roused him. At once, determination lending strength, my murderer was behind him, hands on Gerard's back, propelling the victim forward and tipping him, head first, down the well. Then, with a firm grasp on those two bare ankles, all my phantom had to do was hang on securely until the struggles ceased. It would not have taken very long, on that bitter night, for ice to form on top of the water, holding the body fast . . .

The longer I considered this version of events, the more I

was convinced that it, or something very like it, must be what had really happened. I returned to the kitchen with my brimming pail, well satisfied with my cogitations. After two more trips for yet more water, I was dispatched to the woodpile in the stable, where I was greeted shamefacedly by three of the grooms and with a morose indifference by Hamon. On this occasion I made no effort at conversation, simply filling the basket with as many logs and branches as I could carry before leaving them to their consciences and games of hazard.

Back in the open air again, although my toes and fingers ached with cold, the sun was warm against my face, and I noted that snow was beginning to drop from trees and bushes. Unless there was a dramatic reversal in the weather conditions overnight, my days at Cederwell Manor were undoubtedly numbered, and there could be no excuse to linger after tomorrow. I realised suddenly that I was unsure as to which day of the week it was, and had to think hard before working out that, as I had arrived here on Tuesday afternoon, it must now be Thursday, Thor's Day, as Ulnoth would have called it; Thor, the sender of lightning, the son of Woden, whose realm was Thrudvang and whose wife was Sif . . . Guiltily, I pulled my errant thoughts up short and made the sign of the cross.

As I approached the back door, I heard voices coming from the direction of the main gate, and a moment or so later a man appeared round the corner of the house; a short man, with bushy red eyebrows, skin as brown and wrinkled as an old leather shoe, and a wide, thin mouth which split into a friendly grin as soon as he saw me. His cloak and boots were both well patched, and there was a great rent in one leg of his hose.

'Peace to this house,' he greeted me, at the same time opening his cloak to reveal the tools of his trade suspended from his belt. 'Does your goodwife have any pots and pans that need mending?'

I laughed. 'I'm a widower, friend, and nothing more than a poor chapman taking shelter here until the weather improves.' I jerked my head. 'But come inside and I'll ask the cook.' I led the way into the kitchen and said to Martha, 'Here's a tinker wants to know if he can be of service.' And I emptied my basket of logs into the larger one standing in the corner.

Martha looked up from her pastry-making and regarded the man with astonishment.

'As it happens I do have a couple of pans which have parted company from their handles, but I didn't expect to get them mended for another week or two, at least.' She frowned. 'Are the roads passable already? Ethelwynne, give the tinker a cup of ale.'

The dark little eyes beneath the craggy brows sparkled with anticipation, and the stranger came closer to the fire in order to warm his cold fingers.

'That's very kind, Mistress, and much appreciated. In answer to your question, although it's beginning to thaw, walking's still a very treacherous business. I shouldn't have risked it but for the fact that my host of the past two days has disappeared. Went out yesterday morning, and I haven't seen hide nor hair of him since. I was hoping I might have come across him; that he's managed to find shelter somewhere.

But if he spent the night in the open, I haven't much expectation of discovering him alive.'

An unpleasant thought surfaced. 'Where have you been staying?' I asked, praying that the tinker would say in one of the manor dwellings to the west, but he did not reply, no one else being in the mood to take much notice of his story.

He cupped his hands around the mazer of ale which Ethelwynne handed to him, and drank noisily. When he had finished, he wiped his mouth with the back of his hand.

'That was good. Do I smell hot pasties?'

Martha nodded resignedly. She was getting used to extra mouths to feed.

'But you'd best take it with you into the storeroom while you mend the pots,' she advised. 'We don't often see Sir Hugh in the kitchen, but just in case . . . We already have more visitors than he approves of, on account of the snow.'

'*I* was sent for,' Simeon chimed in peevishly, evidently annoyed at being lumped together with uninvited guests such as myself.

'No offence meant, Brother!' Martha was nettled by his reproach. 'Edith! When you've found the pans which need repairing, take the tinker next door. And here! Give him this pastry coffin.'

I waited a few moments until Edith returned to the kitchen, then followed the tinker into the storeroom. He had not yet started work, but was seated on a barrel, eating.

'You didn't answer my question,' I accused him.

The man, who had his back to the door, jumped, swallowed a crumb of pastry the wrong way and choked. When he finally recovered his breath, he spluttered, 'Hell's teeth! You startled me, friend. What was it you wanted to know?'

I apologised and repeated my question. The tinker crammed the last of the pasty into his mouth.

'A boulder house, built into the side of the hill,' he answered thickly. 'About a mile or so east of here. Belongs to a hermit.'

'Ulnoth!' I exclaimed, my worst fears realised. I seized my companion's arm. 'You say he went out yesterday, before noon, and hasn't returned?'

'That's right. So his name's Ulnoth, is it? That's more than I could vouch for. He gave me food and drink, such as it was, but never a word of conversation. A strange, nervous little man, afraid of his own shadow.' The tinker got to his feet and began to unhook the tools of his trade from his belt, laying them neatly one by one on top of the barrel.

'How did you come to be there?'

'At the boulder house? I was caught in the snowstorm of Tuesday night, as I gather you were.' He grimaced expressively. 'Only you were luckier. You found a warmer, softer billet than I did.'

I smiled. 'I spent four nights with Ulnoth after twisting my ankle. I was comfortable enough, and after his own fashion, he made me welcome.'

The tinker picked up one of the pans and examined it, before stooping once again to retrieve the handle.

'A couple of rivets will see this right, I fancy.' He turned to me. 'You were more fortunate than I was, then. Oh, he fed me, and not badly, either, but he couldn't, or wouldn't, talk. I told you, my feeling is that he was afraid, but of who or what I've no idea.'

I chewed my bottom lip thoughtfully. So much had occurred since my arrival at Cederwell Manor, that much of what had happened previously had been driven from my mind. But I recollected now that Ulnoth had told me he was frightened during that brief, second visit I had paid him on Tuesday, after leaving Lynom Hall. I remembered, too, how he had moaned and rocked himself, muttering all the while, 'Death. Death. Death.' Plainly some event had taken place between my quitting the boulder house earlier in the day, and my return to it a few hours later. It was also obvious that the tinker had no better idea than I what that event could be.

I watched him in silence for a moment or two, as he skilfully proceeded with his work. He had by now removed his cloak and hood to reveal a small, neat head covered with springing curls as fiery as his eyebrows. Becoming aware of my scrutiny, he glanced up and grinned.

'It's comforting to know there's yet another fool wandering about the countryside in the depths of winter. Not,' he added 'that I'd have ventured so far afield if I'd known we were in for weather such as this. My woman told me I was a dolt to go, but times are hard and work was slack in Bath. It's a little town. I don't know if you're acquainted with it. Whereabouts are you from?'

'Wells is my home, but I've a child in Bristol. She lives with my late wife's mother.'

The tinker nodded sympathetically. 'I've four daughters,' he sighed. 'Sometimes you get tired of being ordered about by women. Now and then you need your own thoughts and company.'

I laughed. 'True enough. And you want to be on the move. Being mewed up indoors for too long makes your legs begin to twitch.'

'It does that. But my goodwife was right on this occasion. I walked for miles without meeting another soul and then the weather began to turn. Luckily I was close to the Priory at Woodspring, where there was room to spare in the guest hall. The monks said they'd only had one other visitor in weeks.'

'That would have been Brother Simeon,' I nodded, adding in explanation, 'The friar who's presently warming himself in the kitchen.'

The tinker grunted, but displayed no real interest. It seemed the monks had said very little about Simeon or his visit, and I smiled to myself as I thought how affronted he would be if he knew. His message of eternal damnation unless they mended their ways had probably been forgotten almost as soon as he was out of sight.

There was another silence while my companion began work on the second skillet. Then I asked, 'When did you quit the Priory? The following morning?'

'Ay, on the Tuesday after dinner. It was foolish to leave so late in the day, but I waited until it was properly light. The monks had told me of a big house, Lynom Hall, where my services might be wanted, but somehow or other I took a wrong track and lost my bearings. With night setting in and the sky threatening snow, I was scared, I can tell you. But just as I was beginning to get really frightened, I came out on to a broad road which eventually brought me to the hermit's lodging. A hundred yards or so before I reached it,

I saw another track off to my left, and I wondered if it was the road I should have taken.'

I nodded. 'From that spot it leads south to Woodspring Priory and Lynom Hall. You made a bad mistake there, Tinker.'

'True. But it's taught me a lesson. It's the first and last time I go travelling at this season. What say you, friend?'

I agreed, but absent-mindedly. My thoughts were centred on Ulnoth, who had left home yesterday and not returned. I bade the tinker an abrupt farewell and returned to Simeon, who was still toasting his toes by the fire. I bent over him and laid a hand on his shoulder.

'Are you coming?'

'Where?' he demanded irritably, and settled himself more comfortably on his stool. The rich smell of stew now filled the kitchen.

'You promised to explore the scrubland with me.'

'Well, I've changed my mind,' he snapped. 'I've decided I'll not be dragged outdoors looking for a mare's nest. If you want to go and search, you must go alone.'

His face was set in stubborn lines and I saw that he meant what he said. I was sorry for the loss of his company; two pairs of eyes are likely to see more than one. Nevertheless, I was not to be deterred. I picked up my cloak again and put it on for the second time that morning.

'I shall be back in time for dinner,' I informed Martha Grindcobb, but she, resigned by now to my folly, made no answer.

Chapter Sixteen

I walked along the back of the house in the direction of the stables, then turned left and crossed the inner courtyard, past the fish pond, to the gate set in the wall between laundry and dairy. The sun was mounting in the sky, and every now and then my eyes were dazzled by the sudden glitter, reflected from piles of banked-up snow. At the end of the path across the marshland, the tower swam insubstantially in the morning light. When I reached it, I did not enter, but turned yet again to my left, along the narrow track which led through the scrubland.

At first this was easy to see despite its white covering, for the clumps of sea holly and samphire were widely spaced, with coarse tufts of marram grass in between. It gradually became less obvious, however, overhung by crowding trees and dense undergrowth, and as I picked my cautious way amongst stunted oaks and snaking roots, I was forced to keep my eyes firmly on the ground. But I was relieved to note that, even under snow, the well-trodden path grew slowly visible. People passing and repassing over the years had broken down foliage and branches, leaving a clear, if narrow, track which rose steeply towards the high ground and the broad, rutted road leading eastwards in the direction of Bristol.

The silence felt suddenly oppressive, and I realised how alone I was in this desolate wilderness. The manor was by this time somewhere behind me and out of sight, although now and again I briefly glimpsed the outline of a distant roof as trees thinned and the path began to climb. I also grew more aware of my body's aches and pains as it protested against the treatment it had received in recent days. I began to shiver, and it was not altogether on account of the cold. The ancient gods of the trees seemed very close; it needed little imagination to fancy the Green Man following hard on my heels . . .

I took a firmer grasp of my cudgel and flung the right-hand side of my cloak up and over my left shoulder, making the garment more secure and freeing my ankles, so that whenever possible I could take longer steps. Every so often I raised my voice and called, 'Ulnoth!' but there was no reply.

I was certain, although with nothing to support my conviction, that the signs of life I had noticed yesterday morning from the direction of the scrubland had been made by the hermit. For some reason, he had set out early from home and walked to Cederwell Manor. It would have been a long and arduous journey in such terrible conditions, and it was almost impossible that he would have come so far in search of food. Had he then been looking for me? He knew where I was, for I recalled telling him my destination during that short, second visit to the boulder house on Tuesday. Yet why should he wish to find me? What was it he had been so frightened of? And if he had indeed managed to get as far as Cederwell, why had he not simply entered by the main gate and asked for me by name? There was no gatekeeper, but he had only to make his way around to the back of the house and knock. Why was he so obviously spying out the land before approaching?

I realised that I might never know the answers to these questions, for if Ulnoth had found no shelter last night – and the tinker had testified that his host had not returned – he could well have frozen to death by now. The thought made me quicken my pace and, in consequence, I slipped on a patch of frozen snow and slid to my knees. I cursed aloud. That was my third fall in just under a week, and although my tumble from the tower stairs had not been my fault, I was nevertheless growing careless. My health, particularly my physical well-being, was my fortune, what little there was of it, and I could ill afford to be laid up if I were to earn a living for myself and my child.

Shaken, I stayed where I was for a moment or two, but as I made to rise I noticed that the bushes and small trees to my right had been disturbed, bits of twig snapped off and a passage forced between them. Moreover their covering of snow was lighter than that of the surrounding undergrowth, a soft powdering, the result of the storm during the early part of last night and not the heavy burden of many days' accumulation. I scrambled to my feet and very carefully began to penetrate the scrubland.

Trailing brambles tore at my cloak and hose, but I was too worried now to pay any attention or take heed of the damage they were causing. Something or someone had recently passed this way, beating a path through the tangle of wild vegetation. And there, hanging from a thorn, was a long black thread and, further on, what proved to be, when shaken clear of snow, a thin strip of black woollen cloth. My heart sank at this proof that my suspicions might have substance. I lunged forward, swinging my stick from side to side, only to be brought up short by an obstacle which blocked any further progress.

The man's body was wedged between the iron-hard roots of trees and stems of saplings, having been pushed down as far as it would go to keep it concealed throughout the winter. Had I not formed a theory and come looking, had I not slipped and noticed the tell-tale signs, the chances were that it would have lain undiscovered until spring, by which time, a prey to the elements and the predators of the woods, it would have been barely recognisable. Certainly there would have been too little left of the flesh to show how he had died. The bruised throat, the bulging eyes, the protruding tongue would no longer have borne mute witness to the fact that Ulnoth had been throttled.

For I had no doubt that it was Ulnoth, even before I stooped and turned his face towards me. The bald, almost skeletal head was instantly familiar, as were the thinly fleshed bones. His rusty black cloak was still fastened about his neck, but had fallen away from his body to reveal his much darned, greyish-brown tunic and hose. His hunting knife, however, remained in its sheath, attached to the leather belt around his waist, surely an indication that robbery had not been the killer's motive.

Anger licked through me with a steady and persevering

216

flame, and I swore to bring to book whoever had committed this appalling crime. Ulnoth had been a quiet, kindly and, above all, gentle soul, offering harm to no one. Yet his life had been cut short, not by the forces of nature but by one of his fellow humans. The bruises on his throat were the shadows of two thumbs, pressed hard against his windpipe, and there was no doubt at all in my mind that when the back of the neck was exposed, I should find the imprints of fingers. Someone had seized him by the throat and strangled the life out of him with no more compunction than if he had been a chicken destined for the pot.

Cautiously I straightened my back, vainly trying to avoid further damage to my clothes, and stared down at this latest victim of the murderer who stalked Cederwell Manor. It was impossible that I should move the body on my own, and I must therefore return to the house with news of my discovery, and get help. It would come hard on most of the inhabitants to be faced with yet another death, even though they acknowledged no connection between this one and the previous two. Ulnoth's would be attributed to a marauding thief, abroad looking for sustenance, who had quarrelled with the hermit over some precious morsel of food.

And might not that indeed be the case? I asked myself, as I retraced my steps through the scrubland. But I could not accept the explanation. I had spent four days in Ulnoth's company, during which time I had got to know him, if not well, at least as well as any stranger could. I was certain that he would not have strayed over a mile from home unless for a purpose, and that purpose would not be to forage. He knew all the places close to the boulder house where food could be obtained, even in the worst of winter weather. No, I felt sure that Ulnoth had come searching for me in order to unburden himself of something he had remembered . . .

And yet, I wondered, suddenly hesitant, why should he do so? Why should he seek me out? He knew nothing of the other deaths at Cederwell Manor. How could he? Nor could he be certain that, having reached there, I had remained in the house for the past two days. I might, after all, have travelled on beyond the manor to the cottages ranged along the river's edge, where lived Sir Hugh's tenants and many of his workers. I paused, resting on my cudgel, staring sightlessly before me. Perhaps I had made a false assumption in thinking that Ulnoth had come to find me. But if I were indeed in error, what had he been doing here?

My news was received at Cederwell in exactly the way I had anticipated; dismay at the report of yet another death, but each one, in its own way, attributable to the terrible weather. Lady Cederwell had slipped from the look-out platform of the tower, partly through her own folly in standing on the parapet, but partly, too, because conditions were already treacherous, with ice forming between the crenellations. Her half-brother had walked in his sleep and fallen headlong into the well, a tragedy which might have been precipitated by a treacherous patch of frozen snow. And now the hermit had undoubtedly been attacked and murdered for some scrap of food coveted by another fellow creature, desperate to keep body and soul together in this bitter cold.

Such was the version of events presented to me not only by Martha Grindcobb, heartily endorsed by Ethelwynne and

Edith, but also by everyone else to whom I spoke, including Sir Hugh and Mistress Lynom. (The general atmosphere between these two seemed to have improved very slightly since the previous day, but it was obvious, nevertheless, that suspicion of each other still lingered, although they were careful to disguise this fact from others.) The weather explained everything to their satisfaction, as apparently it did to the rest of the household. The Capsgrave brothers, who accompanied me into the scrubland, bearing a litter, and who assisted in bringing back Ulnoth's body to the manor, were confidently of the opinion that the bad winter was the cause of all. And who could blame them? Who, if given the choice, would prefer the idea that a killer was loose amongst them; a killer who, for aught they could see, might strike again for no good reason?

There was only one person who did not pretend to share the general view, and that was Brother Simeon. He suggested that, as the sun was shining, we take a walk around the courtyard until dinner was ready.

'It's a little warmer, I think, than earlier this morning. Besides, there's no way we can talk in the kitchen. The clack of women's voices is unceasing.'

I readily agreed, so we wrapped ourselves in our cloaks and went outside. The slight thaw was increasing, and some of the icicles beneath the eaves were beginning, steadily, to drip. We directed our feet towards the outer courtyard and circled the fish pond, where carp and pike swam like ghosts beneath the coverlet of ice, or came now and then to the hole made that morning by whoever had fed them, to see if there was anything more for the taking.

'Well?' Simeon asked. 'What is your idea now about these deaths?'

I answered promptly, 'That they are the work of one person and are all connected, although I think Ulnoth's murder to have but an indirect link with the other two.'

Simeon frowned. 'What makes you say that?'

I chewed my bottom lip. 'Because,' I said at last, 'I believe the death of Lady Cederwell and her half-brother to have been for a single purpose. Ulnoth, on the other hand, may simply have seen or heard or noted something that he shouldn't. In spite of his seeming stupidity, he had greater perception than you might think; he was perfectly capable of drawing conclusions from what he saw which were unnervingly close to the truth. It was a kind of sixth sense such as animals seem to have, and which alerts them to danger or evil in their vicinity.'

The friar hunched his shoulders.

'I'll accept your word for that as our paths never crossed. So, what do you think to be the reason for the deaths of Lady Cederwell and Gerard Empryngham?'

I hedged. 'I haven't yet decided.'

'But you have some inkling of the truth?'

'Perhaps. But whether it *is* of the truth or not, I'm still uncertain.'

There was a short silence before Simeon demanded testily, 'Well? Do you intend to share your suspicions with me?'

I shook my head. 'Forgive me, Brother, but they are too nebulous to be told to anyone, even to your good self. All I can say at present with any authority, is that I'm sure the spark which ignited this conflagration was the invitation extended to you by Lady Cederwell. Your presence here at the manor posed a threat.'

Simeon's lips thinned. 'And we all know to whom! Sir Hugh and his paramour!' He fairly spat the last word, as though it were an imprecation. 'And to Maurice Cederwell and his *mignon*!'

I shushed him. 'We have no proof of that calumny now that my lady's letter of accusation has been lost.'

'And whose fault is that, pray?'

'I'm hardly to blame, Brother, if someone pushes me off the stairs and renders me unconscious.'

'You should have foreseen something of the sort. You should have anticipated the possible danger.'

I opened my mouth to reply, then shut it again. It was pointless to argue, and I realised that the friar's sudden burst of bad temper had its origin in my refusal to share my innermost thoughts with him. He had been as deeply involved in the events at Cederwell Manor as I had, and, if I were fair, had played a more important and central part. But I had no desire to expose an imperfect theory to Brother Simeon's incredulity and scorn.

I laid a hand on his shoulder. 'Forgive me, but I need more time.'

'Which is what you do not have.' He shook off my hand with a petulant shrug. 'We shall both be gone from here by tomorrow.' He nodded at the surrounding snow, which was already showing small lakes and rivers amongst its undulations. 'It's thawing apace. The air is several degrees warmer than at this same time yesterday. We have no excuse to trespass on Sir Hugh's hospitality after tonight. You've said so yourself.'

Sadly I acquiesced, thinking, although not saying aloud, that this was one occasion when I might not be able to bring a murderer to justice. There were things I should be doing, but somehow the will to bestir myself had deserted me. I felt tired, my body ached, and I watched with dull eyes as the friar, with a curt word of farewell, scuffed a path through the ankle-deep snow and vanished around a corner of the house, on his way back to the warmth of the kitchen. For a moment, I was tempted to join him. I could comfortably spend the remainder of the morning and the afternoon checking through the contents of my pack and resting, husbanding my strength, ready to set off tomorrow as soon as it was properly light. Within three days, maybe four in this unfriendly weather, going at a steady pace and with no diversions this time to ply my trade, I could be home in Bristol, settled by the fireside with my mother-in-law and daughter. Margaret, who must be worried, would be delighted to see me, and even Elizabeth might hold up her little arms in recognition . . .

Then, or so it seemed to me, God took me by the scruff of the neck and shook me. Certainly my whole body trembled as a gust of icy wind hit me in the face. And yet, a second later, there was not the slightest breeze to be felt, no powdering of disturbed snow on any of my garments. I drew in a deep breath of ice-cold air.

'All right, Lord,' I said grudgingly. 'All right!' And I went back to the house.

* * *

The tinker had finished his task and gone, even before I had returned with the news of Ulnoth's death, the lure of perhaps more work to be had in the riverside dwellings urging him on and making him refuse, however reluctantly, the cook's invitation to stay to dinner. This was now almost ready, as Martha Grindcobb acidly informed me on my arrival.

'What's wrong with you, lad? You can't be still for half an hour together.'

'What have they done with Ulnoth?' I inquired.

'Who? Oh, the hermit. God rest his soul! Sir Hugh ordered that the body be placed in the chapel. Saints defend us! Where are you off to, now?'

'Upstairs, to pay my respects.' I kissed her cheek. 'I'll be down again before you've taken the pasties out of the oven.'

'If you're not, you'll just have to eat yours cold,' she retorted, but her tone was softer and she gave me an affectionate slap on the shoulder.

The litter bearing Ulnoth's corpse had been placed in front of the altar, its poles supported by a trestle at either end. He was still lying on his side as I had found him, but the body was already beginning to lose its stiffness. He must therefore have been killed yesterday, sometime after I had seen him moving through the scrubland. His cloak had been removed and rolled up neatly beneath his head, so I eased it from under him and shook out its folds. The black cloth smelt musty and, strangely, of fruit. I realised that it must have been dyed with blackberry juice. It was as carefully mended and darned as was the rest of his apparel, for, in his own poor way, Ulnoth had been as particular about his appearance as the King of England. There were no holes or rents in his garments, unlike those of many another man who had a woman to look after him.

I stared down at his distorted features and again vowed to bring his murderer to book. Then I went next door to visit Father Godyer.

The chaplain was looking a little better today, his nose less watery and a faint trace of colour in his cheeks. As I entered the bedchamber, he screwed up his eyes and peered towards the door.

'Who's that?' he quavered.

'Roger Chapman. We met yesterday.'

'Have you brought my dinner?'

'No. It's not quite ready. Don't worry, Mistress Grindcobb will send one of the girls up with it as soon as it is.'

'She forgets me sometimes. Well, sit down! Sit down on the edge of the bed and tell me what's happening elsewhere in the house. I get no news up here, you know. I heard more commotion this morning, and something's been placed in the chapel. Is it my lady? I'd like to think she was near me. What's going on?'

So I recounted the history of Ulnoth, which interested him, but caused no distress other than for that of a soul untimely dispatched to meet his Maker. In common with everyone else, the priest attributed the killing to a fight over scarce and precious food.

'And when word of his slaying gets about, as it will surely do, someone else will find a home in the boulder house. It will provide warmth and shelter for another wanderer who's tired of the road and wishes to put down roots. God will not let the hermit's death be wasted.' Father Godyer sighed.

'Although I doubt there's any chance of catching the man who killed him. But sometimes, you know, those who cheat the law of the land come to a worse end than choking away their lives at the end of a rope.' He saw my raised eyebrows and smiled thinly. 'I was thinking of poor Raymond Shepherd, the man I told you about, who defiled my lady. The outlaws beat him to death so violently, that he was recognisable only by his clothes.' His normally mild tones held a repellently vicious note of triumph. 'That is what I call true justice, God's justice,' he added with satisfaction.

I regarded him thoughtfully. He had admitted during our previous talk to feeling more for Lady Cederwell than he should have done; to looking upon her as his real, rather than his spiritual child. Now, I could not help wondering if he had felt a deeper affection than that for her. Had he experienced a physical love for Jeanette Empryngham to which he could never own, not even to himself, but which was all the stronger for being constantly suppressed?

Edith knocked and came in with a tray bearing a savoury-smelling pasty and a mazer of ale.

'Your dinner, Father,' she announced, setting the tray down on his knees. She addressed me. 'Mistress Grindcobb says yours is ready as well, Chapman, and if you don't come at once, she'll feed it to the birds.'

I laughed and accompanied her downstairs to the kitchen, but not without a backward glance at the chaplain as I reached the bedchamber door. His appetite seemed to have returned and he was eating heartily, holding the pastry coffin between his hands and gnawing on the meat with an excellent set of teeth. The gravy was running down his chin. Yesterday, I had thought him a sad, unhappy man; today, I had different ideas.

Brother Simeon pointedly ignored me during dinner. I had plainly offended beyond hope of present forgiveness, so I munched my way in silence through three of Martha's pasties, excellent even if the dried, salted meat proved to be somewhat tough, and devoted myself to my thoughts. These included a view from a window, a russet cloak flung over Mistress Talke's arm, a conversation with Adela Empryngham, the discovery of her husband's body and an unguarded remark. There were other things, too; a man and a woman quarrelling, the name on a dying woman's lips . . .

'You're very quiet, my lad,' Martha Grindcobb accused me. 'What's the matter? Has the cat got your tongue?'

Brother Simeon looked up and said spitefully, 'Oh, the chapman believes that Lady Cederwell and her half-brother were murdered, don't you, Roger? Furthermore, although he won't tell the likes of you and me, Mistress Grindcobb, he thinks he knows the murderer's name.'

I stared at him, horrified, my hand, clutching a half-eaten pasty, suspended in mid-air. This sudden burst of venom on the part of the friar could easily have put my life in danger.

Chapter Seventeen

After a moment's silence, the cook burst out laughing, while Edith, Ethelwynne and Jenny Tonge, whose eyes had grown large with fright and apprehension, managed to smile, reassured by her obvious amusement.

'I never heard such nonsense! Is this true, Roger?' Martha asked, turning to me.

'No . . . That is . . . Perhaps . . .' I floundered, caught off guard and not knowing what to say. If I told the truth, I should be pressed to name my suspect and produce evidence in support of my claim, and I was not yet ready to do so. There were one or two more facts which I needed to garner.

'Well? Is it true or not?' Her good humour was rapidly giving way to impatience. And when I again hesitated over my answer, she walked up to me and waggled a forefinger under my nose. 'Now, you listen to me, my lad! We've had enough trouble here without you trying to stir up more. We all know what happened to both my lady and her brother – and to the poor old hermit, if it comes to that – so we don't need your mischief-making. Let things alone, Roger Chapman, that's my advice to you.' She smoothed down her apron and regarded me for the first time with hostility.

'Luckily, you'll be gone tomorrow if this thaw continues.'

'Now see what you've done,' I hissed at Simeon, as I resumed my seat on the floor beside him. 'You've put me in the wrong with Martha.'

His mouth pouted like that of a sulky child. 'Serves you right! It's not fair to give me only half a story. I want to know what's going on in that head of yours.'

I shrugged and moved away, letting him see my disdain of such petulance in a grown man. It had no noticeable effect, so instead, I switched my attention to the cook. It seemed to me that her protestations were inspired by fear rather than genuine indignation, but was she afraid for herself, I wondered, or for her master, or for some other person? On second thoughts however, I realised that I should get no satisfaction from questioning her, thanks to the friar's intervention; so, when I had finished my meal, I went in search of Audrey Lambspringe.

It was now impossible for me to ask anyone in the kitchen where to find her without arousing fully justified suspicions of my intent. She had not taken dinner with us, so I concluded that she must be one of the company who ate in the steward's room, along with Phillipa Talke and Master Disney. As Lady Cederwell's personal attendant, and as a compliment to her mistress, she might well be included amongst these more august domestic ranks. Consequently, as soon as Jenny Tonge and the other two maids began collecting up plates from the great hall and elsewhere, I loitered in the main passageway, hoping that Audrey might emerge from Tostig's lair. I reasoned that if she were indeed present, she would be the first to leave, the steward and housekeeper, and even Fulk

Disney, being sufficiently superior to her to linger for a gossip over their ale.

My argument proved correct, and she followed Ethelwynne, who was carrying a pile of dirty dishes, along the corridor, scuffing her feet among the rushes and replying listlessly to some remark that the other girl was making over her shoulder. I stepped forward and spoke her name.

'Mistress Lambspringe! Can you spare me a moment of your time?' Ethelwynne eyed me sharply and scurried off to the kitchen, undoubtedly to report to the cook on my present activity. I seized Audrey's elbow and gave it an urgent squeeze. 'If so, will you accompany me upstairs to the chapel, where we can be private together?'

The girl looked bewildered, as well she might, but readily agreed. Without any duties to keep her busy, she was at a loss how to fill her day.

We mounted the stairs together and disappeared from view only just in time. Below us, Martha's voice could be heard calling, 'Audrey! Audrey Lambspringe! Drat the child! Where is she?'

I hurried her forward, whispering, 'Take no notice! Mistress Grindcobb wishes to prevent me from speaking to you, that's all.'

The chapel, to my great relief, was empty save for the hermit's body. I felt my companion recoil a little at the sight of it, but pressed her to enter.

'Poor Ulnoth can do you no harm. Don't look at him if it disturbs you. Come into the confessional.' And I pulled back the curtain of the priest's cell where a narrow stone bench was revealed against the chapel's outer wall.

Audrey sent me a fearful, sidelong glance. I seized her wrist none too gently and forced her to sit beside me, smothering the desire to give her a shake.

'I haven't brought you here for dalliance,' I said impatiently. 'I want to ask you some questions.'

She looked so relieved that I felt slightly insulted. All the same, I knew it was good for my soul. Conceit and self-esteem are both sins, and two that I used to suffer from when young.

'What questions?' she inquired apprehensively.

'Have you any recollection of where everyone was, and what they were doing, the day before yesterday? The day Lady Cederwell died.'

'Oh! I – I don't know! Why should I be able to tell you? It's not my business to spy on other people.'

Audrey was uneasy now, and half rose from the bench. Again, I took hold of her wrist, but with a greater gentleness this second time.

'Whatever you say, I shall repeat it to no one. You have my most solemn promise on that. I'll swear it on the altar if you like.'

She hesitated, still poised for flight, but at last, with a show of reluctance, resumed her seat.

'Why do you want to know?'

I took both her hands in mine and answered solemnly, 'Because I think it possible that your mistress did not fall from the tower, but was pushed or thrown down. In short, that she was murdered.'

To my surprise, Audrey Lambspringe expressed neither horror nor incredulity at this suggestion. Her only reaction was to return the clasp of my fingers and stare at the ground. After a moment or two, she nodded slowly.

'I, too, have considered that possibility,' she said. 'There are those, both inside and outside this house, who would benefit from my lady's death.'

'Can you name them?'

'I believe you know them already.'

'Nevertheless, I should be grateful to have confirmation of my suspicions from an inhabitant of the manor, from someone who knows its people better than I do.'

'And you won't inform anyone of what I have said? I have your word?'

'I've told you, I'll swear to it if you like.'

'There's no need for that. I'll trust you. Well then, as you have probably seen for yourself, Sir Hugh will not be sorry to find himself a widower again. It means that he is free to marry Mistress Lynom. Similarly, Mistress Lynom is at liberty to wed the master.'

'You know of their liaison?'

Audrey glanced up in astonishment. 'Everyone at Cederwell knows of it.'

'Phillipa Talke didn't, I fancy.'

The small, pale face looked frowningly as she considered this.

'I think Mistress Talke must have known,' Audrey finally decided, 'but she refused to take the matter seriously. Sir Hugh and Mistress Lynom have always been friends, you see, and she thought it was no more than that.'

'So the housekeeper could well have killed Lady Cederwell if she believed it would release your master from an unhappy marriage and free him to offer her his hand.'

Audrey grimaced. 'I've heard Cook say that Mistress Talke believed Sir Hugh to be in love with her, but I didn't take much notice. I'd never seen any evidence of partiality on his side, and considered that very likely Mistress Grindcobb was mistaken.'

'I would never doubt anything Martha told me. She has a sharp ear and an even sharper eye. But let that pass for the moment. We are agreed, then, that both Sir Hugh and Mistress Lynom benefit from Lady Cederwell's death, and that Phillipa Talke may have thought that she would. She has surely realised her error by now, but it is her state of mind before your mistress's death that is important. So, continue. These three apart, who else within the manor pale gains, in your opinion, by this killing?'

Audrey wriggled uncomfortably and cast an anxious look towards the chapel door. 'We cannot be sure that it was murder.'

I ignored this remark. 'Who else?' I demanded inexorably.

She bit her lip. 'No one that I know of.'

'I think you're lying.' But my reproach was muted. 'You were close to your mistress. She was miserable and lonely and needed someone to talk to. You were always with her, attending to her wants. Who would she be more likely to confide in? When she sent for Brother Simeon, was it only to ask for his help concerning her husband's infidelity?'

'N–no,' Audrey replied nervously. A blush spread across the delicate features. 'She ... She fretted about Maurice and ... and Fulk Disney.'

'She thought them lovers?'

The pale rose deepened to crimson. 'So she said. She . . . She tried to tell me . . . to explain things to me.'

'Did she also explain that in the eyes of the Church, it is one of the most heinous sins?' Audrey nodded. I continued, 'So you see, do you not, that when I ask you to tell me what you can recall of people's whereabouts the day before yesterday, it's not simply out of idle curiosity? Were you fond of Lady Cederwell?'

'She was good to me,' was the evasive answer. 'She promised me her russet cloak, and that's the truth, whatever some others might have you believe. It worries me to think that she could have been killed deliberately.' Audrey wiped away a tear. 'All right. I'll tell you what I can remember, but it won't be much, I'm afraid.'

In the event, Audrey Lambspringe's recollections proved to be greater than either of us had expected. Because she was left for many hours at a time to her own devices, while Lady Cederwell was at her devotions in the tower, and with nothing more to do than refurbish her mistress's small store of clothes, Audrey was at liberty to note the comings and goings of other members of the household, without herself being much observed in return. Her natural timidity and self-effacement meant that her fellow servants were inclined to overlook her, or discount her presence even when they knew she was there. I had guessed this to be so when I approached her, and for that very reason had hoped to glean some useful information, but I had not allowed for an innate inquisitiveness which meant that she knew most of what was happening, both indoors and out.

On Tuesday morning, Sir Hugh had left Cederwell, riding his black horse, and had not returned until almost midday, long past dinner time, which had upset Martha Grindcobb. She had been forced to keep his food hot over the kitchen fire and, as a result, had burned the meat and been cursed for her pains. When he had finished eating, the knight sent for Audrey and, having demanded the whereabouts of her mistress, set out for the tower. After some twenty minutes, perhaps longer, he had reappeared through the front porch looking, as Audrey put it, as though he had been visited by Old Scratch himself.

'You saw Sir Hugh?'

She nodded. 'I was at the bottom of the staircase, having but just come down from my lady's room.'

'Yet you thought nothing of it? The way he looked, I mean.'

'At the time, no, I did not. It was a bitter day, promising snow. He had gone out without a cloak, and I thought him white and shivering from the cold. It was only later, after my lady's body was discovered that I . . . well, that I thought there . . . might have been a different cause.'

'Did Lady Cederwell visit the tower every day?'

'Most days, as soon as she had finished breakfast, which she always ate in her chamber. Sir Hugh had turned the top room into a private chapel for her, and Father Godyer had consecrated it. My lady spent most of her time there. She said this was an ungodly house and she would not abide in it for more hours than she had to.'

Sir Hugh began to command more of my sympathy than heretofore. He had plainly had much to endure from his imprudent marriage.

I asked, 'And so you were not surprised when your mistress did not return to the house all day? Not even when darkness fell?'

'No.' Audrey pleated her skirt in her lap, her eyes fixed on her unquiet hands.

'What about food? Was she never hungry?'

'She ate very frugally. Some days Martha would send me with some victuals, and at others, my lady would take a basket with her.'

'What did she do on Tuesday?'

'She took a basket.'

'You're sure of that?'

'Oh, yes.' The answer came without hesitation. 'She was going to see poor Ulnoth.' Audrey glanced sideways at the body, then hurriedly looked away again. 'Twice or three times a month, during the winter, my lady would take the hermit a loaf of bread and a flagon of ale. Tuesday was one of those days.'

'Did she always walk there and back? It would be a long journey on foot, and even longer in bad weather.'

'Yes. She said it was a penance, an act of humility. A *gra'merci* to God for having so much when others have been given so little.'

I cast my mind back to that second visit which I had made to Ulnoth, when he had been so frightened. Once my eyes had grown accustomed to the gloom, I had been able to see everything there was to see, yet I had noted no loaf of bread nor flagon of ale. If Lady Cederwell had indeed set out for the boulder house, she had not arrived there. Who or what had prevented her? And why?

Audrey shivered suddenly. It was very cold in the chapel, and without thinking, she moved closer to me. I put my arm about her in a brotherly fashion.

'Did you notice Mistress Lynom's groom, the one they call Hamon, anywhere on the manor that day? He rode, and would, by my calculation, have arrived some while after noon, around the time that Sir Hugh was at the tower.'

Audrey puckered her brow in an effort of concentration, but eventually shook her head.

'No,' she said with a regretful sigh, sorry to disappoint my expectations. 'Him, I did not see.'

I pressed her shoulder gently. 'No matter. There were those whom you did. Can you recall where other members of the household were throughout that day? In particular, during the morning.'

'Martha Grindcobb was in the kitchen,' she answered promptly. 'I was in and out of there three or four times before and after dinner and she was present each time, as were Ethelwynne and Edith and Jenny. Master Disney was away, collecting the master's rents, as he had been for the two days before that. Poor Master Empryngham, God rest his soul—' Audrey crossed herself '– was in his bedchamber, reading. At least, he was when Martha sent me in to him with a cup of hot, spiced ale half an hour or so before dinner was ready.'

'And his wife?'

'No, she wasn't there.' Audrey frowned. 'I don't recollect clapping eyes on her all morning.'

'Where could she have been, then, do you think?'

The thin shoulders rose and fell. 'The bakery, perhaps. Or the dairy or the laundry. Mistress Empryngham was always very busy about household concerns in Lady Cederwell's absence. She resented the fact that Mistress Talke wears the keys at her belt instead of herself. I once overheard Master Steward tell Martha Grindcobb that when my lady and her family first came here from Gloucestershire, Mistress Empryngham wanted Mistress Talke dismissed, because she felt that she should be in charge of the day-to-day running of the house.'

'So, Adela Empryngham was out of your sight all morning. Did she come in to dinner?'

'Oh, yes! She joined her husband in their room and stayed there for several hours. The weather was worsening by that time.'

'I remember.' I shifted my position. The stone bench was becoming uncomfortable. But I had not yet finished my inquisition. 'Mistress Talke and Master Steward, do you recall what they were doing on Tuesday morning?'

Audrey giggled. She was growing used to me and beginning to treat me as a friend.

'I saw Mistress Talke go into Tostig Steward's room on more than one occasion.' She lowered her voice to a confidential whisper, although there was no one to overhear us. 'He keeps a flask of brandy wine in the corner cupboard. I know, I've seen it. He likes a little sip now and then, and so does Mistress Phillipa.'

I could picture it, the two most important members of the domestic hierarchy, gossiping cosily together over a nip of something warming, discussing their latest petty triumph or grievance.

'But was the housekeeper in Tostig's room *all* morning?'

'No. She was around the house, too. She came into the kitchen about an hour after breakfast and said that if she was needed, she would be in the dairy. She was muffled up against the cold, and I saw her ten minutes later, from an upstairs window, crossing the outer courtyard.'

'Did you see her enter the dairy?'

'Yes. But after that, I turned away and went to cover my lady's bed. The next time I clapped eyes on Mistress Talke was when I saw her leaving Tostig's room again, some while after.'

'How long after?'

'I couldn't be certain. But I'd say she'd been with Master Steward for quite some time. She was a little tipsy. It surprised me, for I'd never known her have too much to drink before.'

I made no reply to this, merely commenting, 'You haven't yet mentioned Maurice.'

'The young master!' She considered for a moment, her head tilted to one side. 'He broke his fast in the great hall with Sir Hugh the same as always. Ethelwynne, who waited on them, remarked that he was in a better mood than he'd been for the past two days, and Mistress Talke laughed and said we all knew why that was.'

'And why was it?'

'I suppose because Master Disney would be home that evening.' This time there was no trace of colour in her cheeks. She was indeed growing used to my company.

'Do you think Maurice knew that his stepmother had sent for Brother Simeon?'

'I think everyone knew. My lady made no secret of it. "And when he arrives," I heard her tell the Master, "you will all get your just deserts. You will be called to account by the Church and very likely find yourself excommunicated."'

'And what did Sir Hugh reply?'

'He just laughed and said something like, "If adultery were punishable by excommunication, there'd hardly be a man left in England for the Pope to command. Certainly not the King and his court, by all that I hear." My lady replied, "You should be afraid for your son, if not for yourself," and then she went away. I think she went out to the tower.'

Very possibly, I thought. It seemed to have been her constant place of refuge.

'Is your master fond of his son?' I asked.

My informant gave this her gravest consideration, not answering immediately. But at last, she said slowly, 'Yes. Yes, I think he is.' The admission seemed to surprise her and she frowned. 'They argue a lot, not over anything very serious. Silly little disagreements, like whether or not Master Maurice has borrowed his father's best boots without asking, or stayed in bed too long, or been rude to my lady. But . . . yes, I do believe that they are fond of each other.'

'If Sir Hugh had been offered a choice between the life of his son or that of his wife, which one of them, do you think, would he have favoured?'

'Oh, Master Maurice,' she replied, this time without any hesitation, and once again looked astonished at her own percipience.

I nodded. The picture Audrey painted was one of father and son at odds over something far deeper and more important than the petty quarrels which were their outward manifestation; something which neither would mention or acknowledge openly, but which remained an irreconcilable difference between them. In the end, however, the bond of blood was too strong to be broken. Sir Hugh's pride of family, and the honour of its good name, were all bound up in Maurice, but there was also an obstinate streak of affection in the older man for the child to whom he had given life. He would not allow danger to menace his son if he could help it; and if the removal of that threat marched hand-in-hand with his own more personal desires, who could say for certain what might have happened?

I realised that I must be looking grim, for Audrey was staring up at me, her little face furrowed with anxiety. I smiled at her, laying a hand on her arm.

'All's well,' I reassured her. 'Don't worry that you've said too much, or done harm to any you might wish to protect. Now, can you tell me where Mistress Lynom is to be found? If she'll condescend to give me a hearing, there is something I want to ask her.'

Chapter Eighteen

Audrey looked at me with a mixture of respect and concern for my foolhardiness. An itinerant pedlar did not usually speak so lightly of questioning someone of Ursula Lynom's importance.

'She's probably still in the guest chamber. She was served her dinner there. Ethelwynne was grumbling about it, saying what a deal of extra work it throws upon her and the rest of them, especially with Father Godyer still abed. Mistress Empryngham's none too pleased about it either, for she can't use her own room while Master Gerard's body remains there, and has to sleep in the common dormitory with the rest of us women.'

'Then the guest chamber is where I shall look for Mistress Lynom,' I said. 'And if she's not to be found, I shall search elsewhere. She must surely still be within the manor pale, for I don't think her ready to leave just yet. The thaw isn't sufficiently advanced to make travelling anything but hazardous for the present. Tomorrow may well be a different story. Indeed, I think another twenty-four hours will see Sir Hugh left in peace to make arrangements to bury his dead and consider the life ahead of him, now that he's a widower once again.'

'But what of your suspicions concerning my lady?' Audrey Lambspringe asked reproachfully as I rose from the bench. 'Do you intend to quit Cederwell without finding her murderer?'

'I believe I already know who it is,' I replied. 'In my own mind I'm certain, but whether or not I can persuade others is somewhat doubtful.'

'Who is it?' she demanded. 'Only tell me his name and I will take a knife to him myself.'

I grinned at her. 'Well, well! What a bloodthirsty little creature lurks behind that timid face. All the better if you don't know, I fancy. You'd best leave matters in my hands, for as yet there are still one or two questions to be answered. Which is why I must speak to Mistress Lynom, and perhaps once again to Father Godyer.'

'And what will you do when you have the answers?' The soft lower lip stuck out belligerently. 'Will you then be able to convince the rest of us of what you say?'

'How can I tell? The outcome is in God's hands. It is for Him to decide what happens next. He has brought me here. He has laid the facts before me. When the time comes to confront my villain, I must be guided by His wisdom and hope that He will put it into my head what to do.' I stooped and kissed her cheek. 'Now, I must be on my way and seek out Mistress Lynom.'

I descended the stairs and crept as silently as I could past the half-closed kitchen door, where the clash of dishes and the hiss of steam told of work in progress; of dirty plates being washed and of the preparation of food for the evening meal, still several hours away. I had no wish to be confronted by an irate Martha Grindcobb demanding to know where I was bound or what I was doing.

Out of doors, the noonday sun revealed a rapidly changing landscape. The magical white world of faerie was slowly being transformed into mundane winter browns and greys. Roof slates showed patchily beneath their frosty covering and distant trees thrust twisted, disfigured limbs through the concealing bandages of snow. The ground was still unyielding, but the steps leading to the covered gallery were wet and slippery with melting ice. I trod carefully. I could ill afford another accident.

The platform was also showing signs of the impending thaw, with little puddles of water collecting here and there in the shallow depressions of the boards. The doors to both the guest chamber and the women's dormitory were tightly shut against the cold, and no sound came from within either room. I paused outside the first, hand raised to knock, listening intently, but all was as quiet as the grave. My heart beat faster, anticipating another tragedy, yet another death. Then someone coughed and I heard the faintest sound of movement. I breathed freely again and tapped with my knuckles on the wood.

The rustling noises ceased abruptly and there was silence. Then a woman's voice called, 'Come in.'

I opened the door and stood respectfully on the threshold. Mistress Lynom looked astonished at the sight of me.

'Chapman? What are you doing here? What do you want?' There was an edge to her tone which suggested fear as well as annoyance.

'I've come to beg a moment of your time, Mistress Lynom. It won't take long, I promise, but there is a question to which you might know the answer.' I made no attempt to advance any further.

She took a step backwards, her eyes still wary. I guessed that despite the accusation I had overheard her make, she was not absolutely convinced of her lover's guilt in the matter of Lady Cederwell's death, nor did she believe that death to be either accident or suicide. I also concluded that if she were not a clever dissembler, she was innocent of contriving the murder herself, for she seemed ready to be suspicious of almost anyone on the manor.

'What question?' she asked, and flung out a hand. 'No! Remain where you are.'

'I had no intention of entering without your permission,' I answered placidly. 'But you have no reason to fear me, I do assure you. Lady Cederwell was dead by the time Brother Simeon and I reached here on Tuesday. We found her body together.'

Mistress Lynom drew in a deep breath and then released it on a long, drawn-out sigh.

'So you did. I recollect now.' She shivered. 'Very well! You may come in, but you are to leave the door ajar.' She still did not trust me completely.

I did as I was bidden. The room within was almost as bleak as the women's dormitory, but some attempt had been made to render it more habitable. The bed was covered by a rubbed and faded red velvet coverlet which matched the equally worn bed curtains, and another piece of the same material was thrown across the clothes chest, draping it to the floor. An ornately carved armchair, adorned with a pair of embroidered cushions, offered what little extra comfort there was apart from a tapestry, depicting the story of Tobias and the Angel, which hung against one wall. I wondered what Ursula Lynom thought of her accommodation, and whether or not she shared her lover's niggardly approach to the luxuries of life. Moreover, what would the redoubtable Dame Judith make of it all if she were forced to live at Cederwell with her daughter-in-law?

'Well?' inquired Mistress Lynom. 'What is it that you wish to ask me?'

I hesitated, knowing that she would find my question odd, then plunged.

'Who are your nearest neighbours to Lynom Hall?'

She blinked once or twice, as though she had not properly understood me, then shook her head as if to clear it.

'Who are my nearest neighbours?'

I nodded. 'It may sound strange, but I should be grateful for an answer without being forced to give my reasons.'

She continued to stare at me for several seconds before sitting down in the armchair, her lips thinning to a narrow line. She was no fool, and was immediately able to add two and two and reach the correct conclusion.

'What do you know?' she demanded bluntly. 'Or what do you think you know?'

We eyed one another cautiously while the silence stretched between us. At last, however, I decided to be as frank with her as I could.

'Whatever my suspicions, they have absolutely nothing to do with Sir Hugh. You have my word on that.' I did not pause to consider if the word of a common pedlar had any meaning for her or no.

She returned my gaze steadily. Then, obviously coming to a decision, she determined to be equally plain with me.

'My groom, Hamon, whom I dispatched after Sir Hugh with the buttons I bought from your pack, saw him bending over Jeanette's body outside the tower.'

'And rode back as fast as he could to Lynom Hall to tell you what he had seen. But that was very little. So why, with respect, did you reach the conclusion that Sir Hugh had probably murdered his wife?'

She got up and began to walk up and down the tiny room. In her relief at finally being able to talk openly to someone, she forgot to whom she was speaking.

'It was only that very morning, at Lynom, that we had discussed the hopelessness of our situation.' She grimaced wryly. 'Neither of us is young, and growing older with every day that passes, whereas Jeanette – Lady Cederwell – is—' she caught her breath for a moment '– or rather was, only twenty-one. We could see no solution to our problem, and Hugh in particular was growing desperate.' The knotted fist of her right hand drove deeply into the palm of her left as she turned with a swirl of her gown and began pacing in the opposite direction. 'To add to his woes, he knew from her own lips that she had sent for this Brother Simeon in order to make allegations not only against Hugh, but also against other members of his household. For his own sake, he did not really care. He has a broad back and is perfectly capable of facing up to some strange friar's hectoring and reproaches. But . . .' She broke off abruptly, on the brink, I fancied, of recollecting my lowly status.

'You refer to Maurice Cederwell and Fulk Disney,' I said swiftly. 'To the love that exists between them.'

Mistress Lynom's eyes widened. 'You waste no time, Chapman,' she accused me angrily, 'in ferreting out other people's secrets.'

I shrugged. 'There's precious little secrecy about it, Mistress. Even an innocent like Audrey Lambspringe knows what they are to one another.' I smiled at her look of horror. 'It's impossible to keep such a thing private in an enclosed community such as this one. Servants will always gossip.'

'And not only servants,' she retorted sharply, thinking, I had no doubt, of Dame Judith. 'So,' she went on after a moment, 'I have no need to explain to you Sir Hugh's concern on behalf of his son. This friar's reputation had preceded him. His mission, it seems, is to punish immorality wherever and whenever he finds it.'

'So I believe.'

'Very well! You can understand, therefore, why, although I was loath to believe it, my interpretation of what Hamon had seen was that Sir Hugh, in a fit of frustrated rage, had thrown Jeanette down from the tower.' She took another brief turn about the room. 'I waited all day in increasing anxiety for him to send me news of the "accident", as he would obviously pretend her death to be, but nothing happened. At last, in spite of the darkness and the snow, I set forward for Cederwell with Hamon and Jasper in attendance. The rest you know for yourself, how I nearly gave everything away.' She sat down again, her fingers drumming restlessly on the arms of the chair.

Now came the hardest part of my inquisition, as I had to feign ignorance of what had passed between her and Sir Hugh.

'And what *was* Sir Hugh's explanation of his omission in sending to you with the news?'

Mistress Lynom's bosom swelled indignantly and her jaw hardened.

'As you must recall, he pretended to know nothing of Jeanette's death until informed of it by you and the friar. When he realised that I knew the truth, he had the gall to plead that he was protecting me! *Me*! He accused me of sending my groom to kill Jeanette, and even made up a story that in her dying moments, she had whispered Hamon's name.'

Her initial anger, which by now had lost its spark, was suddenly rekindled and she was on her feet once more, kicking the heavy chair aside with a vigorous movement of one foot. A strong woman in every sense, Ursula Lynom. She would rule Sir Hugh and his household with a rod of iron, but it was very possible that they might all be grateful for it. It would bring back some semblance of order and calm into their disrupted lives.

I said quietly, 'I think you will find, Mistress, that in this instance Sir Hugh was not lying; that he did indeed believe you responsible for Lady Cederwell's murder and was trying to protect you. After discovering his wife's body, he returned to the house and said nothing either of what he had found or of having seen Hamon. The longer the body lay undiscovered, the less chance there was of any blame being attached to you or your messenger. The fact that such an accusation was extremely unlikely to be brought against you, that in the prevailing circumstances his wife's fall would most probably be considered an accident, did not occur to him, so anxious was he to ensure your safety.'

She gave me a sharp glance and then her rather heavy features lifted with the beginnings of a smile. Just for a moment, I could see the handsome young girl she had once been, when Sir Hugh had first fallen in love with her and she, foolishly and wantonly, had denied her heart and married his friend.

'How can you be sure of that?' she asked scornfully, willing me nonetheless to produce a reason.

'Because, Mistress, I think I know who killed Lady Cederwell, and why. However, for now you'll simply have to take my word for that. But if I'm right, Sir Hugh's actions allow of no other explanation. Whether or not you can forgive him for imagining you capable of murder is another matter, and one you'll have to decide for yourself.'

The half-smile deepened. 'I thought him guilty of the same crime, so we must beg pardon of one another. I don't doubt we shall each offer and receive forgiveness.' She sat silent for a moment or two, contemplating a suddenly much rosier future than any she had foreseen for many years past. But then her expression sobered. 'You are certain that you have stumbled on the truth?'

If I resented the word 'stumbled', I was careful not to show it. I nodded reassuringly, but then reminded her that she had not yet answered my original question.

'I have forgotten what it was,' she confessed, staring at me with a puzzled frown, as though suddenly becoming aware to whom she had been speaking, unburdening her innermost thoughts and fears. She gave her head another shake as if to make sure that she had not dreamed the whole.

'I asked who are your nearest neighbours to Lynom Hall. I know you have none to the north along the Woodspring road, for I've walked that way myself. But to the south, now! Is there a farm or homestead easily accessible from the main track?'

It was plain that she would dearly have loved to know the reason behind my question, but after struggling for several seconds with the temptation to demand an answer, she said merely, 'There is indeed a farm some three to three-and-a-half miles south-west of the Hall, land which belongs to a good yeoman named John Armstrong. Is that what you wish to know?'

'Is the farm moated? Or do its buildings lie open to the road?'

The widow pressed a hand to her forehead, trying to picture a holding which she must have passed many times in her life, but of which she had taken little particular notice. It so often happens that the most familiar objects are the least regarded.

'It is moated,' she said at last, 'but I think . . . No, no, I'm sure that there are at least two outhouses which stand beyond the pale, on open ground. They lie southerly again from the main enclosure.'

I gave a brief bow. 'I thank your ladyship.'

She rose to her feet, eyeing me severely, and smoothed down the skirt of her gown.

'I'm not her ladyship yet as you're very well aware. You're a plausible rascal who knows how to make himself agreeable, especially to women. But even so, how you've managed to get me to open up my heart to you, I've no idea.' She sighed. 'If I were only twenty years younger . . . but no, I'm too old for those kind of thoughts. Get along before I embarrass you and do anything I shall later regret. I must find Sir Hugh. Have I your permission to repeat our conversation to him?'

I hesitated, then nodded. 'But I should be grateful if you would tell no one else for now. Keep what has passed between us to your two selves until I am ready.'

'Very well. I shall ensure Sir Hugh's silence. What other proof are you seeking?'

'I am going to speak once more to Father Godyer. After that, I shall have to make up my mind whether to speak or hold my peace. I would not accuse any person unless I were sure of making my accusation stick.'

The chaplain was looking even healthier than when I had seen him earlier. He was still, as Ethelwynne had complained, in bed, but his face was less pinched, and his more vigorous speech suggested that he might be able to resume his duties within the next few days.

'You're feeling much better than this morning,' I said, and he nodded, smiling. He shifted his legs to one side of the pallet so that I could once again sit on the opposite edge.

'Much better, God be praised, and no worse for seeing you a second time. A man gets very bored tucked away up here with no one to talk to.' He sighed. 'But there! I have no right to complain. I am of little importance to anyone in the household now that my lady has gone.' Tears welled up and trickled down his cheeks. 'I came here with her from

Campden, and had known and loved her as a girl.'

'Indeed, you've already told me so,' I answered heartily. 'And a very interesting story it is, Father. How could you not love her when you knew all that she had suffered in her youth? Of the terrible experience which had warped her mind.'

His head reared up at that. 'Who said her mind was warped? Not I, Chapman! That's your interpretation of my words, and a very wrong one! She bore even that adversity as she bore all the rest, with an unshakeable belief in God.'

'I beg your pardon,' I said. 'Perhaps I expressed myself badly. Yet to know that her attacker escaped the full rigour of the law must surely have embittered her beyond reason.'

'There you go again!' he exclaimed angrily. 'Trying to make out that she was on the fringe of madness.'

'Wasn't she? Forgive me, Father, but surely a pretty young woman should have wanted more from life than prayer and meditation.'

'It is obvious that you have never perused the lives of the saints,' the priest chided me austerely. 'Saint Leocadia, Saint Lucy, Saint Eulalia, all were young women willing to sacrifice life itself for their faith. Do you suggest that they, too, were insane?' I shook my head meekly and he continued, 'They never saw their persecutors brought to justice, either, and at least my darling girl knew what had befallen her despoiler. She came herself to look upon his mangled body when it was carried back to her father's house.'

'A young girl could calmly gaze upon a man with his head crushed in? Father, even someone as partial as you must admit that there is something not . . . not quite . . . quite normal in such an action.'

He shifted his legs once more to the middle of the bed, leaned back against his pillows and closed his eyes, indicating that our conversation was at an end. I did not move immediately, however, but sat observing that pallid face and narrow skull, wondering what was going on inside it. There was now no doubt in my mind that Father Godyer had loved Jeanette Empryngham with a carnal as well as a spiritual love, but he had suppressed it, convincing himself that it was a paternal affection he entertained for her. Had Gerard Empryngham, I wondered, suspected the priest's true feelings?

I stood up, 'I shall be leaving here tomorrow,' I said. 'The snow is beginning to melt and the roads should be passable again.'

He made no answer until I was almost out of the door. Then he demanded, 'Well? Have you got what you came for?'

'I . . . I just came to see how you were,' I stuttered, surprised by his unexpected shrewdness.

The priest snorted with disbelief. 'So I thought at first.'

'So what's made you change your mind?'

His pale eyes opened slowly to fix me with a long, silent stare.

'I don't know,' he confessed at last. 'Just an ache in the bones, a warning bell in the head. So,' he persisted, 'am I right, and have you discovered whatever it was you were seeking from me?'

'Yes. Thank you. I . . . I shall see you again, I hope, before I leave.'

The bloodless lips sketched the ghost of a smile. 'That

rather depends on you, I imagine. I shall be here, certainly. I have no plans, for the present, to go elsewhere.' And the eyes closed again, blotting me from his sight.

I hesitated for a moment, opened my mouth to say something more, then thought better of it. I shut the chamber door quietly behind me and descended the stairs. Fulk Disney was waiting for me at the bottom. Insolently, he looked me up and down.

'Ah! There you are! Well met! I've been searching for you everywhere. I was just about to seek you in the chapel.'

'I've been visiting Father Godyer,' I answered shortly. 'What is it you wish to say?'

'Father Godyer, eh?' His eyes flickered slightly. 'You know, I used to wonder about that man and our pious lady.' A prurient smile lifted the corners of his mouth.

'Why do you want me?' I insisted.

'Mmm, now why *do* I want you?' he mused. He disliked me and was trying to make me angry. When he found he could not succeed, he merely shrugged. 'Ah yes! I have a message for you from Brother Simeon.'

Chapter Nineteen

Fulk Disney continued, 'He has been searching for you for the past hour or more, but you seem to have been in hiding.'

'I've passed through the house on at least two occasions,' I answered, 'and made no attempt at concealment. If the friar had cared to bestir himself and leave the warmth of the kitchen fire, he might have found me easily enough. What is his message?'

'That he has gone to the Saxon tower and wishes you to join him there with all speed.'

My heart gave a great lurch in my chest, but I managed to ask calmly, 'Did he offer any reason for his visit?'

Fulk's eyes were little slits of curiosity in his pallid face. 'When I inquired why he was going to the tower, he refused to tell me, mumbling something to the effect that you would understand.' He cocked his head to one side. 'Do you, Chapman? Do you understand?'

'Perhaps,' was my guarded reply, and I made to push past him.

Fulk barred my way. 'Not so fast. You and that friar have been poking your noses in where they're not wanted for the past two days, and now I hear from Martha Grindcobb that you think Lady Cederwell didn't die an accidental death.' He lowered his voice to an envenomed hiss. 'Get out of here, Chapman! Go at once, today! Don't wait for tomorrow, or you may live to regret it.'

I said quietly, 'Are you threatening me, Master Disney?'

As always, that flicked him on the raw. *'D'Isigny!* How many times do I have to tell you?' Then he recollected that there were more pressing matters in hand. 'Leave Cederwell this afternoon! And take that hedge priest with you!'

'What's going on here?' demanded Maurice Cederwell, as he emerged from the passage leading to the great hall and came towards us.

'Master Disney has ordered me to quit the manor immediately,' I said. 'But I take my marching orders only from Sir Hugh. Perhaps you will explain that to your friend.'

I saw Maurice's eyelids flicker and he looked at me intently before switching his attention to Fulk. His arm jerked involuntarily, as if he longed to reach out and touch the other man, but he forced himself to refrain.

'What is the argument between you?' he asked. 'Fulk? What is your quarrel with the chapman?'

Fulk said nothing for a moment, then shrugged. 'Only that he and Brother Simeon have been here too long. It's high time they departed, and the snow is melting sufficiently for them to go at once.'

Maurice's eyes swivelled round to fix themselves on my face. Then he said slowly, 'That is for my father to decide. He will not tolerate anyone else giving the orders. He is master here and we must accept it.'

'Then speak to him on the subject,' Fulk demanded

peremptorily. 'Tell him that these two, the pedlar and the friar, are troublemakers. They know too much, and the sooner we are shot of them the better.'

'How dare you speak to me like that!' Maurice protested feebly, and solely, I suspected, for my benefit. He sent a warning glance in his friend's direction. Nevertheless, Fulk's last words had frightened him. 'My father's in the solar. I'll . . . I'll go and see what can be done.'

'You'll probably find Mistress Lynom with him. He won't thank you for being disturbed,' I advised his departing back, but he took no notice and hurried up the stairs. I turned to Fulk. 'Well, I must find Brother Simeon.'

But he had grown uneasy and moreover his curiosity remained unsatisfied. 'You stay here,' he spat, and again tried to prevent me from passing.

I sighed. I had not wanted to pit my strength against his, for there was no doubt as to the outcome, but his actions left me no choice. Before he had time to realise what was happening, I had picked him up bodily, swung him around and placed him behind me. Then I walked rapidly towards the back door. Fulk let out an infuriated howl and began to run after me, but I turned about and held up my fists.

'Let me be,' I warned, 'unless you want a bloody nose.'

To his credit, my threat did not immediately deter him and he advanced several more paces before deciding that the game was not worth the candle.

'I know where you're going,' he shouted. 'I know where to find you and the friar. Don't forget that! Maurice and I will be after you as soon as Sir Hugh gives his permission to speed you hence.'

I smiled. 'I shall look forward to your company,' I promised, and meant it.

I went into the kitchen and picked up my cloak from the corner where I had dropped it, along with my cudgel and pack.

'The wanderer returns,' Martha commented sourly. 'You and that friar are like a couple of fleas on a griddle. Why can't you both sit still and give us the pleasure of your company while we're working, eh girls? Strangers here are a rare treat at any time of the year, but in the depths of winter . . .' She did not finish her sentence, leaving the rest of it to my imagination, but went on, 'Brother Simeon has gone to the tower and said that, if we saw you, we were to tell you to follow him.'

'I know. He left a similar message with Fulk Disney. Did he . . . ? Did the friar happen to mention why he needed my presence there?'

The cook shook her head and began looking for something on her kitchen table, moving basins and pans, spoons and ladles in growing irritation.

'Not a word. He suddenly got the fidgets and went searching for you. When you were not to be found, he grew even more restless and said he was going to the tower. He charged us most earnestly to ask you to join him there as soon as we saw you again . . . Which of you hussies has taken my meat knife . . . ? It sounds important,' she concluded, 'if he also told Fulk.'

Once more my stomach muscles knotted together in excitement. Or was it fear, because I knew that the summons from Friar Simeon meant that this particular mystery was nearing its solution? I put my cloak around my shoulders and stooped for my cudgel, but it was no longer there.

'Brother Simeon took it,' Jenny Tonge volunteered, noting my puzzled frown and guessing its reason. 'He said you wouldn't mind, and that as the snow is still deep in places, it would help keep him on his feet.'

'Ye-es,' I answered slowly, 'I suppose it might. And youth must give way to infirmity.'

'He's not that old,' Martha said tartly, the colour mounting her cheeks. Obviously, at some time, she had discovered the friar's age to be less than her own. But I had no inclination to tease her on the subject as I might have done, a day or so earlier. I had too much else to think about. I fastened my cloak at the throat and went out into the winter's afternoon.

Sunshine still lit the scene and promised that the better weather was indeed here to stay, for a while at least. As I left the manor behind me, a gull swooped low over the estuary, heading for the open sea, and I noticed that the swineherd had turned his pigs loose again to rootle among the debris washed up along the water's edge; both signs that life was gradually regaining its customary rhythm after being brought almost to a standstill for the past two days. The Saxon tower rose up before me, clear and sharply outlined against the bright blue sky. There was something sinister about it, and I thought of that Eadred Eadrichsson who had been dispossessed of his home and land by Sir Guy de Sourdeval after this country's conquest by the Normans. Had he put a curse on the place before he departed? Maybe.

As I approached, I could see that the door to the tower was standing ajar. Brother Simeon was waiting for me, and my heart began to pound uneasily. The evening before yesterevening – was it only such a short time ago? It seemed much longer – it was the friar who had fearlessly pushed wide the door. Now it was my turn. I flung it open and went inside.

The silence engulfed me. Only the soughing of the wind, as it searched out cracks and crannies between the ancient stones, disturbed the quiet. I paused, straining my ears for the slightest sound. Surely Brother Simeon must have been watching out for me, marking my progress along the snowy path which led from the gate in the manor wall, relieved that I had come at last and that the waiting was over. But why then did he not make his presence known?

I called out, 'Brother Simeon!' but my voice echoed hollowly up the empty stairs. Foolishly, I released my fingerhold on the edge of the door and advanced a step or two within the lower room. Immediately, the door slammed shut behind me, and before I could gather my wits sufficiently to avoid it altogether, my own cudgel, aimed for the back of my head, missed its target by inches and landed full across my shoulders. I staggered forward several paces, my hands reaching for the small table which supported candlestick and tinder-box, and brought it crashing to the floor beneath my weight. Although momentarily dazed by my fall, a sense of danger sharpened my instinct for survival, and I rolled clear of the stick's second murderous descent just in time. Almost without knowing what I was doing, I scrambled to my feet and turned to face my assailant. Brother Simeon, cursing volubly, wrenched the cudgel free from the splintered shards of wood and raised it for a third attempt on my life.

As it whistled towards me, I managed to catch the free end and hung on to it grimly, shaken to and fro like a straw man at a harvest gathering. I had not believed it possible that the friar possessed so much strength, and perhaps in normal circumstances he did not. But he was fighting for his survival and to prevent me from telling what I guessed. He had watched me, for the past two days, edging closer and closer to the truth, and now intended to silence me for ever, just as he had silenced Lady Cederwell, Gerard Empryngham and Ulnoth.

His eyes were full of hatred as we tried to wrest the stick from one another, and then, by a stroke of ill-fortune, I stumbled and was forced to release my hold in order to keep my balance. With a snarl of triumph, Brother Simeon attempted to lift the cudgel yet again, but during the struggle his hands had slipped too far back along the shaft to make such an action possible without first readjusting his grip. In the second or so's grace which this gave me, I leapt for the stairs and bounded up them two and three at a time.

I did not stop to consider the futility of what I was doing, but was impelled by the simple need of the pursued to elude its pursuer. The friar was between me and the tower's only door, so the stairs offered the sole means of escape. But I was also heading into a trap from which nothing but my superior strength could deliver me. Brother Simeon, however, had one great advantage: he had the murderer's instinct to kill, which had been honed, rather than blunted, by his recent activities. With three deaths already on his conscience, he would not hesitate to add a fourth. And he had already tried to kill me once when he, not Fulk, had pushed me from the stairs.

As I reached the first-storey room, I heard him blundering after me, the cudgel rattling against the edges of the steps as he dragged it with him. Once it sounded as if he tripped, probably over the hem of his habit, and he let rip with a string of oaths which would not have shamed a waterman. But he was on his feet again in less time than it takes to tell, and his head appeared clear of the stairwell. I glanced desperately around me only to confirm what I already knew; that there was no hiding place, and nothing in the way of a weapon.

Brother Simeon paused, baring his teeth in an unpleasant grin.

'I'll get you, Chapman. You can't escape. I'm going to have to kill you, you know that, don't you? I'm really very sorry because I've enjoyed your company, but I think you've guessed the truth about me. You're a clever lad, and you would persist in asking questions. And even if you haven't quite managed yet to piece everything together, I shall be forced to dispose of you anyway, now that I've shown my hand.' He sighed gustily and proceeded up the remaining few stairs.

I climbed the second flight of steps to the chapel. Somewhere below me I heard him laugh, a soft whinny of mirth that rose to a great neigh of joyous pleasure as he contemplated the deed before him. The scales of his poor, tired mind had finally tipped him over into madness, and that madness would imbue him with even greater strength than he had shown hitherto. The Devil now had possession of Simeon and would fight on his behalf.

In two strides, I was across the room and trying to lift the ebony crucifix down from the wall, but its weight defeated me. I cast a frantic glance around and my eyes lit on the silver candlesticks gracing Lady Cederwell's altar. I seized one in either hand, intending to use them as weapons with which to defend myself; but, at the sight of Brother Simeon as he mounted the last few stairs, I held them before me in the shape of a cross in order to ward off evil. For his expression, no longer recognisable, was that of some monstrous gargoyle, leering at me and rejoicing in his wickedness. The eyes in the parchment-coloured face were devoid of all humanity and burned only with the lust to kill.

He had dropped my cudgel somewhere on the stairs – the clatter I had heard, but barely registered until now, as it rolled off the steps into the room below – and had drawn from the breast of his habit Martha's missing black-handled, long-bladed knife, which she used for slicing meat. He advanced towards me, arm raised, gripping it like a dagger, but suddenly he faltered as his gaze came to rest on my makeshift cross. The custom of years, those years since he had first assumed, and then absorbed, the character of Brother Simeon, conquered, if only temporarily, the devil which had him in thrall. He took a deep, shuddering breath and lowered his arm a little, but without slackening his hold on the haft of the knife.

Carefully, without turning my head to look behind me, I moved a couple of paces to my rear until my back was against the wall and my head on a level with the transverse bar of the crucifix. Out of the corner of one eye, I could see the white, contorted legs of the ivory Christ, with the nail driven cruelly through the arches of the feet, and I edged a step or two sideways, forcing the man in front of me to gaze upon the agony of his Lord and Maker each time he looked in my direction. I still held the candlesticks in their cruciform shape, but was ready, at any second, to use them in my defence.

'Raymond,' I said gently. 'Raymond Shepherd, listen to me! Put down that knife. It can do you no good to kill me. Martha, the girls, Fulk Disney, Maurice Cederwell all know that I've come to meet you here. You yourself foolishly saw to that. A fourth death, even if you could make it seem like yet another accident, would be too suspicious to be accepted by Sir Hugh.'

I had made a mistake, however, in addressing him by his proper name, for he had listened to nothing I had said after that. The eyes had clouded over, the face gone blank.

'I am Brother Simeon,' he answered coldly, drawing himself up to his full, imposing height. 'A friar of the Dominican Order.'

'No,' I replied, keeping my voice as quiet and as reasonable as possible. 'Brother Simeon was the man you met up with while you were running away after raping your master's daughter; a man of much the same age and build as yourself. You killed him, dressed him in your clothes, mutilated the body and crushed the head until it was unrecognisable, making his death look like the work of outlaws. You then donned his habit, shaved the crown of your head and took his place. But you took more than that. Over the years you began to assume his character. You came to believe that you were indeed Brother Simeon from

Northumbria, although you must have been careful never to return to your parent House. But there was no need. You were doing good work here, in the south. You were bringing souls back into a state of grace and you loved your work. You must have discovered, almost from the first, that you had a talent for preaching, something you had never suspected in yourself until circumstances forced you to it. A simple shepherd, of no account for all of his life until then, was suddenly transformed into a person who was listened to and looked up to with awe and reverence. But one unlucky day you were summoned to Cederwell Manor by Lady Cederwell . . . who turned out to be that unfortunate Jeanette Empryngham despoiled by you all those years before. If she hadn't recognised you, it would have been all right. But she did recognise you, as did her half-brother, Gerard. They had to be silenced or you would lose everything.'

Brother Simeon – for in spite of all I had said, I could not, and cannot to this day, think of him by any other name – curled his lip. He had listened to me with surprising patience, but now made an angry gesture which commanded my attention: it was his turn to speak. His mood had changed yet again and he was for the moment calm, his eyes as blank as pebbles, soulless, without feeling, showing not even the faintest glimmer of remorse. His grip on the knife was as relentless as ever.

'I did not kill the friar,' he said. 'He died in his sleep, that night we spent together in the barn between Campden and Mickleton. God sent him to me in the last stages of exhaustion, to be my salvation. God had need of me. It was all a part of His plan.'

265

'What about the rape of Jeanette Empryngham?' I asked, trying to keep my voice as level and emotionless as his.

'That, too,' Simeon answered. 'Over the years, I have come to realise that it was also a part of God's plan.'

'How—?' I was beginning hotly, but at my change of tone his head reared up and I hurriedly lowered my voice. 'How can you say that?'

'She was a harlot. She deserved what she got, roaming around her father's fields with never a maid to accompany her, often barefoot, her skirts tucked into her girdle, and all the time pretending to be so pious. She was a whited sepulchre,' he hissed, 'and when God put it into my head to defile her in order to free me from my lowly position, He chose an unworthy vessel for His purpose.'

I wondered how long this madness had lain dormant within him. Probably for many years. A steadily increasing belief in his mission to save souls had demanded self-justification for what had happened. So when he thought of the past at all, when, with greater and greater infrequency, he remembered that he was really Raymond Shepherd and not Brother Simeon, he had created his own version of events to cover all the facts, and then buried it deep inside his mind. And now, when at last it was needed, he was able to dredge it up into the light of day. But the rankness of its smell had turned his brain.

Trying to imbue him with a sense of guilt was useless. I was wasting my breath. Nor was he any longer possessed by a sense of self-preservation. He believed that he could kill me with impunity and still walk free; free of suspicion and of the consequences of his crimes, because he was incapable

266

of reason. Any moment now his present, precarious calm would desert him and he would return to the attack.

Hard upon the thought, I saw his expression alter; the spark of insanity was rekindled in his eyes, and his docile, almost friendly smile was replaced by a wolfish grin. Neither the crucifix nor my candlestick cross could offer me any further protection. His fingers tightened around the handle of the knife and he seemed to grow in stature until I had the oddest impression that his head was touching the ceiling. He was between me and the final short flight of stairs which led to the tower's look-out platform, and I could not have reached them even had I wished to try. But my feet seemed to be rooted to the spot where I was standing. My arms felt as heavy as lead and the silver candlesticks had doubled in weight, dragging my hands down to hang at my sides.

I have never, either before or since, felt the presence of pure evil as potently as I did that day, nor have I ever been so transfixed with terror. I was young, I was very tall and strong. I should have been able to overpower Simeon, even armed as he was, without too much difficulty. But I watched him advance towards me and could do nothing to protect myself.

Far away, as in a dream, I heard a door open and shut, the slap of leather-shod feet against the stone treads of the stairs, the sound of raised voices. But the noises meant little to me; they did not whisper the word 'salvation'. I watched the knife rise higher and higher above my head, gleaming in a shaft of light from one of the window slits, and then begin its slow descent. Behind it, Simeon's face spread wide to fill my vision, and all the while, the constriction in my chest grew ever tighter until I could scarcely breathe . . .

And then, suddenly, Simeon was not there any more. He was on the floor, a sorry heap of emaciated flesh and bones clad in a rusty black habit, while Fulk Disney and Maurice Cederwell sat on him, pinning him to the ground, encouraged from the top of the stairs by Sir Hugh himself. The knife had fallen from his grasp a few inches from me, and a horrible whimpering, like a wounded animal, issued from his bloodied mouth.

'Chapman, are you all right? Are you injured?' demanded Sir Hugh, and a moment later his arm was supporting my waist, urging me away from the wall and lowering me as best he could to sit on the unpadded rail of Lady Cederwell's prie-dieu.

For a second or two, the attention of Maurice and Fulk was distracted from their prisoner, and the former had half risen from his knees to help his father. It was enough for the friar who, with more than human strength, rolled clear of their restraining hands, heaved himself to his feet and made for the stairs which led to the look-out platform. There was a brief, stupefied silence before we all went scrambling after him in a concerted rush which hampered our ascent, as we all tried to squeeze past one another, becoming wedged together in the process. And when we finally emerged on to the roof of the tower, we were just in time to see Brother Simeon climb on to the snowy parapet.

He gave one last desperate glance over his shoulder and then, with a scream which would have opened graves, hurled himself over the edge, to his death.

Chapter Twenty

'Now then, Chapman, let's have the rights and wrongs of what's been happening here over the past three days.'

Sir Hugh settled himself in one of the carved armchairs beside the fire, Mistress Lynom ensconced opposite him in another, which had been brought down from the solar. Maurice Cederwell and Fulk Disney sat decorously apart, each man at either end of a bench drawn as near to the leaping flames as the scorching heat would allow. Adela Empryngham, much to her obvious disgust, was forced to occupy a stool, as was Father Godyer, who had quit his sickbed and, swathed in a blanket, extended his sandalled feet towards the warmth, toasting his toes at the same time as the icy draughts seeped in under the doors and made him shiver. Tostig Steward, Phillipa Talke, Martha Grindcobb and the three kitchen-maids, together with Audrey Lambspringe, had also been summoned to the great hall and were ranged on another bench, dragged from the dais by Jude and Nicholas Capsgrave. These two, with Hamon and Jasper, had been sent for to join the company, but were expected to keep their distance from the circle grouped about the hearth. As for myself, I occupied a place of honour close to Sir Hugh and facing Ursula Lynom. Mulled wine had been served to everyone on the knight's express orders, and the smell of roasting meat drifted along the passageway from the kitchen. In spite of the pall of tragedy hanging over Cederwell Manor, supper was to be a festive meal, for the master of the house could at last foresee a brighter future with his chosen woman beside him. Whether or not others shared in his happiness was a moot point, but one which would not concern me. By this time tomorrow, I should be several miles closer to home.

'So,' Sir Hugh continued, slewing round in his chair to look directly at me, 'when did you first entertain suspicions that the friar was not all he seemed?'

Adela Empryngham interrupted, leaning forward to stare earnestly into my face.

'Are you saying, Chapman, that Brother Simeon was really Raymond Shepherd? The villain who raped Jeanette and whom we all thought dead these six years past? How could it possibly be? Are you certain you haven't been dreaming?'

'I'm quite sure,' I answered. 'He made no denial when I charged him with it. But I believe that the knowledge of my discovery, of being forced to face the truth after years of self-deception, finally destroyed his mind.'

'Yet he came to see me,' Father Godyer protested. 'Surely I would have recognised him.'

I shook my head. 'Your sight is poor, Father. Do you recollect, in your chamber, during my first visit to you, I put on your cassock for added warmth? And although your gaze was fixed on me throughout, later you were surprised to find that I was wearing it.'

'Oh dear, oh dear!' The priest rocked himself to and fro

in some distress. 'I have to admit that my eyes are not what they used to be.' He cast Sir Hugh a timid, sidelong glance as though expecting to be reprimanded for this failing.

But the knight was busy with thoughts of his own.

'Gerard!' he exclaimed. 'Gerard recognised him, though!'

'I think he may have done.' I set down my mazer, empty now of its contents, and propped my chin in my hand. 'But he wasn't so convinced that he felt able to speak out there and then, in this hall, the night of our arrival. He said something about not being deceived, about not being able to prove anything "at this moment", but that he refused to keep silent for much longer.' I did not add that, at the time, I had assumed him to be talking of Sir Hugh and Mistress Lynom. It did not seem politic. Instead, I turned to Father Godyer. 'Is it not true, on your own telling, that Raymond Shepherd would have known that Master Empryngham walked in his sleep?'

The priest shrugged his shoulders beneath the enveloping blanket.

'Quite true, yes. It was a widely known fact at Campden. It reached many ears. But I don't understand,' he added pathetically. 'How could Brother Simeon and Raymond Shepherd be one and the same? I saw the latter's body with my own eyes.'

I reached out a hand and laid it on his arm, where its outline showed beneath the blanket.

'And by your own admission, his body was all you did see. You had previously told me that you identified the corpse by the clothes, and when I suggested to you, this afternoon, that the head was crushed in, you did not deny it.'

271

'But they were Raymond Shepherd's clothes!' Father Godyer protested.

'Of course. According to Simeon – for I cannot think of him by any other name – he shared a barn with a Dominican friar, the first night that he was on the run. No doubt they got talking. The friar described his life on the road, where he came from, what he did. And then, again according to Simeon whose word I have no reason to doubt, the holy man died in his sleep. Simeon saw his chance of escape and took it. He changed garments with the friar, crushed the man's head with a stone or whatever else happened to be handy in the barn, and left the body in a ditch. The gamble worked, and everyone believed Raymond Shepherd to have cheated the gallows, but nevertheless to have come by his just deserts.'

Adela Empryngham buried her face in her hands for a moment before looking up with tears trickling down her cheeks.

'If only I hadn't quarrelled with Gerard, if I'd stayed with him on Tuesday night, Simeon – Raymond – wouldn't have been able to lure him to his death while we were all asleep. It's true, isn't it?' she demanded, her voice rising on a note of hysteria.

Martha got up and hurried over to her, clasping the younger woman in a comforting embrace.

'There, there, my dear. You weren't to know. You mustn't blame yourself. Evil is the fault of the evil-doer. It can't be laid to the charge of anyone else.'

There was a general mumble of assent. It is a comfortable doctrine, and one which I more than half believe myself. We are all given the choice between right and wrong in this world. And yet . . . And yet . . .

Mistress Lynom cut in with a question which had plainly been troubling her for several minutes, ever since it had entered her mind.

'But how could this man possibly have murdered Jeanette when you, Roger, were with him even before he entered the manor?'

Everyone looked at me for an explanation.

'I was certainly with him,' I acknowledged, 'when he approached Cederwell late on Tuesday afternoon. But, by my reckoning, he was here much earlier in the day, and that was when he murdered Lady Cederwell.'

'Earlier?' Tostig Steward demanded, voicing the general bewilderment.

'Yes,' I insisted. 'The tinker who was here this morning informed me that he had spent Monday night at Woodspring Priory and so, according to his own story, had Simeon. But neither man recognised the other, so one of them was lying. I could see no good reason why the tinker should do so, and I already had my doubts about the friar. I decided that he could well have left the priory the previous evening, and not very early Tuesday morning as he claimed, provided there was somewhere on the road where he could have passed the night. Mistress Lynom says there is a farmhouse some three miles distant from Lynom Hall which, although moated, possesses two outhouses standing beyond the pale and open to the track which runs south to Woodspring. Furthermore,' I added, nodding significantly at Ursula, 'Dame Judith mentioned having seen a holy man pass by on Tuesday morning before she was taken upstairs to the solar, a long time before I caught up with Simeon on a two-mile journey which should have taken him little over an hour to accomplish.'

Mistress Lynom gave a crack of laughter. 'So the old witch and her prying eyes have some use after all! Who would have thought it?'

Phillipa Talke intervened. 'But none of us here saw Brother Simeon until he arrived with you. How could he possibly have gained access to my Lady without our knowing?'

Sir Hugh nodded in agreement, as did Tostig Steward and Martha Grindcobb.

'True. How do you explain that, Roger Chapman?'

'Very simply. Lady Cederwell met him on the road.' I smiled at Audrey Lambspringe. 'You told me that on Tuesday your mistress took a basket with her to the tower because she was going to visit Ulnoth, as she did two or three times each month during the winter. I should hazard therefore that she met with Simeon on his way to see her, and turned back with him. They went directly to the tower by the path through the scrubland, so avoiding being seen by anyone in the house or stables. At that point, either Lady Cederwell had not recognised Simeon, or neither had recognised the other.' I shrugged. 'We shall never know now, but there must have come a moment when the truth dawned on one or both of them . . . After which, we can only guess at what happened. They were in her chapel and Simeon most likely blocked her escape to the lower floors, so she ran upwards to the look-out platform. He followed and threw her down. As she lay dying,' I added for Sir Hugh's benefit, 'the name she tried to say was Raymond, not Hamon.'

With the exception of the knight, Mistress Lynom and the man so named, my listeners looked puzzled, but no one chose to enlighten them. Instead, Sir Hugh demanded, 'Why had you begun to suspect the friar, even before the arrival of the tinker?'

'For a number of reasons. When I first heard Simeon speak, at the High Cross in Bristol, I asked him if he were from these western parts, but he denied it and said he was from Northumbria. Yet, later, he revealed an exact knowledge of the grading and price of good Cotswold wool; something, surely, that no Dominican friar from such distant northern shires would know much about. Then again, on Wednesday morning, when we discovered Master Empryngham's body in the well, all that could be seen of him were his legs, sticking up, solid and frozen. Yet Simeon knew that the dead man was wearing a nightshirt, which proved to be exactly the case. Furthermore, he was constantly anxious to get away from here, and blew hot and cold on all my attempts to ferret out the truth. He never pretended to think Lady Cederwell's death an accident, but neither did he behave in the way a man of such zeal and fanaticism should have done in the circumstances. In addition, I recalled how he had flinched on first meeting with Mistress Empryngham in the kitchen on Tuesday afternoon. At the time I thought it for a different reason, but later I suspected that it was shock. He had not realised that she and her husband were also living here.'

'But Ulnoth?' inquired Mistress Lynom. 'Are you also laying his death at Simeon's door?'

275

'Yes, although I have no shred of proof that I am right on that score. Nevertheless, I will tell you what I believe to have happened. After he had murdered Lady Cederwell, Simeon hid for a while in the scrubland, probably too terror-stricken to proceed any further. Gradually, however, as he came to terms with what he had done and to accept it as God's will, he would have become aware, firstly, that he was cold and hungry, and secondly that he must put some distance between himself and Cederwell Manor until he could safely approach it at a later time. So he retraced his steps as far as the boulder house, which he had noticed when he passed it earlier in the day. The hermit would probably have given him food and drink, and was no doubt dismissed by Simeon as the simpleton he outwardly appeared to be. But Ulnoth was shrewd, picking up signs and odd words, carelessly let slip, to lead him to the truth.

'I know this because he gave me shelter for several nights after I had hurt my ankle. On Tuesday, after I had left Lynom to walk to Cederwell, I called on him again. He was very frightened, and kept muttering the word "death". Later, after I had overtaken Simeon on the road, and during the course of our conversation, I told him about this. The following day, I was also the one who mentioned to him my belief that there was someone watching the house from the scrubland. Simeon pretended to disbelieve me, but coupled with what I had already told him, he must have been worried that Ulnoth had come to spy on him, as was indeed the case. While I was at the stables getting logs for Mistress Grindcobb, he went to see for himself. He had already committed two murders by this time and was growing used to the idea of killing for his own protection. He would have had no compunction in taking the hermit's life; and when I discovered Ulnoth's body, I also found a strip of black woollen cloth hanging from a thorn, which had not come from any garment he was wearing. Unhappily for Simeon, the next day the tinker turned up and alerted me to Ulnoth's absence overnight.'

Adela Empryngham shivered suddenly. 'What of me?' she asked. 'What of the figure I saw standing in the doorway and which you all thought nothing but a dream?'

I nodded. 'Again I have no proof, but I think it likely that it was the friar, suddenly seized by the fear that you might still recognise him at some future time. He had been with me in the men's dormitory, and ran up the gallery stairs as soon as he had quit my side, intending to silence you as he had done your husband. But God was watching over you. You woke up and saw him. He took fright and ran away, hiding just inside the back door to emerge with the others as they went to your assistance. No easy opportunity presented itself to him again, so you are safe.'

Adela burst out sobbing, and Martha Grindcobb, who had remained close by, once more wrapped the younger woman in her arms, gently rocking her to and fro. I sympathised with Mistress Empryngham, understanding how she felt; for I could have added that I too had survived an attempted murder at Simeon's hands, convinced by now that it was he, and not Fulk Disney, who had concealed himself in the tower and pushed me from the stairs. (His story of seeing Fulk running away from the tower was, of course, a lie.) But as his object had been to rob me of Lady Cederwell's list of accusations against her husband and stepson, I thought it best to make no reference to something which could only cause embarrassment. Simeon himself must have searched for such a paper in order, if it existed, to destroy it; for without it he could not well instruct any episcopal court to proceed against Sir Hugh or his son, the main accuser being dead and no one else likely to proffer evidence in her stead. He did not want any more questions asked about Jeanette Cederwell's death in case the truth should somehow be brought to light.

At last, Sir Hugh heaved a great sigh and clapped his hands to the arms of his chair, dragging himself slowly to his feet.

'Well, Chapman,' he said, looking down at me, 'we owe you a debt of gratitude.' He smiled at Ursula Lynom. 'We've been a couple of fools, my dear. We must trust one another more nearly in future. And now I must sleep on what's best to be done and how much to tell the Sheriff's officers when they arrive. What do you advise, Maurice?'

His son was ready with his answer. 'We have satisfactory explanations for all four deaths, Father. The weather is to blame for everything. Let it rest there.' He glanced round the little assembly. 'With one exception, these are either our own people or Mistress Lynom's. And I fancy,' he added dryly, 'that that will soon be one and the same thing.' He fixed me with a steady eye. 'Chapman, you are the only outsider amongst us. Are you willing to hold your tongue if we make it worth your while?'

I scrambled to my feet.

'I'll hold my tongue,' I agreed, 'but not for money. If I were such a knave, how could you possibly trust me? No,

278

I'll say nothing because our villain has met with his just deserts, and because he must now be standing in the presence of his Maker in the sure and certain knowledge that nothing but eternal damnation awaits him in the bowels of Hell.'

Sir Hugh clapped me on the shoulder. 'You're a good man,' he said approvingly, as people do when your actions chime with their wishes. But I could see nothing to be gained by bringing further sorrow on a household which had already been so sorely afflicted. Besides, Mistress Lynom might soon prove trial enough for most of them to cope with.

So I took my leave the following morning, knowing that I had performed the job which God had brought me there to do, and also with the consciousness of having done no harm to any innocent person. The snow and ice were fast melting in a warmer, more westerly breeze, and I finally quit Cederwell Manor with the inhabitants' good wishes and blessings ringing in my ears. I turned my feet in an easterly direction, for Bristol.

My mother-in-law, Margaret Walker, was busy spinning when I walked in through her cottage door three days later.

'You're back, then,' she remarked without turning her head.

'I'm back,' I agreed, putting down my pack and cudgel with a sigh of relief and looking around for my daughter.

At the sound of my voice, Elizabeth had picked herself up from the floor, where she had been playing with an old rag doll made of cuttings of unbleached wool, and came toddling unsteadily towards me, her little arms held out in expectation. She was not disappointed as I swung her high above my head, watching her face crease into smiles of delight and hearing her excited chirrupings. When I lowered her, the arms wound themselves tightly about my neck, and a soft cheek rubbed itself against mine.

Margaret Walker did deign to look up then, and nodded briefly. But, 'The prodigal's return,' was her only comment.

I set my daughter on her feet and took a handful of coins from the pouch at my waist, laying them on the table.

'A worthwhile journey,' I wheedled.

She snorted, but was slightly mollified.

'Where did you hole up,' she asked, 'during this dreadful weather?'

'A place called Cederwell Manor.' Foolishly I added, 'On the estuary and some good few miles north of Woodspring Priory.'

She was interested at once. 'The friar was on his way to Woodspring. Did you by chance see anything of him?'

'We . . . did fall in with one another,' I reluctantly admitted.

'A wonderful preacher! We need more of his kind in the world. Morals are too lax nowadays. It needs someone with the courage to speak out against the King and his court, the fountainhead of all such corruption.'

I made no reply and fortunately Margaret asked me no more questions, busying herself instead with putting food on the table and fetching ale from the cask. Elizabeth climbed on my knee to share my meal, her soft mouth opening and closing around the tasty morsels like that of a little bird.

I felt a sudden and unaccustomed glow of contentment. I was home with two who loved me and one of whom thought me the most perfect being in the world. The fire burned on the hearth and the door was closed against the wintry weather. Evil and wrongdoing were as remote from that cosy haven as the moon and stars were from the earth.

'I shan't be leaving you again for a while,' I assured Margaret Walker, but she only smiled.

'Perhaps not for a month or two,' she agreed. 'But when the warmer breezes blow and the days get longer, when the spring comes, then it will be a different story. The wanderlust will take you by the scruff of the neck and shake you as it always does.' She stopped spinning and slewed round on her stool to look at me, her face serious. 'I've told you, you should think about marrying again. I'm a lot older than you. I shan't always be here to take care of Elizabeth. Besides, a man needs more than one child if he can beget them. A man needs a son to carry on his line. So think about it.'

I had not heeded her former words, nor intended to marry again so soon. I was young and selfish and wanted to enjoy my freedom. I had mercifully been delivered from the bonds of matrimony after being enmeshed against my will, and until now had seen no good reason why I should voluntarily embrace them for a second time. Later, perhaps, in a year or two, or maybe three, I might be tempted. But, stupidly, reprehensibly, I had not considered what would happen to Elizabeth if Margaret were to die; the responsibility which would fall upon me, the curtailment of freedom.

It was a consideration which continued to haunt me over the ensuing months; a thought which made me nervous and jumpy each time my mother-in-law coughed or complained of an ague. Once or twice I remembered Audrey Lambspringe, a gentle girl who would no doubt prove biddable enough were I to return to Cederwell and offer her marriage. But I did not love her any more than I had loved Lillis, and I resolved that next time, for my bride's sake as well as my own, there must be more than mere liking between us.

Moreover, I knew that I could never go back to Cederwell for any reason whatsoever. I was unable to dissociate the place from the evil spell which, for me at least, Raymond Shepherd had cast upon it. I knew nothing of what had happened after I left. I had made no inquiries and was happy to remain in ignorance. Meantime, spring lay just around the corner and every day the need to be up and doing, to be on the road again, grew ever stronger. I saw Margaret Walker watching me, an anxious expression in her eyes.

I knew that I must marry again, and soon.

WILLIAM K. SANFORD TOWN LIBRARY

00000137808

AUG 1999

William K. Sanford Town Library

Book Due Latest Date Shown

	OCT 0 8 2015
AUG 1 8 2011	
	OCT 2 3 2015
APR 1 5 2012	DEC 0 6 2019
JUN 0 7 2012	1/3/20
JUN 0 5 2013	
JUN 0 5 2013	
11/29	
MAY 1 4 2014	